RECKLESSLY
EVER AFTER

HEATHER VAN FLEET

sourcebooks
casablanca

Published by Sourcebooks Casablanca, an imprint of Sourcebooks, Inc.
P.O. Box 4410, Naperville, Illinois 60567-4410
(630) 961-3900
Fax: (630) 961-2168
sourcebooks.com

Printed and bound in Canada.
MBP 10 9 8 7 6 5 4 3 2 1

To Jess. Gavin has always been for you.

CHAPTER 1

Gavin

GETTING STUCK IN AN ELEVATOR WITH THE SEXY BLOND I'VE been fantasizing about for months should have been a dream come true. But instead, it was a damn nightmare.

Standing before me, dressed in a pair of blue, cloud-patterned scrubs, McKenna Brewer put her hands on my forearms and spoke to me as if I were a kid. "Just breathe, Gavin. I promise we won't be in here long. In through your nose, out through your—"

My throat burned as I growled out the words. "I'm fine."

"Let's at least get this off you." The back of her knuckles grazed my chest as she tugged on the ties of my hoodie. "You're sweating and—"

"*Don't touch me.*" I nudged her out of the way with my shoulder, then moved to the other side of the hospital elevator. There, I pressed my forehead against the wall, silently begging for this to be over.

I'm surprised she even remembered who I was, since we hadn't seen each other in a few months. That tended to happen when you were a recluse like me. Collin and Max, my best friends, both said I had issues—which I didn't deny. But really, it was the introvert in me that avoided crowds and going out.

Plain and simple? I just didn't like people.

When I did see McKenna, I avoided her. It's not that I didn't like her. I just had no idea what to say when I was around her.

She made me feel things. *Weird* things.

Things I'd avoided for years.

Things I was dying to experience but had no idea how to let myself do.

Her small hand settled against my lower back. I jumped at the unexpected touch, ramming my dick against the metal bar halfway down the wall. "Son of a bitch." I curled over at the waist, my hand on my crotch.

"Oh God. Are you okay?"

I turned to face her, teeth gritted. "Been…better."

"Is anything fractured? Do you need me to take a look?"

"Not unless you wanna see my dick," I snorted through my wince.

"Huh?" She jerked her head back, eyes narrowed.

"Never mind," I barked, not meaning to. But nothing said *claustrophobia* like a clingy nurse—good intentions or not. "Just…stay back and give me a sec, all right?" I paused for a minute before adding hastily, "Please."

Her eyes flashed between my crotch and my hands, widening in surprise. "Ohhh."

"Yep." I popped my lips and waited for the pain to ease, eyes to the ceiling, heart racing too quickly. Sweat beaded along my temples, and I shut my eyes, imagining myself in a safe place. The psychiatrist had told me to go there mentally whenever I had one of these…these *episodes*. The irony is that the place where I always went was with the woman standing right there in front of me.

Fucking hilarious how fate worked sometimes.

McKenna had been the star of my dreams for God only knew how many months. I'd done my best to keep my distance until I was right enough in the head to make a move. Or at least I'd tried to. But there I was, freaking out in front of her. Max had been right when he'd told me I didn't have *game*.

I stepped back, only to slide to the floor against the wall. "Fuck me," I mumbled under my breath, hands in my hair. I was a damn mess.

"I called for help." A few feet away, McKenna crouched to the floor, her white orthopedic shoes coming into view. "It shouldn't be that much longer. Heck, maybe it will be a simple factory reset, and they won't even have to call the fire department."

I nodded, unconvinced.

A minute passed. Then two. I was counting the silent seconds in my head.

"Is your, um, stuff okay?"

I looked up at her question, finding her bottom lip pulled between her teeth. "My stuff?"

She nodded, eyes shifting briefly to my crotch again.

"My *dick*, you mean."

Her lips curled into a half grin. "There are more suitable terms to use in front of a lady, you know."

"Guess I'm not a *suitable* kind of man." I propped a knee up, wincing, then leaned over on one hip and rubbed my hand over my chest. My *dick* was the least of my problems right now.

McKenna sat next to me, still managing to keep some distance between us, thank God. I respected that about her. Typically, when I was having one of my moments, people tended to crowd around more, which usually ended with me causing a scene.

"You don't *have* to be suitable to say suitable things. Trust me." She winked.

I grunted and leaned my cheek against the cold wall, eyes locking with hers. My chest grew tighter with every breath, but hearing her talk? It helped.

"For example, a more appropriate term for your stuff would be 'penis.'"

I lifted a brow. "You really gonna do this now?"

She nodded quickly, and hair from her short ponytail fell over her forehead and nose. She blew the strands away, but they landed in the same spot. She'd cut her hair since I'd seen her last.

"Yes. I am, actually." She rolled her shoulders—one, then the other, only to fling her arms out in front of her and wiggle her fingers. My lips twitched as I watched her. Damn cute is what she was.

"There's 'member,' 'groin,' and 'wiener'—although that one might be crossing the line as far as suitable goes. Then there's 'manhood.' That's always been my favorite."

I frowned. Was she serious? Or was she fucking with me?

"Oh! 'Endowment' is a good one too." She crossed her legs, only to flap them up and down like wings. Her energy level was contagious, like Chloe's when she couldn't sit still.

At the thought of my friend's daughter, my chest eased a little.

"I'd prefer to call it my disco stick," I mumbled.

"Of course you would." McKenna rolled her pretty blue eyes. "But from my standpoint, I don't necessarily like pet names for the peen."

I frowned. "You just called it a peen. Isn't that a pet name?"

She shrugged. "It's better than 'beef whistler,' 'wing dang doodle,' 'zipper ripper,' or the 'just-in beaver,' am I right?"

"Did you just call my dick Justin Bieber?"

"No, silly. It's the 'Just. In. Beaver.'" She grinned. Not a hint of a blush covered her cheeks. This girl was shameless.

"Damn. You're something."

"Something *good*, I hope." She shimmied in place.

I couldn't help but grin, loving the way her nose scrunched up as she spoke, but then things went quiet again, reminding me where we were. I rubbed a hand over my newly grown beard just as a creak and a thud sounded above us.

I shot up and pressed my palms against the wall, ready for battle. With a motherfucking elevator. "Jesus, what was that?"

Kenna stood too, calm and completely in control. Hands on her hips, she looked at the silver trapdoor above us, grinning. "Hey! Anyone up there got beer?"

A man laughed and said, "I'll buy you one as soon as I get you out of there, miss. How's that sound?"

Hands shaking, I brought them to my sides and relaxed as I sat on the floor again.

"Sounds great, actually." She grinned, those eyes twinkling like stars in a midnight sky.

I remembered them from the night I'd first met her last fall. I'd nearly knocked her off her barstool at O'Paddy's, the bar Collin, Max, and I always went to after our rugby games. Later that night, I found her sitting against the wall by the bathroom, wasted.

She'd been crying. Knees to her chest like I was sitting now, bawling about a broken nail and a broken heart. Those eyes were all I could see when I'd asked her if she was all right, yet her words tumbled out faster than a hurricane: *Fuck men.*

That's when I'd crouched in front of her, told her I'd take care of her, and helped her to her feet. No questions asked, she let me…then started purring at me like a cat. Told me she'd be able to get over her ex if I promised to be her sexual bandage. Also pretty sure she told me that if she ever decided to have kids, I'd be the one she'd call for the sperm.

"I could really use something stronger than a beer, ya know?" She sat on the elevator floor again, this time across from me, her smile still wide, her voice disrupting my thoughts.

I swallowed hard and wiped the sweat off my forehead with the back of my hand. My pulse continued to race, but my breathing seemed to steady.

Damn it all to hell. Why couldn't I just be normal?

"Hey." She bumped the toe of her shoe against mine, a shadow of a dimple forming on her right cheek. "You heard the man. It won't be long now."

I looked away, not wanting to stare, zoning out on the sounds of the clunking above us instead.

"…claustrophobic?"

"What'd you say?" I narrowed my eyes and looked at her again.

"I wondered if you were claustrophobic. Like, do you have issues with being in tight, enclosed spaces?"

"What gave it away?" I snorted and rubbed my hand over my beard just as the elevator hummed to life, only to die again.

The guy above said, "Well, hell," and I hit the back of my head against the wall.

Breathe, idiot.

"You want me to talk you through it?" she asked.

"I'm fine." I gritted my teeth, barely opening my mouth. Whether I wanted it to or not, I knew a soft voice like hers wasn't going to completely talk me down. This was something I had to do myself. Besides, I'd just seen a doc. The last thing I wanted was someone else trying to pick my brain.

Life in my world consisted of doctors and solitude. Alone time to function and occasional talks with my best friends that never turned serious. Collin and Max didn't have a clue what my life had been like before them. Nobody did, other than my high school girlfriend and the people who'd made me the way I am today.

As long as I lived and breathed, it would stay that way. Because subjecting the people I loved to the kind of pain I'd endured was not something I could deal with.

"Well, if you don't mind, I think I'll just keep talking, even if you don't want to answer. I love to talk. Like, a lot. Sometimes to myself, even," McKenna continued.

As always when she came near, I couldn't stop myself from studying her, her eyes a beacon in the storm. More than anything, I needed to stop, regroup a little, maybe shut my own eyes if I had to. Because relying on someone else to ease my pain meant I'd never truly be able to find my way alone.

Still, the longer I stared at her, the more the raging winds inside me calmed.

"Talking to yourself is fine. Just as long as you don't answer." I cleared my throat. "Isn't that what they say?"

"Very true." She leaned her head back, smiling at the ceiling. "Which is why I don't shut up most of the time. I'm a people person who *needs* conversation."

I wondered what that might be like.

Then shuddered at the idea a second later.

"Just so you know, my sister suffers from anxiety. I know how to help you."

Exhaling, I turned away. I could almost bet her sister didn't suffer from the same shit I did, but what did I know?

"Let's do the question game. That always helps. You don't have to give full answers if you don't want. One word is fine. Maybe two or three if you're feeling particularly generous."

I grunted.

"Grunts are good too." She shrugged one shoulder. "So, what do you do for a living again?"

I waited a beat before answering. "I'm an EMT." Though currently suspended for losing my shit on a coworker. It's why I was at the hospital today. In addition to seeing my psychiatrist again, I'd been taking anger management classes three nights a week.

McKenna scooted closer, though still respectfully keeping her distance. "How come I've never seen you here before? I mean, I don't work in the ER except maybe once a month, but still."

I shrugged and looked at my lap. Most likely because whenever I saw her, I ducked and ran. But she didn't need to know that.

"Were you born and raised here? Is Carinthia your hometown?"

"No." Not technically. If anything, I wasn't really from anywhere.

Foster home to foster home, city to city in Illinois… A person who'd lived in the system since they were ten years old didn't tend to relate to that word—*home*.

"Well, I was born in New Orleans, but moved to Macomb later on. After college, I relocated to Carinthia to be closer to Addie." She shrugged. "I've been thinking about relocating back south though. I'm young and tired of the cold winters. Arizona would be nice, but that'd be even farther away from Addison. I'd be a mess without her."

My gut tightened. *Move? Out of state?*

"My *mother* still lives in New Orleans. Not that I'd move back there for her. More to see my sister, who stays with her because she's the only child who refuses to walk away from those sons of bitches called our *family*." She cleared her throat. "Sorry. TMI. I don't have much of a filter. Addie always says I wear all my secrets on my sleeve." She shrugged and tugged at the hems of her scrub pants.

I looked away and nodded. That was Addie, all right.

Though I'd never held a one-on-one conversation with McKenna before now, I'd found her fascinating— even from a distance. She was funny. Made everyone laugh. Had opinions and wasn't afraid to express them. It was refreshing for someone like me, who tended to run and lock himself away when things got too tough.

"A person can't run from their problems," I said, the biggest hypocrite alive. "Not healthy."

"True…" She twiddled her thumbs, something I hadn't done since I was a kid. "But don't you ever want to start over in life? Be someone else, even if only for a day?"

I didn't have to think about my answer. "No. I like my job." And even though my mind didn't work like everyone else's and my past was shit, I wouldn't change who I was today. Mainly because I had a family in my two best friends and Chloe.

"Not many people can say that. You're one of the lucky ones. I mean, I don't *hate* being a nurse, but it's definitely not ideal either." She reached up and yanked the hair tie from her ponytail. I swallowed hard, watching as her wavy blond hair spilled down around her face, hitting just at her shoulders. The scent of wildflowers had my mouth going dry and my cock twitching in response.

"Hmm" was all I could manage.

"You don't talk much, do you?"

I could feel her gaze on my face, the warmth of her stare, her attention suddenly everything I wanted, even though I tried to fight it. "No."

"Well, I do, if you couldn't tell already."

"You already said that."

The elevator jerked. I pressed my palms flat against the floor, my knuckles going white.

Like it was no big deal, McKenna kept talking, while

moving closer and crouching so her knees touched my feet. "Talking is my thing, you know? My way of dealing with stress and life. I tell people what my thoughts are, and I don't keep them inside. Like I said, TMI is pretty much ATT for me."

"ATT?" I asked.

She bumped my foot with her knee. "It stands for 'all the time.'" She winked at me. "And you don't have to, but if you ever decided you wanted to get *unfiltered*, then you should hit me up sometime. Swing by when I'm at Addie and Collin's place visiting. Or…I could stop by and see you."

I nodded, failing to ignore the way my heart raced at the thought of her in my house. In my bed even more. I cleared my throat, just in time for the elevator to lurch again. "Fuck." Without thinking, I reached for her hand and yanked her forward. She landed chest first on my knees with an *oomph*. Other than her lips parting as she stared up at me, McKenna barely flinched.

"Shit. Sorry." I jerked back and scrubbed a shaking hand over my face.

Instead of calling me a freak, slapping me, or screaming for help, I felt her sit up, her movements slow against my jeans. Soon, she was straddling my thighs, the heat of her breath washing over my hands too.

I swallowed as she pulled them down from my face, then blinked as she whispered, "Movement's a good sign, trust me. Those movies that show elevators plunging people to their deaths are fictional for a reason."

I groaned at the image she created in my mind.

Each time I swallowed, each time I tried to breathe, I felt less and less oxygen in my lungs, my breaths squeezing my chest as if hundreds of ropes were knotted around my heart.

The elevator began to move, only to jerk to a stop once more.

The guy hollered down at us—"Almost there"—yet his muffled reassurance did nothing to ease my anxiety.

Kenna's warm body scooted closer, her chest to mine, her soft hands on my cheeks. All thoughts of pushing her off me grew suddenly null and void. Not when her nearness was the only thing keeping me from losing it completely.

"When I was a little girl, my dad used to tell me stories about brave princesses rescued by their princes."

I cringed. "I'm no prince."

The side of her mouth kicked up. "And I'm no princess either. Lucky you." Her lips twitched, but the expression did nothing for me this time. "Take a deep breath, Gavin," she whispered. "Breathe for me."

"No." I squeezed my eyes shut.

She dropped one of her hands from my cheek and squeezed my fingers in between our stomachs. "Eyes on me. Don't look away."

My throat burned, but I managed to do what she asked.

"Tell me something. Tell me your biggest secret."

The elevator lurched once more, and the guy on top mumbled something over the noise.

Breathe. Just breathe.

"Tell me a secret," she asked again, this time adding, "Please."

I shook my head.

"Why?"

My jaw locked at her question. Still, I didn't respond.

"Are you afraid I'll hold it against you after all this is done?"

"No. Not because of that." Because the only secret I could share in that moment would be about having her naked in my bed, and now wasn't the time for that.

Her face fell, indecision wavering in her eyes for a second. She searched my eyes, seeming to decide on something before she finally said, "I guess I'll just have to distract you another way."

Then she kissed me.

CHAPTER

McKenna

IMPULSE DECISIONS: I WAS THE QUEEN OF MAKING THEM. AND the second I decided I wanted to kiss this bun-wearing, sexy-bearded, eyes-the-color-of-grass, forbidden man, I knew there was no going back.

My mother always told me my impulsivity would get me in loads of trouble one day. That being the petulant child with big dreams and no brains would only make said trouble worse. But as my tongue slipped between Gavin St. James's lips and I felt him relax against me, I told that woman to go straight to hell because this impulsive decision was the right one.

For the first time since our elevator had skidded to a stop, the tension in his body eased, and a new emotion seemed to overtake him. He moaned and tangled his hands in my hair, tugging me even closer, like he couldn't get enough. Teeth clamped down on my bottom lip, and my lady parts warmed, begging for friction. But it wasn't the time to step over the line. Gavin had the kind of injuries I couldn't tend to.

Still, distracting him was something I *could* do. And clearly, this was the best idea ever.

I think.

His beard tickled my skin with every moment of our mouths. Over and over, our tongues tangled, even after the elevator began to move again. For the briefest of seconds, I thought about pressing the stop button just to keep the momentum going. But with his arms wrapped tightly around my waist, I knew we were out of time. What kind of woman kissed a guy and stayed anyway?

Okay, so lots of women kissed and stayed. Just not me.

He growled as he pulled me even closer, the hardness beneath his jeans giving me exactly what I craved. Once more, the elevator jerked to a stop, and a tiny *Thank you, yesss* echoed in my brain.

I should've stopped him, warned him that we had six floors to go, maybe less. That as soon as the elevator began to move again, this would all be a distant memory. Yet the second his fingers slipped into the back of my scrub shirt and grazed the skin beneath my shoulders, I knew I was done for.

Goddamn. Now I could see why my best friend had warned me away from him. This guy was a pent-up ball of aggressive sex in the making. And exactly my type.

"Kenna," he whispered, the sound so right that I couldn't help grinding my body against his even harder. He kissed my chin, taking his sweet time before he found my lips again. Addie would kill me if she knew I'd let this happen. But Addie had the perfect life and the perfect man, so sue me if I liked taking the long road to something that lasted more than one night. Although from the way Gavin kissed, I could tell he was a "take me, have me, keep me" kind of guy—and that alone should have had me rocking in a corner. Still, even though my mind told me to run, I couldn't help but think about bringing him home with me—something that rarely occurred.

Most of my flings didn't get past my car or a dark alley. Sometimes a bathroom, when I was feeling particularly impatient.

A shiver raced through me at the thought of a full night with him, forcing me to rub over his erection even harder. It's like I was eradicating my normalized ideas and taking what I could get for the next few minutes.

Sweat coated my back, and his fingers trailed over the dampness in an expert move. I lifted my hands and undid the tie holding his hair, sighing as the strands nearly melted through my fingers. Fabio had nothing on this guy's locks.

Itching for more, I touched his chin, tightening my fingers through his beard. He pulled back, looked me dead in the eye, and through staggering breaths, said the one thing I didn't want to hear.

"I've always wanted you, Kenna. That's my biggest secret."

"Crap." I jerked off his body, then pressed my hand over my mouth, gaping, annoyed with myself, and terribly horny.

"What's wrong?" he asked, fear gathering in those gorgeous green eyes. Eyes that I'd come to know from a distance. Eyes that still haunted me whenever I dreamed of them and the night we'd first met in November.

It was the night my best friend, Addie, met Collin, the love of her life. And this man's best friend.

I shook my head. "Gavin, I can't—"

The man above hollered down, interrupting me. "You're good. Have you out in seconds."

I cringed, facing the elevator doors and willing them to open and suck me out whole.

Gavin *liked me*, liked me. And that was *not* okay.

Stupid impulse control.

Wordless, Gavin stood too, just before the elevator reached the second floor. Two floors to go. Then this would all be behind me. For good.

Something tickled my back as Gavin moved in close, reaching under my shirt, along my spine. I felt the clasp of my bra being undone and hanging open. Regardless of my regret, I couldn't help but grin at that. Damn, he was stealthy. How had he done that without my knowledge?

Quickly, I redid the clasp and lifted my head, just in time for the doors to open. But instead of being able to run, like I'd planned, we came face-to-face with my supervisor and three other nurses.

"Um…hi, all." I cleared my throat and tried taming my hair. "We, uh, had a bit of an elevator malfunction." I jerked my thumb back, cringing, because really, what else was I supposed to say?

Gavin moved even closer to my back, his hands settling along the sides of my waist, while his very large erection poked the top of my ass. I shivered, and my stupid, ridiculous lady parts tickled in betrayal too. *Not good, Kenna. Not good at all.*

I stepped out of his hold and stared at the floor, heat filling my face.

A nightmare—that's what this was. A *sexual* nightmare, to be more specific.

"McKenna." His dark voice had my skin prickling with desire and panic.

Ignoring him, I smiled at Emma, the curves-for-miles nurse who always had my back, while my supervisor—a huge flirt named Bonnie—reached for Gavin's arm.

"Are you all right, sir?" Bonnie batted her lashes, tugging him out into the hall. His stare veered back to mine, urging me to come with him. The vulnerable expression made my heart skip a beat.

More than anything, I *did* want to go with him, but I shook my head, knowing it was wrong, and turned pleading eyes toward Emma. Like the heroine she was, she pushed around the others and stepped into the elevator next to me. She stared back and forth between *him* and me before she nodded in understanding and said, "I've got you, babe." Then she tapped a button to shut the elevator doors, blocking my view of the man I'd *almost* wanted to break my rules for.

"It smells like sex in here." Emma flung her long, red braid over her shoulder and tugged at the end.

"W-we didn't..." My lips parted, embarrassment rendering me speechless for once. Though if we'd been given another ten minutes, I'm pretty sure that *not*-happening sex totally *would've* happened. Or at least a dry-humping orgasm.

"I was teasing." She grinned, her hazel eyes raking over me. "Though you are looking pretty flushed right now."

I exhaled, willing my body to cool. "Can you hide me for a little while?"

"No problem, sweetie." Emma was new at Carinthia

Medical Center—twenty-five and quite possibly the smartest woman I'd ever known. She should've been a doctor, but she'd been divorced by one instead. Married at nineteen; cheated on and divorced by twenty-two. Yet she was ten times stronger than I was, despite being two years younger. She was also my savior when Addie was too busy with her man for me.

"Thank you." I squeezed her hand and blew out a breath.

The reality of the last half hour hit me square in the chest.

Good God. What had I just done? Gavin was the former marine with…PTSD? I didn't remember exactly what Addie had said about him, other than that I should steer clear because he was too fragile to be messed around with.

Secretly, though, I'd held him at hero stature for a long while. Mainly because he'd practically carried my drunken ass out of O'Paddy's bar eight months back when I'd overindulged due to Paul—my ex who'd not only cheated on me, but also destroyed my trust in men.

Gavin, whose ass was so perfect I could still see the image of it as I'd seen it through his living-room window while he ran on his treadmill. Totally by accident, of course. I wasn't *that* creepy.

Seriously though… Who ran half-naked on a treadmill with their curtains wide open for the world to see?

"Penis…" I sighed to myself, forgetting I wasn't alone.

"Penis?" Emma jerked her head back, a smug look on her face.

"Long story." I waved her off.

Again, I reminded myself that Gavin became

off-limits the second my best friend decided his best friend was her forever. She knew what I was like—the term *man-eater* was an adequate description. And Gavin? Well, he needed someone stable and good—a partner in all things in life. He was a forever kind of guy, and I was…not that.

At least, not anymore.

CHAPTER 3

Gavin

"But it's Lee-Lee's last night of work. You've gotta go, man. Support her." Max sat next to me on the couch in my living room, laying the guilt trip on thick.

"The last time I tried *supporting her*, I got punched in the face and foamed by a fire extinguisher." I looked down at the floor, a cold beer in my hands as my best friend and neighbor rambled about my lack of a decent excuse. Going to that scuzz-bar where she worked and dealing with a bunch of scuzz-people was not my idea of a good time. "And I'm tired."

"Aww, poor baby Gavvy. Sitting on the couch all day took it outta you, didn't it?" Max noogied my hair like the asshole he was. I knew he meant well by trying to get me out of the house, but I wasn't in the mood. Not tonight.

I shoved him away and leaned forward to set my beer on the coffee table. "I'm not going."

He stood, pointing his finger down at me. "Ten bucks and a hot blond says you are."

"What're you talking about?" I leaned against my couch cushions, arms spread along the back.

"McKenna. She's coming too. I know damn well you've still got a hard-on for her."

Schooling my features was impossible since Max knew about the elevator situation. The last time I'd gotten drunk, I'd told him all about it. That's also the night he admitted to having a thing for the little sister of our other best friend, Collin. I didn't think Max would go there though. The bro code said sisters were off-limits. But he tended to get what he wanted when he wanted it, even when it wasn't right. He and Collin both did, actually.

Then there was me, the guy who didn't ask for anything more than what he desperately needed. "So?" I asked.

"*So?*" Max shook his head. "Are you kidding me, man? Now's your chance to tell her how you feel."

I stood from the couch and walked over to the sliding glass doors that led to the big wooden porch connecting my duplex and the one Max shared with Collin. The sky was black, like my head space since those elevator doors separated Kenna and me two weeks ago. Obviously, what we'd done in that elevator meant nothing to her.

She hadn't tried to contact me since that day. Sure, the phone worked both ways, but I wasn't a chaser. No matter how badly I wanted something, I never went after it. Fear of rejection stuck with a person, no matter how old they got.

I shouldn't have been as surprised as I was. That's the thing. According to Addie, Kenna was the female version of the man standing in front of me. She didn't do relationships, and she didn't sleep with the same man twice. Nothing wrong with that. Hell, I loved a woman who took control of her sexuality. It just wasn't for me.

Still, the stupid part of me thought that she might be different with me. The way her body responded to mine, the way she ran her fingers over my face and through my hair...

I pinched my eyes shut at the memory, needing a hell of a lot more beer to get me through this night.

"Not really in the mood to be around people, Maxwell."

"Are you *ever* gonna be in the mood to be around people again? Doubtful."

My nostrils flared as I inhaled. I loved the guy, but he stepped on my toes harder than anybody else. Collin at least knew when to lay off, but not Max. The pushy bastard wasn't satisfied until he got his way.

"Probably not." I shrugged, grabbed the remote off the coffee table, and sat back again. "Besides, Kenna wanted nothing to do with me then, so what the hell makes you think she'll want me now?"

"Jeez, man, you need to quit being a baby. The girl is a runner. Likes to play with her food, remember? Who says you can't enjoy being the meal for once? That's all I'm suggesting."

He scooped my beer off the table and walked it to the kitchen. I watched as he dumped the liquid into the sink and then tossed the bottle in the garbage.

"That was my last beer." I glared at him.

He smirked at me through the breakfast nook. "And guess where there's an endless supply?"

"The liquor store," I grunted, kicking up my feet as a knock sounded on the door.

"That's probably Colly." Max rubbed his hands together like a kid as he ran through my living room to the door. "He'll get your ass going."

Lip curled, I turned my attention back to the Cubs game. I didn't need to deal with this tonight. Or any other night.

"Hey." Collin's voice echoed through the half-empty room. The only things of merit I had in this place were my couch, my bed, a dresser, the TV, a desk, and my coffee table. Simple. It's how I liked to keep my life.

I looked up, spying the little thing squirming in his big arms. The bitterness inside me melted at the view of Collin's daughter—my pseudo-niece.

"Avvy," she squealed.

I grinned, secretly loving how she'd said my name before anyone else's. I wasn't sure if I'd ever be a dad, mainly because I knew I wouldn't be good at it. The idea of having a kid rely on me all the time was some seriously scary shit. Plus, there were diapers, and all the crying, and their lack of communication… I didn't deal with it well. Hell, most days I could barely take care of myself. Still, the idea of being a father didn't seem as crazy as it used to.

"Hey, baby girl." I waved, and Collin set her on the floor. She raced to the couch and crawled onto my lap. Her tiny arms went around my neck, and I held her close, finally comfortable holding her now that she was mobile. She smelled like baby lotion, Collin's aftershave, and Addie's perfume. A combination that reminded me of family.

Collin sat on the coffee table and frowned. "I'm about ready to take her to my parents' house. She wanted to stop by and see you first." He leaned over to tug on her tiny, curly pigtails—Addie's work, no doubt.

I nodded and kissed the top of her head, only for her to pull back and cup my cheeks with her hands. She jabbered something I couldn't understand, eyes like her dad's, wide and filled with happiness. My heart twisted in my chest at the view. Something about this girl always melted me like butter.

"Max says you don't want to go," Collin said, kicking his feet out in front of him.

I shrugged. "I'm tired."

"You're always tired, Gav." Max sat down next to me again and poked Chloe in the stomach. She giggled, and all three of us smiled, the sound an instant mood-lifter.

"It's just one night. We all want you there for Lia's sake. Something is up with her, and I need you guys' help to figure it out." Collin let out a tired sigh.

On cue, Max cleared his throat and stood, his eyes flashing to the back of Collin's head, then widening with guilt when they met mine. I frowned. If I didn't know better, I'd think *he* was the reason Lia had gotten all weird lately.

"Not happening. Tell her I said hi though," I said.

"Fine. Beaner, let's roll. Uncle Gavin's got brooding to do." Max reached for Chloe, but she shook her head and tugged me closer. Her cheek was on my shoulder, and her fingers tickled my neck.

I flipped Max off from over Chloe's shoulder.

Collin scowled at me, like always. I loved the guy, but he and I had some underlying issues. He used to think I wanted Addie—which I did. But it'd been brief and passed the second I realized how serious the two of them were. Still, Collin had trouble trusting. I did too, another reason why relationships weren't my strong suit. Deep down, though, I wanted what he had with Addison.

"Come on, Chloe." This time Collin reached for his daughter, and she bolted from my lap, only to latch her arms around his neck. He smiled as he patted her back.

"Beaner, I'm hurt," Max piped in. "You go to your daddy, stick to Uncle Gavvy like glue, but you ignore me?" He made a goofy face at her, and she instantly reached for him, a sucker for us all.

The kid didn't stand a chance growing up with three weirdos like us.

When they reached the door, Collin was the first to turn my way. "Tomorrow. We can all hang out. Go to O'Paddy's or something. Maybe watch the Cubs next preseason game together. How's that—"

"Maxwell, Collin, good to see you, boys."

I froze at the sound of McKenna's voice from the porch. Collin might've said *goodbye*, or *see you later*, but my ears were buzzing with the sound of *her* voice.

"You gonna save me a dance tonight, Maxwell?" she asked.

I balled my hands into fists.

"Now, Kenna. You know you're too good for me." Max—always the ladies' man.

She giggled, then said something under her breath that I couldn't hear. But it didn't matter. My feelings and emotions were changing the longer she stood outside my door. Something inside me flashed like lighting striking through my body.

Damn. I knew exactly what I wanted to do, even if it

was the last thing I needed. But if I didn't do it, I'd never be able to get over her.

A minute later, Max poked his head back into my apartment, giving me the all clear.

"I'm in," I said.

His eyebrows rose in question, while a half smile quirked his lips.

Ignoring his knowing look, I finished with, "I'm gonna take a shower. I'll be ready in fifteen."

Fuck it. It was time to be McKenna Brewer's food.

CHAPTER 4

McKenna

FIVE SHOTS—THAT'S WHAT IT TOOK FOR ME TO LOSE MY inhibitions. Now I was on the dance floor, grinding all over the hottie known as Maxwell Martinez—a safe bet. A safe guy. The type of man I wouldn't need to grow attached to because I knew he wouldn't grow attached to me. In a way, Max was a masculine version of the person I'd grown to be. Free to find and screw whomever we wanted. No worries about commitment.

Still, any chance I could get, I found myself glancing at the angry beast of a man called Gavin. I hadn't known he'd be here. The guy never went anywhere public. Or maybe I'd hoped he'd show, and *that's* why I agreed to come out tonight.

Truth be told, I wanted to see him again. See if what had happened in that elevator was a fluke. It scared me that I hadn't been able to stop thinking about him since that day, get the image of those eyes out my head, the feel and taste of his tongue from my mouth. He was incredibly addicting after a single kissing rendezvous.

"So, who're you trying to make jealous?" Max leaned in closer, his hot breath running over my ear as he spoke. Sweat trickled down my spine as we moved to the slow beat of "Pour Some Sugar on Me."

"Nobody. Just needed to get away from that table," I said over the music, glancing again at Gavin, who sat at our table across the room. "All that Addie-Collin lovey stuff makes a girl wanna vomit." The sight of Gavin, on the other hand? Yeah, vomiting was the last thing on my mind.

He sat with his chin against his chest, eyes on me as they had been all night. I licked my lips, my face hot, yet I couldn't look away. His long hair hung over his cheeks, and the muscles of his upper arms pulled against his T-shirt sleeves as he folded his arms. And that beard… Sweet Jesus, it'd grown even longer in two weeks.

Now, more than ever, I wondered how it might feel between my thighs.

I wasn't trying to make him jealous. I was trying to show him that what had happened between us meant nothing. More so, I was trying to prove that to *myself*.

After clearing my throat, I focused on Lia, Collin's little sister. "Lia looks happy. I'm not sure she's ever looked less than moody before." I motioned toward her with my chin as she set down—surprise, surprise—more shots on our table.

"She's far from moody," Max said, loosening his hold on me.

I smirked at Max, whose eyes were fully locked on our subject. "Ah, it's like that now, is it?"

"Like what?" he asked, still distracted as he ogled Lia.

"You and her."

His mouth opened then closed when he looked at me again, the words seemingly stuck in his throat. Before I could call him out on what was so obvious, Lia was right there with us, ramming into his shoulder with a force that was in no way accidental.

"Lia!" Max called after her. She'd bolted down a dark hall, hands balled into fists at her sides. He pulled away and took off after her, leaving me alone on the dance floor.

I winced, wondering if she was pissed about the two of us dancing. The guy was clearly in love with her. Anyone with eyes could see it. The next time I saw her, I'd have to clarify that Maxwell and I were strictly friends who liked to flirt. That's all.

Head high, I wandered around a cowboy and his girl who had been dancing next to us, nodding as he tipped his hat at me. This wasn't just a place for country folk, but a melting pot for every breed of human. Bikers, punk rockers, the occasional hippie or college group... You name it, this tiny bar had it.

As I made my way from the dance floor, I looked toward the bar, wondering if I'd be better off sitting there than at the table. It's not like Addie was sober enough to have a conversation with me. And neither of the guys sitting there seemed to even like me.

I could leave, sure, but taking an Uber or riding in a taxi always freaked me out when I did it alone— especially after indulging like I'd done tonight. Not only that, but I'd been hoping to find a little action. Something to curb the itch that had only intensified in the two weeks since Gavin and that damn elevator.

Decision made, I headed toward the bar, picking the seat next to some guy who looked around the same age as my little sister, Hanna. My guess was that he was around twenty-two. Freshly graduated from college maybe? A businessman with that blazer, but an innocent smile that lit up his face. Fresh. Young. Eager. Another type that would likely love to give me the one night I needed.

"Hiya." I purposely rubbed my leg against his, leaving it there.

Right away he sized me up, his eyes flashing longer than necessary at my cleavage. The girls behaved properly in my push-up bra, but the rush I normally felt from a good ole perusal wasn't hitting me like it usually did.

Guess I needed another drink.

I ordered a vodka lemonade, heavy on the vodka. The guy next to me pushed my hand away when I tried to pay—a sure sign he'd noticed me noticing him.

"What's your name?" I asked, running the tip of my sandal over his ankle. Forward was my middle name, and this guy looked like he needed a little help with the let's-get-laid project I was trying to initiate.

His smile grew wider, showing me a perfect set of Mommy-and-Daddy-bought teeth. I looked down at his pants, expecting slacks to match his blazer, and found a pair of distressed jeans instead. He was vulnerable but willing. My favorite type.

"I'm Bryce."

I smiled and held my hand out to shake his. He took it and brought it to his lips, but my shoulders fell when the tingle didn't spark further than the back of my hand.

Praying I was just slow to the game tonight, I continued with my introduction. "I'm McKenna."

"That's a beautiful name for a beautiful woman."

Same line, different day. Still, I had one goal. It started with an *O* and ended with a *gasm*.

"Thank you." I moved in closer, ready to close the deal. "Wanna get out of here?"

His eyes grew wide, but he nodded quickly before he turned to talk to the guys right next to him at the bar. The three of them high-fived while I downed the rest of my drink. Bromances between college guys really got on my nerves.

A few minutes later, I was following him through the bar, only to be stopped short when a warm hand latched onto my upper arm.

"Kenna."

That familiar, rumbly voice made my pulse spike faster than the seduction techniques of the guy's hand I was now holding. The one whose name I couldn't even remember.

I smiled at my hookup and told him to wait for me by the door. He glanced at Gavin but nodded, slapping me on the rear before he went.

Jerk.

"Did he just smack your ass?" Gavin growled, his eyes bloodshot and that long hair sticking to his sweaty face. He looked like a surfer with that wild, windswept hair. One who'd just hit the ocean hard. Yet those eyes—so green and filled with concern—turned my stomach into knots.

"Maybe I wanted him to." I shrugged.

"You're going *home* with that guy?"

"What's it to ya?" I asked, suddenly dizzy. I wasn't one hundred percent sure if it was his proximity making my head spin or the alcohol. Either way, I did know one thing: a single sentence from his mouth paired with the hint of jealousy in his eyes, and I was an instant ball of putty, ready to be molded by his hands.

Eyes lit with sudden fire, Gavin backed me up against a nearby wall. With his hands at his sides, his body went flush with mine. I gasped as his erection pressed hard against my stomach. "There's no point in going home with a boy when you can go home with a *man*."

My eyebrows shot up, and I couldn't help but grin. At the same time, my body began to sway, leaning into his even more. "Are *you* a man, Gavin?" I bit my lip.

Something flickered in his eyes. Fear? Vulnerability? I couldn't tell. Still, he searched my face, looking for something that almost had me running, until Blazer Boy Bryce stepped back into the picture.

"What's up? You ready?" Ignoring Gavin, the guy focused solely on me.

Against me, Gavin's body grew stiff, but I managed to step around him. "Change of plans." I shrugged one shoulder. My eyes grew heavier by the second, but my heart still raced in my chest. "I've found someone else for the night." I reached back and pulled Gavin's hand in mine, squeezing. "Sorry," I added for good measure.

"Whatever." The innocence I thought I'd seen earlier in this college boy's eyes switched to something ugly. Menacing. His lips curled. "Slut."

Before I could think twice, I slapped my hand against his cheek. He stumbled back and fell on his ass. *Wimp.* "Watch your damn mouth, Dick for Brains."

Gavin yanked me back toward the table. "This bar," he mumbled. "Fucking fights…"

I had no clue what he meant—nor did I care. Stupid, slut-shaming assholes would be the death of me.

Palm throbbing from the hit, I tucked my hand against my side, glancing back at the guy as he stood, now surrounded by his friends. I flipped him off before stepping closer to Gavin's side.

With one hand splayed across the center of my spine, Gavin bent over Collin and tugged at the collar of his shirt. "We gotta go."

Collin leaned back, bringing Addie with him. "What happened?" My best friend's head hung low for a second until she lurched forward over Collin's lap and puked all over the floor.

My eyes widened, but not at the puke all over Collin's lap. "Oh, hell." Blazer Boy Bryce and his buddies were on the prowl, likely looking for me.

Side by side, they skirted the edge of the dance floor like some nineties boy band. If I hadn't been suddenly scared to death, I'd have laughed. Thankfully, they didn't see us, but it wouldn't take them long if we didn't hide—or all run away together.

"Um, Collin?" I poked his bicep, holding my breath to avoid smelling Addie's vomit.

"*What?*" he snapped, pulling his girlfriend close as Gavin dropped a bunch of napkins on his lap. Collin tied Addie's hair up into a ponytail and wiped her mouth with one of the napkins. Whether I was anti-relationship or not, I had to admit that puke-wiping boyfriends were incredibly sweet.

"Um, so, I kind of smacked a guy. Now he and his friends are on their way over here."

Collin glared at me. "You're a damn nurse, Kenna. Why the fuck are you going around smacking people?"

Gavin jumped in. "It was either she smacked the fucker, or I would've beat him down completely."

A thrill shot through me at the thought of Gavin protecting my honor.

"Besides that, I'm only a nurse on the days I work." I grinned. Or tried to. My bullshit meter was a little off tonight.

Gavin moved in front of me, drawing away Collin's glare. "We need to go. Now."

Collin sighed, gaze locked on Addie's face as he said, "I know." He stroked her hair out of her eyes, his touch soft, his tone gentled. "Stay right here, you two. I've gotta go get Max." Then he lifted my best friend and set her in the booth, urging me to sit across from her. Gavin shifted in next to me seconds later, his thigh brushing against mine.

When Collin moved to walk away, Addie reached for him, only to fall face-first into the booth, passed out. I snorted at the view, which earned me another evil eye from Collin. I hadn't seen my best friend this drunk in... well, ever. It was definitely funny.

"Goddamn bar," Gavin grumbled, lowering his hands to his lap. His pinkie finger grazed my bare skin in the process. I froze at the sensation, suddenly remembering the way he had pinned me against the wall by the bar.

Holy hell, did I want this man.

The question was, did he want me?

I hadn't bothered to connect with him after the elevator, anxiety and fear of Addie my main reasons for keeping away. But being here with him tonight felt like fate. The unavoidable kind that there was no escaping.

Slowly, I lifted my head and studied his brooding profile. Eyes drawn together, lips pursed, Gavin looked like he was ready to commit murder. It was the sexiest thing I'd ever seen. I'm not sure what that said about me as a woman, but I didn't care.

As though sensing my stare, Gavin turned to me. One bat of his thick lashes, and all the rage he'd been carrying slipped from view. Instead, his eyes filled with that vulnerability I suddenly craved from him, accompanied by heat, curiosity, and maybe a little fear.

Gavin had every right to be wary of me. I wasn't the type of woman he needed. He was broken, and I hated to fix things. *But* I could give him what he wanted sexually, if he'd be open to it. Deciding to take a chance, I moved in closer, thanking God for the fact that Addison was too out of it to notice.

He glanced at my mouth, waiting a beat before he lifted his hand, taking me completely by surprise. "May I?" He motioned to my ear, a total gentleman.

I nodded, having no idea what he planned to do until I felt his fingers graze the top of my cheek. Carefully, as though I were made of glass, he tucked a lock of my hair behind my ear, watching the movement, eyes laced with concentration, full bottom lip tugged between his teeth. The sensation sent goose bumps shooting up and down my arms.

"Cold?" He smiled, almost teasing. A different sort of Gavin than I'd come to know. Relaxed and nothing like the man I'd been trapped in an elevator with. I shook my head, my lips parting, so far from cold that I couldn't even get the words out.

"Hmm." He lowered his hand to my neck, trailing a

line from my ear, down farther, until his fingers grazed the V of my shirt. "This okay?"

I nodded and arched into his touch, bravery taking hold as I leaned closer. "I wanna go home with you tonight."

He sat for a moment, entranced, stoic. My vision was a little blurry, but I was well aware of the heat in his eyes, aware of what I was asking.

I was very ready for everything those green eyes promised.

"Okay." He leaned closer.

And then I kissed him again.

CHAPTER

Gavin

SOMETHING SOFT AND WARM SNUGGLED AGAINST MY SIDE. I didn't want to open my eyes, too scared it was all a dream. But then I yawned, and I felt it move. My cock jerked in awareness too, just in time for my eyes to shoot open.

Oh hell. Not a dream. Not. A dream. At all.

A leg was thrown over my waist. Smooth, completely naked flesh was pressed against my thigh. McKenna sighed, and her hot breath tickled my skin, reminding me of the way she'd first responded to my touch in the back seat of that cab.

After we left the bar, we had the taxi driver take us to a gas station. There we got a bottle of peach schnapps and secretly drank it in the back seat like a couple of teenagers, only for her to crawl on my lap and ride me through my jeans. Just the thought of that had me growing harder and made me want her all over again.

"Mmm, what time is it?" she mumbled, rocking her hips against my leg.

I reached down, tempted to begin a repeat of the night before. "It's noon."

She flew up and out of my hold, only to lean back against the headboard. Wide blue eyes scanned the room, terrified, before they landed on me. "Shit."

I frowned. That wasn't the reaction I'd been hoping for. "What is it?"

Her wild hair fell over her nose, and when she huffed, bits and pieces flew everywhere. Before I could stop myself, I sat up too, reaching to brush the blond strands away. God, she was beautiful. Why the hell had I waited so long to work up the courage to do this with her?

"I-I gotta go."

"Why?" I frowned. "It's Sunday."

"Um…" She looked around the room until she spotted some of her clothes, our empty bottle of schnapps right there in the middle of it all. Covering her breasts with one arm, she jumped out of bed, that ass of hers on display as she bent over to grab her clothes off the floor.

"Want to grab breakfast? I can take you home afterward." I stretched out my arms, a rare smile on my face. Last night, I'd used muscles that had been dormant for a long time. Now all I wanted to do was use them again.

She shook her head, still not looking at me. "No. Addie, sh-she'll take me home."

"I doubt she's in any shape to go anywhere." Nerves long gone, I stood too, moving to stand behind her. She'd pulled up her skirt and panties, but her bra and shirt were still missing.

Slowly, carefully, I settled my hands on her naked

waist and nuzzled my nose against her neck. She smelled like flowers and my cologne, a combination I could get used to.

"Gavin, I don't think…"

I froze, my lips hovering over her pulse. *Shit.* I knew that voice. I also knew what the rest of her sentence was probably going to be. *This will work.*

"Please, don't." Desperation was suddenly my middle name. Max would have my ass, but I couldn't let this go. Not yet. "Spend the afternoon with me. I'll make us a late breakfast. Or I can take you out for lunch. Either one is fine by me."

I tried to swallow the lump in my throat. After an amazing night together, she was ready to bolt?

She sighed, the sound like a death sentence to my heart. If she walked away, I wouldn't chase her. Food. I'd been her motherfucking meal for the night. That was all. But did that keep me from trying?

"Breakfast, huh?"

"Just breakfast." I turned her around to face me, needing to see her eyes. They always managed to tell me everything her words didn't. I tipped her chin up with a finger, smiling…until I saw the emptiness in her stare. *Shit.* This was worse than I'd originally thought.

"Okay. Breakfast." With a small nod, she patted me on the chest and turned to grab the rest of her clothes from the floor.

My sex life was scattered and infrequent, my experience with woman almost null and void. Before I left for boot camp, I'd had lots of opportunities, but one-night stands had never been my thing. What I did know, without a doubt, was that a friendly pat on the chest couldn't be a clearer sign. Kenna wasn't interested in anything beyond last night.

"Bathroom?" She held her clothes to her chest, a weak smile on her lips. She was uncomfortable, nothing like I'd thought she'd be. Which had me regretting every moment we'd spent together, no matter how amazing it was.

I cleared my throat. "Down the hall to the right."

"Thanks." She avoided my eyes as she moved around me, putting a good foot between us in the process.

My gut tightened once she was gone, and I let go of a heavy breath, refusing to think the worst. To keep myself focused, I went to the kitchen, fumbling with the coffee.

Five minutes passed, according to the clock on my microwave, but she still hadn't finished. I frowned, already done with my first cup of coffee. Something itched at me, telling me to go check on her. With her cup of coffee in hand, I made my way to the bathroom. The door was open, but when I looked inside, she wasn't there. Thinking she'd gone back to my room, I swung a left, finding the window wide open.

The one thing left behind? A torn piece of leather, maybe from a boot.

My shoulders fell as I walked over to look outside, the disappointment in my gut growing tighter. I set the mug aside and leaned out the window, my hands on the sill. I looked toward the street, my skin grazing over the ripped material still stuck in the window frame. Dark, muddy footprints led away from where she'd obviously jumped out, continuing down the sidewalk until they were out of sight.

Christ. The girl had pulled a Cinderella on me.

CHAPTER 6

McKenna

FOR THE FIRST TIME IN ALL THE YEARS ADDISON AND I HAD been friends, I'd been lying to her.

Normally, we had a chick-flick night with ice cream and wine every Friday while Collin worked. But for the past three weeks, I'd told her I was on night shift at the hospital, claiming that someone was out on maternity leave and I'd been covering for her.

The real problem was that I was playing Addie—and probably myself—by doing anything and everything imaginable to avoid her next-door neighbor, aka the guy I was somehow developing real feelings for. Feelings that Prick-Head Paul was supposed to have eliminated in me for good.

But tonight, exactly one month since Gavin and I had hooked up, I was totally going to surprise her—and prove to myself that the avoidance game had gone on long enough.

Only her new Civic sat in the driveway, thankfully.

That meant she was home alone. All I had to do was sneak to the front door, avoid peeking into her neighbor's window to see if he was running on his treadmill, and then *boom*, things could return to normal.

With a couple of nineties rom-coms tucked inside my purse, and a fresh carton of Ben & Jerry's in a bag hanging off my forearm, I was determined to make up for lost time.

I knocked twice, like always. Once to make my presence known, and the next to make sure Max wasn't in there screwing one of his many flavors—though I didn't see his car. Unlike every other time I'd stopped by, nobody answered…at least at first. But then I heard it—a grunt, followed by "Fuck me" and then "I'm coming, hold on."

"Oh God." I took a step back, looking over my shoulder toward the driveway, more than ready to run.

No, no, *no*. I knew that voice.

There was no time to escape, because a second later he was there. And quite frankly, my legs weren't capable of moving. Because the moment that door whipped open and I saw him standing there, I was screwed with a capital *S*.

"McKenna…" He said my name on an exhale, while his hypnotic green eyes raked over me in one long, agonizing swoop. His cheeks grew bright red—making him look bashful and adorable, not a tough guy like his friends tried to be. When he bowed his head, I took a second to look him over too, frowning when I noted a clump of black, sticky, gooey stuff clinging to the ends of his lashes and a smearing of something shiny and red on the corners of his lips and clinging to his beard.

"H-hi." I cleared my throat, attempting to remember why I was there in the first place. His intensity tended to make me forget pretty much everything.

"What are you doing here?" He folded his arms over his massive chest. The same chest I'd touched... The same chest I'd stroked, nibbled, kissed...

I blinked. "W-where's Addie?"

He frowned and that beard of his shifted, conforming with the movements of his jaw. "Grocery store. She asked me to watch Chloe for half an hour."

"*You?* Watch Chloe?"

"Yeah. Me." His eyebrows drew together as he propped one hand against the doorframe, a dare in his words that said *Challenge me, and you will lose.*

I highly doubted this man could ever beat me in a match of wits. Regardless, he had me mesmerized, as always. His hotness, his coyness, the vulnerability I knew he embodied... *Total. Human. Catnip.*

I swallowed, watching his forearm flex. Gavin was humongous in every sense of the word. I might have been a little tipsy when we had sex, but the delicious soreness between my legs the next morning proved that big was worth it.

My face grew hot at the memory, my mouth opening and closing like a dunce's. Who was I? Where was I? And why the hell did I have an unexplainable urge to drop to my knees before him?

Because you like him.

I frowned and held my chin high. "Mind if I come in and make sure you didn't tie the tyke up?" Without waiting for a response, I ducked under his outstretched arm, holding my breath as I did. Unfortunately, the air in my lungs did little to block the heavenly, masculine smell he emitted. Spice, pine, soap… The combination made my lady parts tingle and my thoughts spin in remembrance.

I didn't do men for more than a night. Not anymore. Not since Penis-Head Paul. So, what was my issue? One and done, that's the way it was supposed to be. Not third time's a charm, damn it.

Ignoring his *are you kidding me* expression, I headed into the living room, finding the coffee table filled with all things princess. Crowns, feather boas, fake earrings, and… "Is that makeup?"

He cleared his throat. "Yeah, um, give me a second, would ya?"

I grinned at him, watching as he bowed his head— this time rubbing at the clingy black goo on his eyes and, yes, the red lipstick on his beard.

Oh. My. God.

He'd let the kid put it on him?

Be still, my beating heart.

"Sure. Take your time." My lips twitched as I watched him rush down the hall. The bathroom door shut a second later, followed by some seriously explicit content as the water began to run. I giggled, knowing exactly what he was doing. Washing it off.

Something tugged on the leg of my pants, forcing me to look down. I couldn't help but smile wider when I found the little lady who had enamored my bestie—and maybe even myself—standing at my feet.

Chloe was dressed in jammies, yet she wore a fancy crown.

"Hey, kiddo." I crouched in front of her, touching her shoulder. "Are you having fun with Uncle Gavin?"

She nodded wildly, her eyes bright and blue like her daddy's. She pressed her tiny hands over her mouth a second later and giggled, looking over my shoulder. I stood and turned, finding Gavin shirtless and using his T-shirt to dry his face, the abs of that gloriously flat stomach making my throat run dry.

My knees grew weak at the image, and I plopped onto the edge of the chair, trying to curb the shaking in my hands. Jesus, I needed to get it together.

"Beaner. Grab your pretty princess stuff and put it back in the bag before Addie gets home, okay? Remember our secret? No telling her about the makeup."

Her head bounced up and down and she hauled the stuff into her arms.

With my bottom lip pulled between my teeth, I watched him sit on the coffee table in front of her, holding out the bag. As a team, they piled up all of the stuff and stowed it inside. Seconds later, Chloe ran down the hall, her feet pattering against the floor.

I looked at his lap, briefly scanning his long legs tucked under a pair of mesh basketball shorts. They came to just above the knee and were navy blue, the letters *USMC* written along the edge. "You wanna sit on my lap?"

"Um…" *Sweet Jesus, yes! Yes, please!*

"You keep staring at my shorts."

"Oh, uh, no. I was just…" I looked away and nibbled harder on my lip, the temptation far too…tempting. If I sat on his lap, I might not be able to get off so easily this time. Not just in the sexual sense—though Gavin was very skilled at making a lady come—but in the emotional sense too. Because, well, I wasn't as strong as I wanted to be, and being in his arms was something

I'd vowed not to do again. Mainly because I'd liked it so much.

"I'll pass."

"Hmm." He nodded, elbows on his knees, hands dangling out front.

Surprisingly, Gavin seemed unaffected by my presence now that he'd cleaned up. Bored, almost. And as much as I didn't want to admit it, that nonchalance sent my ego spiraling into a hole. The guy was far more immune to my charms than I'd thought he'd be, which bothered me more than I wanted it to. If anything, he was acting like our one-night stand had never happened. Which was weird. Because everything I'd come to know about this guy from Addison was that he was all-or-nothing about life relationships—friends, family, and lovers.

Oh…and he was picky, which could've been why he was acting unbothered by my presence. Maybe he wasn't as taken with me as I'd thought.

I chewed on my thumbnail, trying to keep myself in check, but a crash sounded behind me, breaking my thoughts. I'd never been more excited about a Chloe act of trouble in my life.

"Beaner, no." Gavin jumped up from the couch and grabbed the little nugget as she tried to climb into her high chair. Somehow or another, she'd snuck back into the room. Showed just how *in*attentive I was to kids.

"You're gonna get hurt, kid." Gavin tucked her against his side, and she all but melted against his chest. With a grin on her face, she met my gaze from across the room.

I narrowed my eyes. Little stinker did that on purpose. The girl was playing him to a T…and because of it, I'd never adored her more. Apparently, she was going to take after her pseudo-auntie Kenna after all.

From the back, I watched as Gavin's shoulders and muscles moved, secretly thanking all the gods in the world for the fact that he hadn't bothered to put on a shirt yet. With practiced ease, he picked Chloe's high-chair tray off the floor with one arm and set her inside with the other. He cursed under his breath as he fumbled with the buckle.

I sat on the armrest of the chair, watching. "She's not gonna fall out once you put the tray on. I wouldn't bother with that."

He froze. "It's safer to keep her buckled."

"It's not *necessary*." I stood and moved to the chair across from them. "Once you get the tray on, she's stuck. Ask Addie and Collin. They do it all the time."

"You're kidding, right? The *nurse* is telling me I shouldn't care about safety?"

"I do care about safety. I'm just saying the buckle isn't entirely necessary if you are right there with her." I pulled my ice cream from the bag, then popped the lid off my container. No thoughts to my madness, not caring if he saw my dirty little habits either, I dug two fingers into the mass of chocolate and coffee bean good-ness. I shoved the ice cream–coated digits between my lips and moaned at that first bite.

"You're like a damn porn star with that stuff."

I blinked, meeting his heavy stare. "This is nothing, trust me."

Chloe babbled loudly, yanking his attention away. "What is it, kiddo?" he asked as she tossed a handful of crackers across the room. The rainbow Goldfish crunched against the wall and rained down the plaster like a waterfall. Seconds after that, her hands were in the air, reaching for me—or, more so, my half-hidden B&J's.

I grinned. "Girl's got my taste buds."

"You're not related." Gavin frowned, scooping out another handful of crackers, only for her to toss them against the wall again. He shut his eyes, clearly frustrated. He was as good with kids as I was, it would seem. Which was not good at all. Still, when a tot tossed crackers across the room, that usually meant she didn't want them. Common knowledge.

"So? I'm a woman, and she's a girl. Our taste buds are inevitably going to share some similarities, right?"

Standing, I moved around the table and to the left of her high chair. Digging my pinkie into the chocolate portion of my B&J's, I pressed it to her mouth. She opened right up, smacking her lips and clapping when she was done.

"I sure as hell hope my niece doesn't have your *cravings*." He shook his head.

I snorted out a laugh. Who would've thought that broody-pants Gavin St. James had an actual sense of humor?

He grumbled something else under his breath and took Chloe out of her chair once she was done snacking on my ice cream. She clung to his neck with one arm and tucked a thumb in her mouth, her signature move.

He moved around me and went back into the living room, only to set her in a little chair with light-up buttons that played music. She bounced her legs, waiting as he scoured Netflix. Once he'd stopped on some show with a giant, talking bunny, he kissed her on the forehead and went back into the dining room to clean up the Goldfish mess. While he was occupied, I grabbed my ice cream and headed into the kitchen to put it in the freezer.

I hustled back into the living room, for some reason afraid to leave him alone with the kiddo, even though he seemed to have things under control.

Chloe's gaze was still glued to the TV when I rounded the corner, but Gavin was nowhere in sight. Part of me wondered if I should hang with her, but another part was curious to find out where Mr. Beastly had wandered off to. Because I didn't claim to have perfect pseudo-parenting skills, I went with my gut and followed *him* instead.

My curiosity got the best of me as I meandered down the hall. I stopped to look up at the pictures on the wall, finding some of Gavin and the guys, along with Chloe, or Chloe and Addie, or Chloe and Collin. I trailed my finger over one particular picture. A blond lady with Chloe's smile and round nose. It was her biological mother, Amy, the one who'd died a few months after Chloe was born while the guys were finishing their second tour of duty in the marines.

What little I knew of her was that she was a good person who loved her daughter to pieces, unlike my own mother. That was yet another reason why babies were not welcome in my uterus. No way would I subject a kid to my ability to screw up like she had.

"I only met her once."

I jumped at the sound of Gavin's voice, but I didn't take my eyes off Amy's picture. In her arms sat a tiny bundle of pink. Chloe Bean—or Beaner, as Gavin, Collin, and Max affectionately called her. Addie was determined to remind Chloe who the woman was, and how much she had loved her.

"She was beautiful." I smiled wistfully.

Gavin leaned against the wall next to me, arms folded over his chest. His body was like a furnace, yet his breath was cool against my cheek as he yawned. He smelled like cinnamon toothpaste, as though he'd just brushed.

An odd sensation ran through me at the thought. Was he planning on kissing me? Is that why he'd brushed his teeth? And could I push him away if he did? Was I sadistic enough to want him to kiss me after I'd worked so hard to avoid him? Hell, my favorite pair of boots was now in the county dump because of how hard I'd fought to run away from him.

Escaping through a window hadn't been one of my finer moments.

"Beaner's lucky she has so many people who love her. I'm glad she's not alone." His voice cracked as he stared at the floor. His feet were bare, yet they looked clean, healthy. Everything about Gavin, other than his long hair and beard, said perfect order. Control.

I looked down at the chipped nail polish on my feet and my stained yoga pants. I was a hot mess of disorganized and disgusting.

"She's very lucky." I cleared my throat, the topic too close to home. No way would I tell him that my family life growing up had been like something out of an unhappily-ever-after Cinderella story. The wicked mother. The absentee father. The only difference was that I got an amazing stepbrother and stepsister out of the deal.

"Collin will always miss Amy, but he loves the hell

out of Addison. They're sickening." Gavin smiled as he said this, longing in his eyes.

My chest warmed at the view and I pressed my hand over my heart, willing the sensation to skedaddle. Clearing my throat, I said, "Personally, I think it's unhealthy to be so attached to someone. You should be your own person. Live your own life. The thought of finding a soul mate goes against human nature." I shrugged. "I try to tell Addie that all the time, but I'm pretty sure it goes in one ear and out the other."

He took a step closer, brows furrowed. "You don't believe in love?"

"Maybe I used to." I looked at the floor and sucked in a cleansing breath. "Believe in it, that is." The topic of love used to make me uncomfortable. But talking to Gavin about it was relatively easy for some reason. "Or rather, I used to believe in the *idea* of love." Yet along the way, the motto *forever is for penguins, not humans* had become my go-to phrase. From there on out, I'd vowed to make myself superficially and temporarily happy instead.

"That's sad."

I frowned. "How so?"

He leaned in closer, his body nearly flush with mine. Desperation filled his gaze as he lowered his head until his lips were mere inches from my mine. "Because sometimes, McKenna, the things we fight against are the things that are best for us."

I shivered and leaned against him. "Gavin…"

As if his proximity hadn't almost brought me to my knees, he shrugged one shoulder and took a couple of steps back, sticking his hands inside the pockets of his low-slung shorts. Because I was a masochistic son of a gun, I quickly zeroed in on his protruding hip bones, wondering what it might be like to touch him there just once more.

I refocused on his mouth, finding a frown pulling down the corners of his lips. It was almost as though he knew what I was thinking, feeling, remembering…

My throat burned in irritation as I swallowed. "I-I'm not fucking you again."

A muscle in his jaw ticked, and his frown turned into a quick, unnerving smirk. "Fine by me. I'm not looking for another fuck-and-run anyway."

I cringed, guilt somersaulting in my stomach. Before I could respond—apologize, even—he took off down the hall toward the living room, shoulders pulled back and head held high. Why the hell did this man have to be different from all the others to me?

What I needed was to remain calm, unpretentious even. Because if Gavin knew how much he affected me, he might think we had a chance together. Which we didn't. I mean…

No. Absolutely not.

"Well, good," I called after him. "I'm glad we settled that. Because I'm a just-friends kind of gal anyway, St. James. Permanence isn't my thing. And now that we've slept together, I think it's best that we, you know, keep our distance." Then why was I chasing him down the hall, trying to make known what he obviously already knew? And why was my traitorous heart skipping as I watched him swoop Chloe into his arms as though he were her prince?

"Fine. Distance. Whatever you want." He nodded at me as he passed, his arm bumping mine.

"Yeah. Distance. Fan-tabulous!" God, why was I being so loud? And why was I yelling it at his back like a six-year-old?

From Chloe's room, he hollered for me. "Hey, *Brewer*? Come give a guy a hand."

My shoulders fell. I'm not sure why they did. Because disappointment was *not* racking my body as I stepped into the room and saw that all he really needed was diaper help.

"I haven't ever…" I motioned toward the changing table, hating how I was worried about my lack of maternal skills in front of him when that had never bothered me before.

"You're serious?" He frowned.

I squirmed under his intense gaze but managed to close the distance between us. "As serious as anyone can be when not wanting to look and sound like a freak."

He urged me forward with his chin, his patience and the fact that he wasn't laughing earning him bonus points. Not that I was keeping score.

"Come on, then. We'll master this together."

Hands flexing at my sides, I watched and learned from a nonexpert who looked, in fact, like an expert. "That doesn't seem too hard," I said.

"It's more time-consuming than anything." He shrugged and hummed something under his breath. "Especially when she's wiggly."

It was strange, changing diapers with a man I'd slept with but never actually had a relationship with. Life was constantly a surprise in the making. Especially when it came to Gavin St. James.

CHAPTER 7

Gavin

THERE WAS SOMETHING ABOUT THE SMELL OF SAWDUST THAT made me forget the thoughts running through my head. And today, I needed all the distraction I could get.

McKenna Brewer was like a fly that wouldn't stop buzzing in my ear. And now that I knew how she felt in my arms, it sucked even more to want someone who didn't want me back. I guess, in a way, it was a blessing that my doc had told me I needed to get a hobby other than rugby. Had she not, I most likely would've been at home, pacing the floors and punching my fists through walls.

During our initial appointment, I'd told my psychiatrist I played intramural rugby.

Her response had been a headshake and a few words about *violent sports* not being the answer. How I needed something to keep me Zen because my job was stressful enough.

About a month later, I saw an ad in the paper for a land auction. The old shack where my uncle—my dad's estranged brother—had lived in Arlo by the Mississippi River. The place where my life first started going to shit. It was up for sale.

That day, I told my psychiatrist about what had happened to me as a kid—the whole story, though she already knew the logistics. She'd nodded and asked me how it made me feel to know that the home was there, but my uncle wasn't. I told her another truth. That I wanted to buy the motherfucking place myself, then gut the insides, leaving just the frame and walls, only to rework it into something good and right. Something I could be proud of and call my own.

That was the day I finally picked my hobby. Also the day I spent my entire savings on a piece of shit run-down shack that'd been haunting me for years.

I didn't have a damn clue how to fix up a house, but buying it, then demolishing that shed where I'd spent so many nights, made me feel as though I had control again. Not to mention something to work toward. Plus, I took to tools and nails easily. Working with my hands and doing something—other than sitting around feeling sorry for myself until I went back to work—was the final step I needed to find myself.

I walked over to the card table I'd set up in the middle of what used to be the kitchen and spread out the blueprints. Two bedrooms, one bath, a kitchen, a porch, and a living room—perfect for when I needed an escape from the duplex. I didn't see myself moving far from Collin, Max, Chloe, and Addie anytime soon, but it was nice to have something to fall back on.

The sun had set a while ago. And according to my cell, I'd missed dinner. There were also three missed calls from Max. The guy needed to know where I was every second of every day lately.

I texted him back, saying I was fine, just busy, then turned off my phone and pocketed it.

Yawning, I rubbed my hands over my eyes and reached to switch off the battery-powered lanterns I'd been working under. Then I made my way outside, only to be stopped short by a tiny *mew*.

"Damn cat." I muttered under my breath and headed toward the box he liked to hide under just to the right in the grass. I'd left the box there in case it rained and I wasn't around to let the cat inside.

The tiny orange-and-white thing had taken up shop at my place a few weeks back and couldn't have been more than two months old—abandoned or lost, I didn't know. I couldn't exactly turn him away, being so little, so I'd fed him, let him stay inside when I wasn't there, and adopted him in a way. Even bought a little bed, some toys, and a litter box for him. The guys would die laughing if they knew I'd taken in a kitten.

I hadn't seen the cat for a few days and thought maybe he'd gone back to wherever he'd come from.

Guess I was wrong.

He purred and rubbed against my leg when I lifted the box. Unable to stop myself, I picked him up, only to find his front left paw covered in blood. "Shit, buddy. What happened?" Using the flashlight on my cell, I went back inside and grabbed a semi-clean shop towel to wrap around his paw. He hissed at my touch but didn't try to bite me.

"What am I supposed to do with you now?" I scratched the back of his head, frowning harder when his little blue eyes shut. *Christ.* I couldn't leave the kitten alone when he was hurt, and I didn't have anything here to clean up the blood.

I grabbed the old box and set a work towel inside it. With a gentle hand, I tucked the cat in and didn't think twice as I put him in my truck. Collin would have a conniption if he knew I was bringing an animal home. But I wasn't a dick, and the kitten obviously needed help.

Twenty minutes later, I'd barely made it onto my front porch when a voice called my name from next door. "Gavin, hey."

My shoulders went stiff while my heart picked up its pace. Where the fuck had she come from? Not knowing if I should run and ignore her, or turn and show my face, I stood there and waited for her to continue.

"How are you?" McKenna's voice was soft, yet scratchy, almost as if she were sick.

Because I couldn't help myself, I turned to her, trying to keep the box still in my hands. "Fine. You?"

From under the porch light, I took a good, long look at her face. She seemed tired, with pale cheeks and dark circles under her eyes. But that didn't keep my heart from racing.

She shrugged, then looked at the ground. "I'm okay, I guess."

My throat burned as I swallowed. She wasn't okay. But she'd made it clear she didn't want a relationship with me. That didn't mean we couldn't be friends, and didn't friends check up on one another? "You sure?"

Her head jerked up. Wide eyes met mine in confusion, maybe with a bit of hope too, which was weird as hell. "It's…been a bad day is all."

"Hmm." I nodded, then cleared my burning throat. "So, uh…you got a sec? I could use some help with something." No, I didn't need her help. I could deal with this on my own. But she looked so damn sad, and I didn't like it.

"From me?" She frowned.

"Yeah." I rubbed my free hand through my hair, then added, "If you have time, that is."

"What do you need help with?" And just like that, her sadness slipped away. Perky, upbeat Kenna was back.

I was opening my mouth to tell her when the little thing inside the box starting meowing. Her eyes zeroed in on the box. "Is that a cat?"

Nodding, I reached inside and rubbed the top of his head to get him to stop with the noise. Instead, he started scratching at my fingers and meowing louder. "Ouch. Damn it, yes, it's a cat." I pulled my hand out and shook off the pain.

"I love kitties!" She clapped and went to peek inside, but I yanked the box back, not wanting her to get scratched or bitten.

"It's hurt."

"Oh." She frowned. "Well, we should take him to one of those overnight pet hospitals."

"No." I stuck my key into my door lock. "Too expensive." Especially for a guy who was suspended from work and trying to remodel a house. If I couldn't get the kitten fixed up on my own tonight, I'd take him to the shelter tomorrow. Let them deal with him.

I shouldered my way in, leaving the door open behind me.

"What are you going to do with him, then?" she asked.

Not answering, I set the box on my table and yanked off my shirt, tossing it onto the arm of my living room couch. I smelled like ass and needed a shower, but first I had a cat emergency to deal with.

"What are you doing?" Kenna's voice caught from behind me.

I reached into the box for the cat. "My shirt stinks."

"So, what…you just rip it off like that?"

"What else do you want me to do?" I tucked the little orange tabby to my chest and headed to the bathroom. There, I grabbed a bar of soap and a couple of towels, along with some peroxide and antibiotic cream. I wasn't a vet; I was an EMT. But injuries were injuries, and this thing needed treatment.

Her feet padded behind me as I headed into the kitchen. "Well, I mean…you just…"

"I just what?" I laid out a big towel on the counter and set the cat on top, holding him still with one hand. When I was sure he wasn't going to escape, I urged Kenna to stand in front of him while I filled a big bowl with hot water, laid it on the counter, then placed the soap and cream down next to it.

"You just got half naked and started snuggling a kitten. It's…it's not right, okay?"

"What?" I glared back at her from over my shoulder. "I'm hot and I stink. What else was I supposed to do?"

She groaned and moved over, the scent of her skin smacking me in the face like an instant reminder. *Not mine. Not mine. Not mine. Friends. Friends. Friends.*

"Ugh. You're such a man." She elbowed me in the ribs, which ended up being more of a love pat, also causing the neckline of her shirt to fall off one shoulder.

I grunted, then took another step to my left so she could get closer to the cat—and farther away from me.

"What happened to him?" she asked.

I frowned. "Not sure. I found the little guy in my work boot one day when I…" *Shit.* I couldn't tell her where I'd been.

"When you what?"

I ran my finger over the cat's head, trying to find an excuse. "When I was at my ex's house helping her put up a shed." It was the only thing close to the truth I could come up with. Technically, my ex was not really an ex, more of a girl I went on a few dates with after we got back from Afghanistan. She lived in the same town as my fixer-upper, but she had no idea about my place. I hadn't talked to her in six months.

"Oh. I didn't know you had an ex."

Something in her voice gave me pause. The tone. The question. "Why would you think that? Because I don't flaunt women like Max does?"

She reached for the rag and dropped it into the warm water, squeezing the excess liquid out in the sink. "No. I just meant…I didn't think you dated around."

I didn't. Still, there was no reason for Kenna to know anything about my personal life. Not when she wasn't willing to give me more than occasional companionship. It had taken me nearly six years and two tours of duty to tell Collin and Max the truth about my upbringing—the foster part of it. Not the bad shit. I wasn't one for talking about my past.

"I'm not from this area originally." That's all I could

give her. All she deserved. Sharing things with her would be too easy, and I'd grow attached. And getting attached to McKenna Brewer wasn't something I could do. I had to remember that.

"Oh. Okay. I didn't mean to pry. Sorry."

Shrugging, I pulled the rag from her hand and finished wiping the cat's paw. There was a nasty burr stuck between his toes, and thankfully, once I pulled it free, the cat started moving his paw around again. Still, I wasn't going to take him back to my place and release him. Not tonight. Staying here with me was the safest option for him.

"I'm a cat person, you know." McKenna hopped up on my kitchen counter and tugged the hair up off her neck. I watched as she smiled and reached down to rub the cat behind his ears. He purred against her palm and mine.

"I don't do animals at all. Too messy and expensive," I said.

"But what about this one?" She reached for him and lifted his body to her face, rubbing her cheek against his fur.

Tugging at my beard, I watched, completely mesmerized by the woman, as always, while she shut her eyes and giggled. *Lucky cat.*

"I'll take him back where I found him once I know he's okay."

Her blue eyes opened, searching my face. "I think you should keep him."

My throat clogged at the vision. The cat was rooting through her hair, snuggling on skin I was dying to get my hands on again. "No."

"But he's so cute." The corners of her lips pulled down into a pout.

"Then you take him."

Annoying thoughts started ransacking my brain as I watched her coo at the animal. McKenna working next to me at my river house, feeding the cat when I couldn't get to it, feeding me her beautiful body all over my floors when I was feeling needy. Because with her, I'd likely be needy all the fucking time.

I shook my head, ignoring a future that was untouchable and refocusing on the here and now.

"I would, but my landlord is really adamant about pets." She poked my thigh with her toe. "But your landlord has a tiny minion for a daughter who would absolutely love having a cat. It's a childhood rite of passage: get an animal to torture and love." She scrunched up her nose. "Imagine that as the Humane Society slogan."

I chuckled, her energy contagious.

Her feet were bare, the flip-flops she'd worn now on the floor. Heels banged against the cupboard, reminding me of my heart, which was beating like a monster inside my chest.

"Seriously, St. James. You *need* to keep this cat. Imagine the number of women you'd score if you had one of these. A dude with a cat is an instant panty-melter."

I dropped my used supplies into the garbage and used my towels to wipe up the wet mess. Then I leaned against the counter and said, "I don't need a cat to get some pussy."

She tossed her head back and laughed—the sound so loud that the cat hissed and jumped off her lap onto the floor. I watched him scurry away, not even worried about where he went. As much as I didn't want to admit it, the thing had been growing on me for a while. I was kind of glad I'd decided to bring him home with me. But I wouldn't be telling Kenna that.

"You, dear sir, are funny." She jumped off the counter with a flop and patted my shoulder. *Another shoulder pat.*

Still, I couldn't stop watching her. My eyes followed every move she made. When she bent over to grab her shoes, strands of her hair slipped over her face and the scoop of her shirt hung low, revealing a yellow bra. Pretty, silky, just like her hair.

"So, I take it you've got it from here?" she asked.

I blinked, the image locked in my mind. Because I couldn't speak, I nodded and motioned a hand toward the living room. She smiled with a touch of something soft in her gaze. And before I could pull her back against me and beg her to co-parent this goddamn cat, she was gone from the room and out the front door.

There were no formal goodbyes. No *I'll see you tomorrow* or *Call me.* Just two people in passing, helping when needed.

With my heart in my gut, I went in search of my new roommate. In my bedroom, something as loud as a motor sounded from under the comforter. And there on the pillow next to my spot was the cat.

"You're a sneaky son of a bitch," I mumbled under my breath as I headed toward the shower. I'd never admit it aloud, but I was secretly glad I wasn't alone tonight.

CHAPTER 8

McKenna

I LOVED SEX. LIKE, A LOT. BUT FOR THE FIRST TIME IN FOR-ever, I couldn't bring myself to go through with it.

Don't get me wrong; the guy I'd gone out with tonight was hot as hell. Twenty-two, played semipro baseball, and looked like he'd fallen straight out of *GQ*. He'd bought me a fancy dinner, opened my doors, and even told me I looked like a goddess in a halter top. I should've been flipping ecstatic about a sex date.

Yet all I could think about was how wrong his hand felt on my ass when he pulled me against him in the hallway outside my apartment door. And how he smelled like expensive department-store cologne. His face was baby smooth, and his hands were even smoother than my own, weirdly. Plus, during dinner, he told me he hated cats. And with cats, my mind had conjured up the image of Gavin, shirtless, cuddling that kitten in his kitchen three nights ago.

That alone had ix-nayed the sexiness of the guy.

"If you change your mind, I'll be in town for another two weeks."

I took the small piece of paper he offered me with his phone number on it and tucked it into the back pocket of my jeans.

"Thanks, sweetie." I leaned up on my tiptoes and kissed his cheek. His hazel eyes were hooded and hopeful when I pulled back, but he didn't push for more.

After closing the door, I leaned against the wood, eyes to the ceiling. I could've at least gotten some oral out of the deal. I didn't *have* to go all the way with the guy. Still, just thinking about letting a man touch me gave me a sick feeling in my gut—a twisting knot down low that felt…wrong.

"Ugh." Annoyed with my overthinking brain, I went to my room and grabbed a pillow and blanket, ready to binge on *The Walking Dead*. Nothing said *not sexy* like flesh-eating zombies.

As the hour ticked by, though, that same knot in my stomach twisted into something feral, as if one of the walkers on TV was chewing my insides to bits. A cold sweat broke over my forehead, and a bout of chills racked my shoulders, arms, and back. When a set of brown teeth mowed down on a neck, my dinner lurched up into my throat. I stood up as fast as my body could take me, barely making it to the trash can in the kitchen. Over and over, I heaved, trying not to smell the fried food I'd dumped in there the night before.

By the time I finished puking and cleaned myself up, the *Walking Dead* episode had ended, leaving me on the floor with my head pressed against the tile.

"Holy shit." I panted, somehow managing to roll over onto my back. The ache in my stomach increased, even though I'd just vomited out everything. I was having cramps that rivaled every period in the history of periods too.

When the pain got to be too much, I cried out, curling forward with my hand on my abdomen. I glanced down at my lap.

A few minutes later, when I was pretty sure I wasn't going to pass out on the floor, I managed to grab the straps of my purse up on the kitchen counter and pull it down to my lap. I flipped through its fifty million pockets until I found my phone.

It was 11:00 p.m. on a Saturday. Addie would either be asleep or doing the unmentionable with her boyfriend. Decision made, I dialed a different number and brought the phone to my ear.

"Hey! How was the date?" Emma chomped down on something, a chip or who knows what, from the other end. I squeezed my eyes shut, cringing at the noise. The sound brought the vision of vomit back into my mind.

"Sweet Jesus, hold on." I dropped my phone to the floor and grabbed the trash can to hurl once more. Only this time, nothing came out.

Moments later, I scooped up the phone, lowering myself back onto the cold tile. "I'm dying."

"Jeez, you sound like it. What's up?"

On their own, my eyes shut. Speaking burned my throat so badly that I had to whisper. "I think I've got food poisoning or something. Ate some bad sausage."

"That's what she said." Emma giggled.

"Ugh."

"Sorry, no more jokes. You need me to come over?"

"Fluids." I coughed, cringing, the nurse in me thinking the worst. "Need them."

"I'll be there in ten."

Exactly eight minutes later, Emma was inside my apartment, helping me off the floor. Never was I more grateful that she lived close—and had a spare key to my apartment.

By the time I made it to the car, with Emma holding me against her side, I was a shaking, hot mess of *holy-shit-I-really-am-dying*.

"No wonder you didn't get any tonight." With gentle hands, Emma leaned over and brushed some hair off my forehead as I finished buckling my seat belt.

"Worst. Consolation prize. Ever."

She snorted, and I groaned in return, resting my forehead against the cool glass of the window. She pressed the gas pedal down and upped the AC. Within fifteen minutes, we were in the ER.

"Here we go, patient zero."

Eyes narrowed, I glared at Emma from over my shoulder as I sat in a wheelchair. "Very funny."

Her auburn brows rose in amusement, yet her freckled nose scrunched at the same time. "Love you too, stinky breath."

Not soon enough, I was in a room, hooked up to an IV and having blood drawn. I'd called Addie on our way to the hospital. A visit to the ER was something she'd want to know about. Plus, she was like my sister.

She asked me if I needed anything. I said, *Nah, I'll be good*, and she claimed she'd have lemons for my water at the ready in the morning, knowing they were the only things that settled my stomach when I was sick, oddly enough. I might have sucked at choosing men, and my parents were truly disasters, but I'd somehow managed to strike gold in the best-friend department.

The doctor walked in a good forty minutes later. He was one of the newer physicians I'd been creeping on from afar. A definite hottie, but not one I'd gotten to work with yet. Thick brown hair, tall frame, and dark eyes—Italian, maybe? Not that it mattered either way. I didn't date the guys I worked with.

"Good evening, ladies." He nodded at Emma, then focused on me. "I heard you had some bad food."

"I think it was the lettuce. Maybe the sausage." I shuddered at the thought, rubbing my hands up and down my arms.

Emma snorted. I flipped her off when the doctor wasn't looking.

Doctor Hottie hemmed and hawed and marked something on his laptop before looking at me again. "Well, you've obviously eaten something that has not agreed with you. Hopefully, the bag of fluids and anti-nausea pills will help."

Too tired to talk, I nodded and shut my eyes.

"But it also says here that you're a little anemic. Are you taking any iron supplements or vitamins?"

I frowned, one eye opening "No. I had no idea."

Nodding once, he said, "It could be the baby. Lots of expectant mothers suffer from anemia. I'm not too concerned, and the medications we gave you for the nausea are not going to harm the baby's health, but when you come to the hospital, it's always a good idea to be up front about any medical conditions you may have, and that includes pregnancy."

"Um, excuse me?" My heart raced, and my eyes popped wide. The skin on my palms slickened with sweat as I dropped them onto the blanket. "I'm not *pregnant*." I shuddered and sat up straighter, poking my finger out at him. "You're pretty funny, Doc." I looked at Emma, laughing louder. "He's a damn riot, isn't he?"

Emma's lips were parted, yet her face was pale as she glanced over the doc's shoulder at his laptop.

"Emma…" My smile fell.

She glanced at me and pressed a hand over her mouth.

"Were you unaware of your condition?" Doctor Hottie asked. "My apologies."

I whipped my head back and forth between Emma and the doc again. "I am a condom *freak*, Doctor." And the night Gavin and I hooked up, he was actually the one who brought up protection, while I…

Wait.

Oh shit.

Gavin?

I shook my head no. "There's no way I'm pregnant. Can you, I don't know, do an ultrasound? Run another test or something?"

With wide eyes, Emma came to sit by me on the bed. "Jesus," she whispered, her lips curving into a disturbing smile. I say *disturbing* because she should not have been smiling. At all.

"It says right here that you are." The doctor tapped a finger against his laptop screen. "The hormone levels are not the strongest, which indicates you're around five weeks. Have you been taking your birth control pills on a regular basis?"

"No. It messes with my weight too much."

"No method of birth control is ever fully effective, miss," he continued, his brows furrowed.

"I'm not pregnant. I can't be."

"Yes, Kenna." Emma settled her hand over mine. "You're very much pregnant."

Tears stung my eyes as I looked at Emma and then the doc. "Please tell me you're kidding. Tell me I'm on some sort of TV show where you prank people. I'll forgive you if that's the case. Hell, I'll probably laugh with you. Just…tell me you're both lying to me."

The doctor cleared his throat, drawing my blurry gaze back to his face. "Once your IV has run down, you're free to go home. I'll have the nurse come in with your discharge papers as soon as possible. An anti-nausea pill prescription as well. And if you'd like some pamphlets on pregnancy, I can—"

"No. Oh God, no." As if my body were weighted down with lead, I fell back in the hospital bed with a thump.

Jesus. This wasn't happening. I wasn't pregnant. I *couldn't* be pregnant.

Warm fingers grabbed mine, squeezing. "You're going to get through this," Emma whispered. More tears sprang to my eyes at her tone, and a sob burst from my throat.

"Oh, honey, don't cry," she whispered, running a hand over my forehead.

How was this possible? I mean, I knew how it was *possible*, but how could I have been such a damn moron to let it happen?

"Gavin…" I cried harder as I said his name. The universe was clearly against me. Someone out there was trying to torture me. I didn't want a baby right now—if ever. I didn't want to have a baby daddy either. Especially not a guy who was probably as messed up emotionally as I was.

"Is he the father?" Emma asked as she rubbed her hand up and down my arm.

I nodded once, no doubt in my mind. "There hasn't been anyone else." Not since *that night*. And I'd had a two-month dry spell before Gavin. He was the only possible candidate for the job.

Snot puddled inside my nose, burning like the ache in my heart. God, I knew nothing about babies, and I didn't have a maternal bone in my body, thanks to my mother. She was cold and angry and, quite frankly, didn't look at me as anything but a germ on her shoe. That's why she'd shipped me off to live with my father in Macomb when I was a teenager. Not even when she remarried and adopted my stepbrother and stepsister did she ask me to move back to New Orleans. One week during the summer and an occasional weekend during holidays… That's all I ever got from her. Instead, I lived in a house with a man who was rarely home because working was so much more important than raising a kid.

I couldn't bring a child into the world. Especially if I'd be the same way my parents were with me. What if I wanted to give up? What if I created a kid who turned out just like me? Unable to settle, picking the wrong partners, and making the wrong, impulsive decisions? I mean, sure, I grew up and all, but that wasn't *all* my parents' doing.

Two hours later, when I was settled in my bed at home, a stack of untouched *what to expect* pamphlets lying on my end table, I couldn't stop the tears—and I wasn't a crier. My thoughts went back and forth as I wavered over my options.

Yet the question that plagued me most was *How the hell am I going to tell Gavin?*

CHAPTER

Gavin

"Please, take them to her. She has food poisoning and needs these lemons, but Chloe's extra car seat is in Collin's parents' car."

My best friend's girl was evil—standing at my doorstep with a bag of lemons and a sad story about a sickly woman I was trying to forget.

"She was in the hospital, Gav."

I rubbed a hand down my face, trying not to flinch at the word *hospital*. "Fine. I'll take them."

Addie wrapped her arms around my waist and hugged me, her voice muffled against my shirt. "Thank you, thank you, *thank you*."

There weren't many people I'd do anything for. My boys and Chloe were it, for the most part. It was only within the last five months that Addison had jumped into that small circle too.

"Is she all right?" I asked.

Addie stepped back and shoved the grocery bag into

my hands. "Yeah, she sounds really tired. I plan on going over there once Collin gets home from work. I'm worried about her though."

My shoulders tensed. "What happened?"

"She had a date last night and wound up getting food poisoning."

My gut tightened. "A date."

With her head tipped to the side, Addie searched my face. "Yeah. A date."

"Hmm." Jealousy lodged in my chest. I grabbed the keys off my kitchen table to avoid letting it show.

"You okay?" Addison asked, always the observer.

We walked out the front door, and I locked it behind me.

"Perfect." *Far from perfect* was more like it. Pissed. Agitated. Affected when I had no right to be. But I wasn't willing to tell Addie that her best friend had me all messed up emotionally.

Besides, I had a date this coming Thursday—a girl Max was hooking me up with. Someone who would be *perfect* for me, he'd said. I was trying to move on. I *had* to move on.

"Collin and I are going away next weekend to visit my mom, by the way."

"Your mom?"

Addie nodded and looked at her hands. "Yeah. She, um… She's sick."

I knew that. Collin had mentioned it. But from what I'd heard, Addison didn't have much of a relationship with her parents.

"I'm sorry." I squeezed her shoulder.

"Thanks." She shrugged. "Do you mind swinging by

once or twice to check on Max and Lia? They're going to be watching Chloe for us."

"Yeah, sure. No problem." I twirled my keys around my finger and smiled.

A few minutes later, I was on the road, following the directions to McKenna's place. I hadn't been there before, but I knew where the complex was. It sat on the edge of town, just before the turn onto the interstate I took to Arlo, the small town where my river house was.

When I pulled into the apartment complex's parking lot, I sat for a while to try to calm my nerves. No doubt Kenna was waiting for Addie, not me. Would she tell me to leave once I got to the front door? Maybe she wasn't even dressed. Addie should've called and told her I was coming.

"Fuck." I tugged on my beard and blew out a breath as I got out of my SUV. If she was really sick and needed these lemons, I had to help her, whether she wanted me as a friend or not.

After buzzing at the door, only for some guy to let me inside in passing, I headed to apartment 117 and knocked twice on the door. Nerves had me rocking back and forth on my heels as I waited. Call me a chicken, but the thought of dropping the bag and running came to mind just as the door cracked open.

"Gavin." Her eyes were wide, and tears filled the corners as she pulled the door open all the way.

I flinched at the sight of her. Pale face, red, bloodshot eyes… She looked like hell.

I went right in, my doubts eliminated about her needing me—or not wanting me there.

Forgetting our just-friends rules, I dropped the bag

to the floor, kicked the door shut, and pulled her to my chest, stroking a hand up and down her spine. Against me, she relaxed, as though her entire body was on the verge of collapsing.

I pulled back enough to see her face. "What happened?"

She opened her mouth as if to speak, but then began to sob.

"Hey, talk to me." Not thinking twice, I scooped her in my arms and carried her to the couch. She didn't fight me. Instead, she cried harder, sobbing against me, clinging to my shirt.

A shit ton of thoughts ran through my head. Had she gotten bad news from the doctor and not told Addie the truth? Was something else wrong with her? Worse yet, had someone hurt her? I growled softly at the thought and held her tighter. What if the fucker last night did something to her? Addie said Kenna had been sick, but what was she sick from? I'd kill the asshole if he'd dosed her with something.

The longer Kenna cried against me, the more I lacked the words to speak. I didn't comfort people well, except for Chloe on occasion. I didn't know how—had never been taught. It was another reason why I shouldn't want Kenna the way I did. Not when I didn't even know how to make her feel better.

"Are you still sick?" My voice cracked. *Jesus, Captain Obvious.* "I mean, can I do anything to help?"

Her sobs finally stopped, but her arm stayed wrapped around my neck. "No," she whispered.

That breathy word grazed hot against the side of my throat, and I couldn't help but squeeze her closer. But instead of talking or trying to figure out what to do, I let her lie against me, let her hold me too. Because that's what friends did, right? Held each other when things got tough.

Ten minutes later, her breathing evened out. And because I couldn't stand the thought of letting her go, I sat there, stroking her blond hair, rubbing her back, doing everything I could to soothe her without pushing the limit.

McKenna

My eyes were swollen when they reopened an hour or so later. Not that I was surprised. I'd basically lost it the second I saw Gavin standing at my door.

Gavin, the father of my child.

Sweet Jesus, what the hell was I going to do?

Of course, I couldn't find it in me to tell him the truth. I'd barely been able to wrap my own head around the idea. I would tell him soon though, very soon. I just had to figure out how and when.

I'd expected him to maybe put me in bed or leave me alone on the couch. What I didn't expect was to be in the same position I'd been in before I fell asleep: warm and safe in his arms.

Snuggled against his hard chest, I couldn't help but sigh. Being there with Gavin... It could be my home, if I let it. I knew he wanted more from me. He'd told me straight up in that elevator that he liked me. But now, in the middle of the biggest crisis of my life, was not the time to ponder the impossible.

"You okay?" he whispered hoarsely.

"I'm okay." Or as *okay* as I could be, given the circumstances. "Thank you for staying with me."

He absently twirled a lock of my hair around his finger. "You scared me."

Slowly, I sat up, nonchalantly moving onto the couch beside him. The intimate touching was making my already-aching heart even wearier. "Sorry. It's just that sometimes when I'm sick, I get emotional." It wasn't a huge lie.

He cleared his throat and leaned forward onto his knees, running his hands through his shaggy hair. "Do you need me to get you anything else? I brought lemons for your water. Soup or crackers, maybe?"

"No thank you." My stomach tightened at the simple thought of food, reminding me I wasn't completely okay from last night's food disaster.

What I really needed was for him to stop being so sweet and loving and so…Gavin. It only complicated things more.

"I'm not okay, actually." I sucked in my breath, gathering courage I didn't think I had. With my hands on my hips, I stood, unsure of where to go from here. For weeks, I'd been pushing him away, and I hated myself for doing so. Not only was it rude and selfish, but also incredibly immature. For now, though, I needed space. Some time to think and be alone, figure out what I wanted, most of all. "I think you should go, Gavin."

The shock in his gaze was a good sign—the kind that said he was too stunned to respond. But seconds later, when my courage was shot full of adrenaline, he shook his head and moved to stand in front of me, breaking down the barriers I'd just barely built. "I want to stay and help you. Please. Let me."

I flinched at his sentiment. Nobody had ever stayed. Not my mother, my father, my exes. What made him any different?

My throat ached as I swallowed, yet I held my chin high and said, "No thank you."

"But you're sick. I want—"

"I smell like puke." I turned my head away, annoyed with my own invalid excuses.

"McKenna, look at me." He tipped my chin up with his finger, eyes wide and filled with an emotion I couldn't recognize as he searched my face.

"I am looking." And I was—with so much more than just my eyes. That was the problem.

I was looking through my heart and my head, which were battling each other. My head said *run*, my heart said *stay*, and the baby in my stomach...

"Oh God."

This time, I made it to the bathroom before vomiting. I heaved into the toilet, and my head spun as I pressed my hands against the side of the bowl.

"Whoa." Gavin mumbled from the doorframe.

"Leave me alone," I groaned, nudging his arm back.

"You need help. Let me—"

"I don't need your help," I cried, heaving again. "Go away. Please." Tears from vomiting and crying filled my eyes. My throat singed, as if it were filled with razor blades, clawing at my insides from my chest to my throat, then delving straight into my heart.

"Kenna, please..." A hand pressed against my lower

back as he crouched down beside me. That's all it took for me to lose it.

"I don't want you seeing me like this. Please. Just go."

"But—"

"I said *leave*." Tears dripped down my cheeks, passing the dip of my chin. I shut my eyes, embarrassed and hating myself for becoming the bitch I strove not to be. I wasn't my mother. I never would be. But in that moment, I felt exactly like her.

I'd never hated myself more.

A sigh came from my right, but I didn't look at Gavin's face, too scared to see the disappointment I knew would be there. He was a good man, unlike anyone I'd ever met. And the more goodness I saw in him, the more I wanted him. In a weird way, I already had him— at least a piece of him. But this baby inside me was not going to make me do an about-face on relationships.

I'd learned the hard way, watching my own parents' marriage fall apart. Children did not heal people. Nor did they bring them together.

I heard him leave—the way his shoes hit the wooden floor in my hallway, the sound of the word *fuck* in the living room. The door clicked as he let himself out and I flinched, hearing everything. Feeling it all inside my chest as I broke down and sobbed. I cried until no tears remained, until I lay down on the tile and fell asleep, all by myself…exactly the way it should be.

CHAPTER 10

Gavin

EVERYTHING ABOUT HER WAS WRONG, EVEN THOUGH SHE WAS exactly the type of woman I would normally go for. Smart, funny, sweet…a brunette with gray eyes and dimples, beyond gorgeous. Hell, she even laughed at my stupid joke, when I managed to tell one. Her name was Sienna. Max had gone out with her once, but she wasn't his type. Unlike a lot of the other women he went out with, they'd managed to stay friends.

Had I not been hung up on a certain blond, I would've thanked the hell out of Maxwell for hooking me up with this woman.

I really fucking hated how my mind worked.

Still, I was out of the house, not thinking about Kenna's rejection, on Thursday. Not thinking about how broken she'd looked when I left her crying in her bathroom. Though the longer my date lasted, the more I wondered if Kenna was okay. If she was drinking enough water. If she was eating enough, or if she was still throwing up. I'd have to call Addie again, though I was pretty sure she suspected something, since I'd been calling twice a day about Kenna.

"So, you're an EMT? That's what Max told me." Sienna moved in closer, clearly interested. The lights above our restaurant table only made her look more beautiful.

"Yeah." I was usually a man of few words. But the way I was behaving tonight, she probably thought I was the closest thing to a mute there was. I needed to end this now. Tell her I wasn't feeling it. That she deserved better than me. But the words wouldn't come out, and instead, I sucked down the rest of my beer.

I tugged at my beard and leaned back in the booth, needing space. She frowned, obviously disappointed, but didn't say anything. Not like a certain someone would.

I should have appreciated that. Not being pushed. But I realized how badly I craved it. From Kenna.

The rest of the dinner passed in awkward silence. I found myself looking at my cell phone a hell of a lot more than I should. I felt like an asshole about it, even apologized, explaining how my *friend* was sick and I was worried about her.

After the check was paid, and we headed out the door, Sienna took my hand as we walked across the parking lot.

"I had a really good time tonight." Her smile was soft and pretty, but she didn't make my heart beat faster.

"You did?" Because I was more than positive I'd fucked everything up. Maybe she was just being nice. Or maybe I wasn't trying hard enough.

"Yeah, I'd love to go out again sometime."

"Hmm."

She frowned at my answer, leading me to her car. We'd met at the restaurant. She told Max she felt safer doing so. And because I was all about making someone feel safe, I'd agreed.

"Are you heading home after this?" she asked as we stopped in front of her car.

I nodded.

"Do you maybe want to watch a movie or something?"

It took me a second to realize what she was asking. And because I knew Max would be pissed if I didn't try harder, I said, "Sure. My place?"

Her smile grew wide. "I'd like that."

I nodded again, a little stupefied over why she still wanted to hang out. In the end, she followed my Suburban, parking along the street outside the duplex.

Twenty minutes later, we were on my couch, scouring Netflix. She'd grabbed a folded blanket off the floor by her feet and laid it over our laps. Beneath it, she reached for my hand and squeezed as she pulled it onto her lap.

I tried like hell to enjoy the sensation, the soft feeling of her skin against mine. Tried to make myself feel something—*anything*—for this woman. This was the first date I'd been on in months, and with a pretty great woman at that. But nothing felt right.

A quarter of the way through the movie, Cat—which is what I'd decided to name the cat—jumped onto our blanket.

Sienna gasped and jerked toward the other end of the couch, causing Cat to arch his back and hiss. "You have a cat?"

"Yeah, I do."

"Well, can you lock it up?" Lip curled, she shooed a hand toward the hall. Her reaction was the first sign that this was not, indeed, the woman for me.

"Are you allergic?" I asked.

"No. I just… I don't like them. They're too hairy."

Someone knocked at my front door just then, saving me from saying something asshole-worthy. Cat jumped down, beating me to the door, and out of the corner of my eye, I watched Sienna stand and grab her coat. Apparently, cats were deal breakers for her.

I swooped Cat up and tucked him to my side. He purred, nuzzling against my stomach. I grinned. A woman who didn't like cats was a deal breaker for me too.

The knock grew more insistent. I looked out the window and froze.

Kenna.

~m~

McKenna

Addie squeezed me tighter, the scent of her strawberry shampoo soothing my frayed nerves.

I'd come over to have pizza with her, Chloe, and Collin, but one bite in and I was done for. The nausea was so awful that I barely made it to their bathroom in time to be sick. It would seem the food poisoning I'd been diagnosed with had turned into all-day, every-day morning sickness.

Like the perfect bestie she was, Addie had followed me into the bathroom, then held my hair and stroked my back. But she was silent the entire time, and I knew from that alone she had suspicions. It only took her one question to turn me into a blubbering mess.

Do you know who the father is?

Part of me wanted to lie, mainly because Addie had warned me away from Gavin from the beginning. And since Pisser Paul had come and gone, she knew my stance on relationships. Still, a person could only tell so many lies before getting caught up in them. So...I told her everything. From the elevator, to the kiss *in* the elevator, and how I'd run right afterward. Then I told her about the night we'd spent together five weeks ago, after Lia's last night at Jimney's, and the next morning when I'd jumped out the window, ripping my favorite leather boots in the process.

Then I cried. Again.

"You know condoms are not always effective. And for as active as you are sexually, I'm surprised you aren't on any other contraceptive."

I cringed, wishing she were wrong. Because I wasn't as head-in-the-game as she thought. I was a half-asser in all things in life, someone who made reckless mistakes. For instance, sleeping with a man I knew I shouldn't have slept with.

"Birth control and I don't mesh." I blew out a quick breath, thankful she wasn't going to nag me about Gavin being the father. Still, I didn't like that she was shaming me at all.

I pulled back, putting distance between us on the bed. Trying to stave off my tears, I looked around the room that now belonged to her and her boyfriend.

"Still, Kenna..."

"What, you think I planned this or something? I

wasn't exactly in the right frame of mind that night." But then again, I wasn't *that* drunk either. Peach schnapps be damned.

Her eyes widened. "What? No, no, no. God, no, Kenna. You know I didn't mean it like that. I—"

"That's what it felt like. You of all people know I don't want anything serious right now, relationship-wise. And a baby? That's *never* been in my plans. I want to travel more. Get my master's. I'm not cut out for *this* life." I jerked my hand around her room, only to let it slap against my thigh.

"What *life* do you mean, exactly?" Her eyes narrowed.

I stood from the bed and walked over to her dresser, picking up a four-by-six photo of her and Collin from sometime last fall. They were in Chicago together, cuddled up on the sidelines at one of his rugby matches. She was dressed in a hoodie, and Collin wore those tiny shorts and no shirt—even though the temperature was freezing, from the looks of it.

"I want more than *this*, Addie." I showed her the picture, shaking it slightly, then set it back down.

"So, you're saying that since I don't have an actual *job*, I'm lower than you?"

It was my turn to cringe. *Crap.* I really needed to reengage my mouth's filtration system. "No." I turned to face her. "That came out wrong. I'm sorry."

"Well," she scoffed, "you know this wasn't how I'd planned on my life turning out, but I'm happy with it, and I don't really care what other people think. Including you."

I sighed, too tired to fight. "Addie…"

She lifted her chin, staring down her nose at me. I knew that look, that fire in her eyes. My blowtorch of a best friend had been lit.

"What I meant was…" I held my breath, then slowly blew it out. "I didn't plan on having kids."

Her shoulders fell—whether from relief or disappointment, I wasn't sure. "We've never wanted the same things in life, Kens. But we've always agreed on supporting each other's decisions, no matter what happens." She moved closer, all five foot four of her standing in front of me, pride in her dark eyes. "And just so you know, I did get that job for this fall at the preschool in Matoona. And I *like* staying home with Chloe. And Collin doesn't care what I do, as long as I'm happy. He's not like my father, or my mother, or anyone else I've ever met. He doesn't pressure me—"

"He wants to get married, doesn't he? Isn't that pressure enough?"

Her smile grew softer, but she didn't answer right away. My best friend—who loved children and wanted a brood of them someday, along with a happily ever after—had always feared marriage.

"He does. And I want to marry him too. It's just taken me a bit to decide that. But Collin has waited for me. Been patient with me and my decisions. And as crude and rude as he can be, he'll always support me in whatever I choose. Just like *Gavin* will likely support you no matter what *you* choose."

I sighed to myself, finally seeing her point. It was a wonderful, torturous kind of hell to have such a smart, supportive, loving best friend.

The two of us had known each other since college, but we'd never compared our lives. We just lived them side by side, there for each other when need be. Addie had a domineering, controlling, asshole father and a mother who'd never stood up against him, while I had a mom who wanted nothing to do with me and a father who always forgot about me. The difference between Addie and me was that I didn't strive to find someone in my life to make me happy. At least *I thought* I didn't. But she craved it. That warm, fuzzy kind of love that gave someone a sense of purpose.

Collin was her purpose. And he was hers.

"Listen, this"—she pressed her hand against my flat stomach—"isn't the end of the world. I can help you with whatever happens, whether you decide to raise it on your own or give it up for adoption. I'm here, okay? I'll support you."

"Why?"

She jerked her head back as if I'd hit her. "Why what?"

"Why would you do that for me?" My eyes swelled with more unshed tears.

Slowly, she shook her head, looking stupefied, yet her gaze never left my face. "You're really asking me that?"

I shrugged, at a loss for words.

"Because, Kenna, no matter what happens, you and I are lifer friends. You got me?"

My lips trembled. As if someone had pulled a plug, draining all my emotions into one dripping waterfall of sadness, I lost it. Gushing tears, sobbing—*lost it*.

"Aww, don't cry." She smoothed a hand down my back as she hugged me close again. I wasn't that much taller than her, but I felt tiny in her strong arms.

A few minutes into my sob fest, soft footsteps sounded along the floor behind us. I sniffed, embarrassed by my weeping, and pulled away to see Chloe toddling into the room, followed by her daddy. She reached for the edges of my shorts, then stabbed a thumb into her mouth. Her wide eyes met mine in that way only a toddler could. Big, honest, and hopeful.

Could I do this? Raise a kid? Be a mom? I had never planned on it. But the idea seemed less daunting as I looked into this little girl's eyes.

Collin cleared his throat as I looked up. Clearly uncomfortable, he rubbed a hand up and down the back of his neck. "Sorry. I was gonna tell you ladies that I'm taking Chloe for ice cream."

Addie kept her arm around my shoulder as she turned. With her other arm, she reached over and ran a finger through Chloe's curls as she said, "Sounds good." She looked my way. "You want to come along?"

"Thanks, but fourth-wheeling it with you guys on a Thursday night isn't my idea of a good time."

I couldn't help but smile as I watched Collin walk over and scoop up his daughter. He might have bugged me with his bossy tendencies, but I couldn't fault him for it that much. He'd been through a lot. At least he had two other men in his life, along with Addie, a super-supportive sister, and decent parents to help him.

"We'll meet you in the car." He bent to kiss Addie's temple. Next to her, he looked like a gushing giant—which he pretty much was when it came to my best friend. I'd never doubted his love for Addie; I just doubted the way he went about loving her.

He was nothing like lumber-sexual Gavin, though their height and weight matched. Gavin was quiet and broody, yet thoughtful. Collin was broody and broody, and loved my best friend as though that were his only job in the world. Gavin wasn't quite as agitated about the world as Collin was, and when Gavin looked at me…

"Shit." I gasped at the thought, leaning over to press my hands to my knees, remembering how much he seemed to like me. Thinking back on it, Gavin looked at me the way Collin looked at Addie. How was that even possible? We barely knew each other.

"You all right?" Collin asked.

Addie answered for me. "She's okay. Just still dealing with that stomach thing."

"Five days later?" His voice rose in disbelief, and Addie's hand froze between my shoulder blades. I held my breath, and I could hear her doing the same.

"Dada, bye-bye," Chloe squealed, saving me from having to explain something I was not ready to explain.

"Okay, Beaner, let's go." God. That kid was my Wonder Woman in Diapers.

Once the front door clicked shut, I righted myself— along with my head. "You can't tell Collin."

"About the baby?" Addie bit her lip.

"Yes. Please don't." I blew out a breath and leaned back against her dresser. "I need to tell Gavin first. It's only right."

She nodded in agreement. "Are you going to…you know, go over there tonight and tell him? I think he's home."

I knew what needed to be done, that I couldn't wait any longer than necessary. I already felt like a bloated cow, and according to my monthly cycle, I was only about five weeks along. Someone would pick up on it sooner or later, and I couldn't ask Addie to keep the news from Collin for too long either. They had a no-secrets policy, something I still didn't fully grasp. And again, Gavin had a right to know.

"I think so."

"Are you sure you don't want me to stay behind, just in case something goes wrong?"

I shook my head. "If he blows up on me, I'll know what needs to be done."

"And if he doesn't…?"

The hope in her eyes could have been bottled into something that changed the world. My best friend still believed in my happiness, way more than I did.

"I'll be fine." I kissed her on the forehead and smiled, not feeling the positivity I tried to emit. If I was being honest with myself, I think I was more scared he'd accept the truth. Then in turn, would he push for more? With me? I'm not sure if I was ready for that either—if I ever would be.

I walked Addie outside and said my goodbyes, inhaling a giant breath before I swung right toward Gavin's place. Rolling out my shoulders, I didn't take the time to think about what I was about to do and just did it, knocking on the door with a hell of a lot more bravery than I felt.

A few minutes passed, and he'd still not answered, yet I heard noises inside—voices, more than one. My chest grew tight, my heart racing too fast, yet instead of leaving, I knocked harder. I'm not sure why. Maybe I needed to see what I already knew was there?

Affirmation that proved I was right to not want more with a man?

Rooted in place, I knocked one final time. And then the door opened.

CHAPTER 11

Gavin

"MCKENNA..." I STARTED.

Kenna stood fixed on the other side of the threshold, looking worse than she had two days ago. Uncombed hair, pale complexion, dark circles under her eyes, which were bright red. Yet even haggard, she was still the most beautiful woman I had ever seen.

"Hey." She tucked a lock of hair behind her ear. "I was wondering if we could—"

"I think I'm going to take off, Gavin." Sienna came up beside me, eyes widening a little at the sight of McKenna. I cringed, wondering if I should do introductions, only for Kenna to jump in first.

"You're busy. I'll come back another time." She backed away, eyes welling with tears.

"Wait, please. Don't go." She was the reason I was breaking. She was also the reason I was struggling to pick myself up again. One night with this woman, and I was a mess. She was the unattainable lover I could never have again.

But she was here now…

Sienna touched my shoulder, then smiled politely at Kenna. "I was just leaving. Please, do stay." She looked at me, knowingness in her gray eyes. "And thank you for tonight, Gavin. I'll talk to you soon." Then she was gone. A woman who was textbook perfect, but not for me.

"I'm sorry," Kenna said, watching Sienna get into her car from over her shoulder. "I didn't mean to mess up your date."

"You told me to leave" were the first words out of my mouth. I didn't expect to be so pissed. But I was. "In your apartment, when you were so sick, you told me to leave and…" I took a breath, letting it come out in a rush as I struggled for words.

Kenna sighed and kicked the tip of her shoe against the porch floor. "It was a bad day."

"You've had a lot of those lately," I grumbled.

She shrugged, then looked inside my apartment. "Do you mind if we talk?"

"About?"

"Us."

I froze, unsure if I'd heard her right. "Us?"

She nodded. "Yeah."

If I let her inside, if we *talked*, there was a ninety percent likelihood that she'd run away again. Question was, could I keep doing this? Let her in, only for her to push me away? I was already tired of it—the games, the *yes*, the *no*, the *I can't*. Which is why this talk of ours? It would have to be on my terms, not hers.

"How about tomorrow night?" I asked, trying to stay

strong but struggling every second longer we stood there, so close, yet so damn far away.

"Tomorrow," she repeated, her blue eyes holding mine.

"Yeah."

Just then, Cat came out of the house, purring as he rubbed himself in between Kenna's legs. I lifted my head, finding her gorgeous, wide smile, and all the air in my lungs grew heavy, burning. I pressed my palm against my heart, wishing it'd stop with the fucking reactions.

"You kept him?" She bent over to pick him up. Pulling him to her chest, I watched as she snuggled him close, wishing she was holding me instead.

"I did." I smiled. "Named him Cat." I could have told her why I kept him: that I was lonely and tired of being that way, that more than anything, I wished she were in the bed next to me at night instead of him. Though I suppose he could stay too, at the foot of the bed or something.

But I didn't say any of that.

I couldn't.

Not when her words kept running through my head.

Go away. Please.

My chest grew tight at the memory. Too many people had said similar shit to me, and it wasn't something I could just get over. Not anymore.

"That's a very original name." She rubbed her cheek against Cat's nose, eyes shut. Her hair fell over his face, and he batted it away with his white paws.

"He likes you." I stuck my hands in my pockets.

Her smile decreased a little, but it still packed a punch, one that hit me straight in the gut this time.

"I like him too."

Inside my house, my cell phone rang. It was likely Max, asking about how my date went, but it was enough to spook Kenna. "Tomorrow night, then. That will be better for me. I have to work all day, then maybe I can, um"—she tucked some hair behind her ear again as she looked at me from under her long side bangs—"come by and cook us dinner?"

I should've said no. Maybe told her I wasn't in the state of mind to get head-fucked by her some more. What I needed to do was work on my house, as I'd planned, and concentrate on getting myself ready to go back to work on Monday. Yet telling her no didn't exist in my limited vocabulary.

"Sure." I held out my arms and grabbed Cat, setting him inside my place and pulling the door shut behind me as I stepped farther onto the porch.

"Awesome. What's your favorite meal?" she asked.

"Not picky."

"You're a meat-and-potatoes man? Fish? Pasta?" She nudged me in the ribs with her elbow as we started walking down the driveway toward her car. Our arms were close, fingers closer. My body was humming for her, desperate to pull her close.

"Hmm. Whatever."

"I'll surprise you, then."

I followed her with my gaze as she opened the car door, not asking questions when she got into her seat and waved goodbye.

—⁓—

McKenna

I couldn't concentrate on my shift the next day, not that there was much to concentrate on. The patients were cranky as hell in orthopedics, and the other nurses were bitchier than the ones I typically worked with in the ICU. But they were short-staffed, and I was feeling generous.

Thank God I got two breaks.

What I needed was a toilet. And some coffee. For the first time in days, my stomach was grumbling for something real and nutritional. It was either a blessing or a curse, and I wasn't sure which yet.

To get to the cafeteria, I had to pass the ER. I tried to avoid that place—the GSWs, the heart attacks… I might have been a nurse, but I preferred the slower paced departments. My ultimate goal was to work in an office, because the stress and hours of a hospital were becoming too much for me. This job was the epitome of stressful, but I couldn't go back in time and tell twenty-year-old me to step away from the dream, that reality tended to be crap. Still, I loved helping people, cranky assholes or not.

Thankfully, the ER seemed to be quiet for the most part, other than a scuffle down the hall between a cop and a guy in cuffs who was puking all over the floor.

"Yeah, not cool." I had veered off to the left when my cell rang. Frowning, I looked down at the screen. Addie was calling.

"Hey, girl. How are things in Minnesota?"

"Kenna? Oh, thank God you answered. Are you still working?"

"Well, hello to you too. And yes, I am."

"Seriously, McKenna. There's been an accident."

My body went stiff. "What happened?"

"Apparently Lia and Max took Chloe to some pizza place, and she fell off a basketball game thing and broke her arm."

"Shit." Forgetting my break, I headed straight toward Peds. My guess was that Chloe was still in the ER, but X-Ray was closer to the pediatric unit than anywhere else, so I'd take the chance there first. "How long ago?"

Addie blew out a heavy breath, and I could tell she was holding the tears back. With her mom being so sick, she didn't have time to deal with this.

"We just got the call ten minutes ago. Collin can't get a flight out until tomorrow morning, so he's pretty worked up."

I cringed, imagining a worked-up Collin. "She'll be in good hands. Max and Lia are here, and aren't his parents too?"

"Yeah, but he hates that he can't be. Both of us do. This is his baby girl."

And yours too, I wanted to say.

Unconsciously, I lowered my hand to my stomach, wondering if I'd be the same way had the roles been reversed. "I'll check on her as much as I can, okay?"

"Thank you." She sniffed.

If I could hug her, I would, but I couldn't, so I did the next best thing and distracted her. "Oh. I've got news."

"What kind of news? Because I can't take any more bad stuff right now."

"No. This is…different news. I'm cooking dinner for Gavin tonight at his place."

She coughed. "Come again?"

Swallowing hard, I stared at the floor outside the X-ray room. Maybe this wasn't the best conversation I could offer. Still, I wasn't graceful when it came to something that made me worry, and my worry over my best friend *and* Chloe were making me extra shaky. "I *said* I'm making dinner tonight for Gavin. At his place."

"Wow. Okay, then. This is good news. I take it you told him everything after you left our place and things are going to work out with you two?"

I sucked in a deep breath, holding it for a second. "Well, technically—"

"…and you have no right to talk to me like I'm lower than you, you rotten bitch. This is my fifteen-month-old niece. I *will* be in that X-ray room with her, whether you like it or not."

My eyes widened as a pink-and-purple-haired woman zoomed by me, raging mad and stabbing a finger in the air. On a stretcher next to her was a familiar-looking, curly-haired toddler with wet eyes and pouty lips: Chloe. An X-ray tech pushed her through the door, and the world's bitchiest doctor walked five feet ahead of them.

"Um, I've got an emergency to get back to. Call me later?"

"Okay, love you, Kens. Please let me know what you find out."

"Will do, babe."

I hung up quickly, sticking my phone into the pocket of my scrubs. Not wasting any time, I took off after the four-person crew, eyeing the doctor with my world-famous glare. Of course Dr. Johanna would be the attending doctor tonight.

"Lia!" I grabbed her elbow before she could head into

the X-ray room. "You okay?" Collin's sister's eyes were red and wet, her lip curled like that of an evil warrior as she stared at Dr. Johanna, who was retreating toward the ER. I squeezed her upper arm and urged her inside the room before closing the door. It was part of my silent promise to be there for both Chloe and Lia.

She wiped her wet cheeks and nodded. "Yeah, I'm fine. Just worried is all. And that doctor…"

I cringed. "Yeah, Dr. Johanna can be a tad bit over the top sometimes." And that was putting it mildly.

Hands shaking, Lia brought them to her mouth and nodded, glancing only briefly at me before focusing on Chloe.

"What happened?" I asked.

"She fell off a hoop game, trying to make a basket. It happened so quickly. Max and I were kissing and—"

"Kissing?" I quirked a brow, confused.

Her face paled. "I, um, yeah…"

I nodded, eyes narrowing a bit. If she and Max were together, I had to wonder if this was a secret they'd be taking to the grave. As far as I knew, this wasn't something anyone else was aware of.

"I'm not judging, Lia. Accidents happen all the time. I just want to make sure you're okay."

"I'm okay. Max is a bit shaken up, but I'm good now. Better."

"Other than Dr. Wonderful, you mean?" I rolled my eyes.

Lia snorted—as did the X-ray tech—then bit down on her lip as she turned to look at Chloe again. The little girl was sniffling and crying as they moved her to the seat, but never once fought the tech as she adjusted

Chloe's little arm one way and another to get the right angle for the shot.

"Are you pregnant?" the tech asked Lia, who quickly shook her head no.

The lady looked at me next, the same question on her tongue. "Oh, uh, I have to get something across the hall," I lied. "I'll wait for you outside the room."

Not bothering to look my way, Lia said, "Okay." And I left to stand in the hall outside of the room.

Across from me on a tiny love seat was a couple waiting outside the ultrasound room. The man's hands were on both sides of the woman's stomach, while he put his mouth against the baby bump and silently spoke to it under his breath.

They were smiling. So...*happy* and accepting of what they'd created. The guy pressed his palm over the middle of the woman's stomach next, the move so natural I struggled to look away. The lady set her hand over the back of his knuckles, telling him to hold still, that if he moved he wouldn't be able to feel it kick.

My throat grew tight at the view, and tears burned in my eyes. There was so much to love about that beautiful moment, yet none of that would be for me.

Was it wrong of me to not want this baby—this child that was half Gavin's, half mine? Was I a bad person to feel zero connection to it? Granted it was a tiny, minuscule blip, but it had a heart, one I helped to create. Still, nothing about that idea made me tingle like an expectant mother should when thinking of her unborn child. Instead, all I could see were the ways I'd screw a child up. How my mother would tell me *I told you so*.

Maybe Gavin would be a great father. Or maybe, like

me, he didn't want kids either. I'd seen him with Chloe, though, seen the love in his eyes when he held her. But did that mean he wanted to have a child of his own? There again, what if he did want that? Would he hate me because I didn't? Or would he want this baby and offer to raise it without me?

My stomach churned as countless thoughts ran through my mind.

Kids were forever, a responsibility there was no escape from. I could barely take care of myself, let alone a tiny person. In the end, this baby would be coming in a little over eight months. Only time would tell whether I was strong enough to be the person a baby would need.

First, though, I needed to tell Gavin.

CHAPTER 12

Gavin

MY HANDS WERE SHAKING AS I PUSHED AWAY FROM THE laptop. This night was turning into an all-out fucking disaster. Not only had I just gotten the call about Chloe breaking her arm, but I'd received an email from the county saying my permit hadn't been updated when I started work on the innards of the house. Now, I had to pay fines out my ass before I could work on it again.

Not wanting to waste another second, I ran next door to grab the things Chloe needed at the hospital—most importantly, her favorite blanket—and took off. Max was a damn wreck on the phone, but finding him outside Chloe's hospital room, head pressed against the wall, cussing, was the last thing I'd expected from my normally joking best friend.

My boots thudded to a stop next to him. He didn't look up when I said, "She'll be all right." I patted him on the shoulder, taken back to the last time I'd tried to comfort another man: Collin after he'd learned about Chloe's mom dying in a car accident while we were stationed in the Middle East.

"I fucked up, man."

I shrugged, finally meeting his eyes. "It happens."

"No…" He paused. "I mean, I really fucked up. A lot. Me and Lia, we got distracted…"

My eyebrows rose. "How so?" Though I was pretty sure I already knew. This morning, I'd learned how serious he was about our best friend's little sister when I found her in only a T-shirt inside his apartment.

He leaned his back against the wall and pinched the bridge of his nose. "Just…I wasn't paying attention. Couldn't stop kissing Lee-Lee and…" He shrugged.

"What are you more worried about?" I asked, folding my arms over my chest. "Colly finding out about you and Lia, or Colly going off about Chloe getting hurt?"

When he looked away, I knew the answer. Hooking up with your best friend's little sister was bad, yeah, but being on watch while your best friend's daughter broke her arm? That was ten times worse.

We went into Chloe's hospital room after a while. Lia was snoring away on the bed, holding Chloe asleep against her chest. A tiny, purple cast covered the little girl's arm, and I had to look away because seeing her hurt made my throat go tight.

"We're gonna stay the night," Max said. "Lia and I don't wanna take her home, not knowing what to do if she wakes up screaming. They offered, so we said yes."

I nodded, not blaming him. If Collin were here, there's no doubt she'd be home, but Max and Lia and I never took chances with this little girl.

"Where are Colly's parents?" I asked.

He winced. "On their way."

More than anything, I wanted to hold Beaner close

like Lia was, while promising to never let anything hurt her again. But I was almost positive that if I did, Max would've fallen over the edge of guilt-insanity he was teetering on. Things might have been different if the two of them *had* paid better attention, yeah, but it could've happened to anyone. There'd be no blame cast.

I sat on the edge of the bed for a little longer, just talking to Max, pretending it wasn't weird when he'd go over and rub his fingers across Lia's head, or lean down and kiss her every couple of minutes. I'd witnessed a change in the guy lately. And even before the truth about him and Lia was out, I'd known whatever they had going on had become their new normal.

"When's Colly coming home?"

Max shrugged. "Tomorrow sometime. He can't get a flight out until then."

I yawned and looked down at my cell phone. It was almost five thirty, but I had some things to take care of at my house in Arlo before I went home to have dinner with Kenna at seven. Had to grab the stuff I'd left there for Cat, now that I'd taken him in, then drop off some more tools that I had stored away in my Suburban. I wouldn't be able to use them until my new permit got approved next week, but I was tired of hearing them bang around in the back seat. "I've got some things to do so I'll be out for a while, but if you need me, call."

Max leaned forward and hugged me with one arm. "Thanks for bringing the blanket."

"Course. I'd do anything for that little girl." I walked over to still-sleeping Chloe and kissed her temple before leaving the hospital.

CHAPTER 13

McKenna

I WOKE UP SOMETIME AFTER EIGHT TO TWO ARMS PULLING ME off Gavin's couch. Soft footsteps thumped beneath me on the floor, jostling me slightly against a chest as we walked down a dark hall. When I turned my head to settle against his shirt, I inhaled, smelling Gavin's scent. I'd grown to enjoy it way more than I should have lately.

Not bothering to fight him, I'd played like I was asleep. The embarrassment over me falling asleep on his couch while I waited for him to come home so I could cook dinner felt a bit clingy. I was an emotional mess of hormones as it was, and the last thing I needed was for him to look at me with pity and set me off.

Once he was out for the night, I'd leave, this time through the door. Yet the second he laid me in his soft, cozy bed and covered my body with his warm blankets, I realized how hard my escape would be.

The lights flickered off, and I heard the rustle of clothes and a belt clinking against the floor. On my side and facing away from him, I could easily open my eyes, knowing he wouldn't see my face. But I kept them closed, willing the moment to be a dream. Or the moment to hurry up so I could leave. The ease with which he handled me and did this whole bedtime thing was far too couple-ish for a girl with commitment phobia.

"I know you're awake."

I stiffened. The mattress sank as he moved to lie next to me. But instead of getting under the covers, he stayed on top and pulled a separate blanket over himself. I bit my lip, having no idea how to respond.

"I'm so fucking sorry I'm late. I'm a jackass."

"It's okay." He wasn't *that* late. And it's not like I was waiting out in the chilly air or anything. Besides that, he'd warned me.

When I got to his place a little before seven, I'd texted him that I was there. He'd told me to use his spare key under the doormat to let myself in. Apparently, he'd had something come up but would be there within the hour. I told him that it was okay, I didn't mind waiting, but twenty minutes into doing so, I'd fallen asleep. Pregnancy exhaustion was a total bitch.

"Chloe broke her arm today, and I've been worried about her. Then I had something else come up, and I lost track of time trying to work through it all."

Part of me was dying to know what he'd had to *work through*, but I didn't have a right to know anything about his life. I was his…friend? Acquaintance? Oh, and let's not forget the mother of his child.

"It's just been a shitty day all around," he finished.

"I'm sorry your day was shitty." I pressed my hands

between my cheek and the pillow, keeping still. If I spoke any more or rolled over to face him, I'd crack and tell him everything. Sure, that had been the original plan for tonight. Cook him dinner, only to sit him down after and break the news once his tummy was full and his eyes were half-shut. I was going to tell him not to worry, that I'd thought it over, and he didn't need to take any responsibility for this child.

But now, with his soft voice, his proximity, and my half-sleepy state doing mushy-gooey things to my already whacked-out hormones, I could barely string two words together.

"It's not okay. I'm so damn sorry I'm late." My biggest fear came true as he moved to lie close to my backside. He didn't wrap an arm around my waist, nor did he make a move to snuggle in any way, but he did reach up and pull some of my hair off my shoulder.

Gavin was on the verge of a major cuddle moment.

And I was too needy to push him away.

"It is. I promise." I'd fallen asleep on his couch like Goldilocks, yet felt no shame in being cuddled in his bed with lies that could break us both.

If there was such a thing as a person who deserved to go to hell, other than the obvious bad people, I would be the prime candidate.

A heavy breath escaped him, and I could feel it across my shoulder and neck. I shivered, unable to stop myself from arching my back and getting closer. His hand skimmed my waist, just beneath the bottom of my shirt.

He leaned over and kissed the back of my head. "Go to sleep. In the morning, I'll take you to breakfast to make up for tonight."

I nodded once, barely moving as he turned away from me. My shoulders fell in disappointment.

"And, Kenna?"

"Hmm?" I didn't trust my voice.

"Please don't leave in the middle of the night."

"What if I have to pee?" I pulled my bottom lip between my teeth, trying not to grin.

He chuckled softly. "Then go. Just no more Cinderella moments, okay?"

I narrowed my eyes. Cinderella? As in… "Oh, my boot."

"What'd you say?"

"Nothing."

"Hmm."

Several minutes later, with his warm back pressed solidly against mine, I found my nerves easing and my guard lowering further. "She'll be okay."

"Who?" he asked, his voice crackly with sleep.

"Chloe. The break was clean. And since she's so young, even if she does wind up needing surgery, it'll heal quickly."

He shifted in the bed, turning toward me again. "How'd you know she broke her arm?"

"I was there. I worked today, remember?"

"Shit. I forget everything."

Slowly, my bravery took over, and I turned onto my other side to face him. In the dark, I could just make out the outline of his cheek, his beard too. I clutched my hands together so I wasn't tempted to reach out and touch him. Ever since my trip to Maine last winter, I'd developed a weird thing for lumber-sexual men. I think it was because my ex wasn't hairy in the least. If anything, Paul had less hair than I did.

I squeezed my eyes shut at the thought of *him*. Somehow, I'd managed not to think about the guy for a solid month…yet one night in bed with another man— even clothed—and my thoughts conjured up Paul.

"Can't sleep?" Gavin searched my eyes in the dark.

Our faces were still a few inches apart, yet I felt closer to him than I should.

"Not really." That was a lie. Because if I shut my eyes, I'd no doubt fall asleep in a heartbeat, something I struggled to do at home. In the bed I *used* to share with the ex. Before he started sharing beds with a *couple* of someone elses.

"Me either."

"Why?" I asked, because I was a glutton for punishment and suddenly wanted to know everything about this man—the man I wasn't supposed to want to know.

"Got a lot on my mind."

"I'm a good listener." I smiled. So did he. It was rare, and I could barely see it in the dark, but I knew it was there. A smiling Gavin was pure brilliance.

"I go back to work on Monday, for one."

I frowned. "What do you mean, go back to work?"

He rolled onto his back and looked at the ceiling. "I've been suspended for a month for…losing my temper."

"No shit?" I laughed. Which wasn't the most appropriate reaction, but I couldn't help myself. It was what I did when I didn't know how to react to certain circumstances.

"Not funny," he grumbled.

I snorted again, then slapped my hand over my mouth, because, hello? *Rude much, Kenna?* "I know it's not funny. I'm sorry. It's just…when I don't know how to react to something, I laugh. Like, it's a stress-management thing. It's an actual condition." I brought my thumb to my mouth and started biting on what little nail I had left. "For instance, when I first started out as a nurse, a man came into the ER, which is where I did a lot of my training, and he literally had a rash from head to toe. It was the most disgusting thing I'd ever seen, yet when I looked at him, I had no idea what to say. I, like, froze up. And because of that, I wound up laughing. I laughed so hard, I started to cry. It was…awful."

"Laughter is a mild form of hysteria."

"What do you mean?"

Gavin sighed, letting his hands fall to his sides. The backs of his knuckles grazed the front of my thighs in the process, but he didn't move them closer, nor did he move them away.

"Take, for example, when someone laughs at something really hard. They say it was 'hysterical.' There's a fine line between laughing and crying. That's the reason why people cry when they get happy, like when you go to a wedding."

"Mr. Psychological is in the house." If I could have *whooped* in that moment, I probably would have—but, tact. I needed to learn it. Who knew Mr. St. James could be so insightful?

"A person's mind isn't great at deciding which reaction is appropriate in certain situations," he continued, ignoring my smart mouth. "Which is why you laughed at the man with a rash, and why you laughed when you learned I'd been suspended."

Through a yawn I said, "That makes sense." More sense than anyone had made for me on any subject I'd struggled with. "Growing up, I always looked at things a little differently than most."

"Yeah?"

I nodded. "I was shipped away to live with my father as a teenager because dear old *Mom* called me the socially unacceptable child with the loud mouth and no impulse control."

"So? I like that you're impulsive."

He rolled back to face me again, laying a hand on my hip. Grinning, he squeezed it lightly. I moved closer, instead of away, letting our hips press together. For once in my life, I was determined to let intimacy win out.

"My parents didn't see it that way. Mother dear took me to three separate psychiatrists until one finally diagnosed me with impulsivity."

"Had to be hard." His smile faltered.

"It was. Mom wanted me to be the perfect southern daughter. But I didn't fit into her life plan. That's why she shipped me away, remarried, and adopted my stepsiblings."

I couldn't stop myself from doing some things in my life, no matter how many times I was told the behavior was unacceptable. I spoke out loud at inopportune times, saying random stuff that made no sense to anyone but myself. I also picked at my scabs, bit my nails down to nothing, and rubbed at my nose and my eyes constantly. I had tics, I guess you could say.

Luckily, I'd grown out of most of them, other than biting my nails obsessively. But sadly, I'd pushed those tics into other areas of my life. I talked too much and still said inappropriate things. And my life decisions were impulsive. For instance, I was really bad at picking boyfriends, which I'd finally figured out with Paul. If Gavin knew about all my strange quirks, he'd probably run for the hills. Which would be perfect. Well, if I wasn't carrying his child.

"I'm sorry you went through that." He studied me through the dark. It was as if he had super X-ray vision and could make out every inch of my face, every line, every freckle. With Gavin, I felt exposed.

"Why were you suspended?" I finally asked, needing to break the moment.

Just like that, his intensity disappeared and in its place was a mask of…nothingness. The same one I put on constantly myself. Guess we had more in common than I'd thought.

"A guy was running his mouth at me."

"And let me guess…" I poked him gently in the ribs. "You had to show him *who's boss*, right?" I grinned, trying to play it off as a joke, but he didn't respond to it that way. Didn't bat an eye or show even a shadow of emotion.

Cringing, I propped my head up on my hand, bringing our faces closer. "I'm sorry. You know I was kidding. I'm sure you had a great reason for—"

"Breaking his nose with my fist?"

"Oh." I cringed again.

"Yeah, *oh* is right," he scoffed. "Took two guys to pull me off him, and if it wasn't for the fact that he was sexually harassing one of the female EMTs, I would've gotten into a hell of a lot more trouble than I did. Four weeks of suspension is enough as is."

"Jesus." I hadn't heard about that. Then again, the EMTs ran in their own circles outside the hospital. They were our delivery people; at least, that's what the nurses tended to call them.

"Not really something I wanted advertised. Besides, he was fired—with compensation, if you can believe that—while I was put on unpaid leave."

"Bullshit." I narrowed my eyes. "Sounds to me like you were trying to defend that woman, yet you got the shit end of the deal."

Gavin's brows furrowed as he spoke. "In the world of adulting, you apparently have to go to a supervisor to report certain behaviors." His voice became mocking as he finished. "Fighting with your hands in a workplace environment is deemed the most irresponsible thing a person in the medical field can do."

I snorted, remembering that night Gavin and I hooked up. Remembering my fist plowing into that preppy kid's face because of what he said to me. "It sounds like you've had some experience with Jayla in HR."

A real smile graced his lips, sending a shot of warmth into my chest. "She's never been a marine."

"And she also wasn't raised by a father who fought for money on the weekends at an illegal underground club, while leaving his daughter at home alone—from age thirteen to seventeen—in a one-bedroom shack in the worst part of a town. I would've totally punched that bastard too."

Gavin mirrored my position, propping his head on one hand. He moved his hand from my waist and pressed his palm against my cheek. His grin was gone, replaced by silence and a locked jaw. "That really happened to you?"

"Maybe." I shrugged, hating how easily I could blurt things out with him. It reminded me of Paul. But with that asshole, I'd believed in false promises about *never letting someone hurt me again.*

Gavin, on the other hand, didn't offer me false possibilities of protection. Instead, he offered me ears and a nod—and a little bit of himself too. "I had a pretty shitty upbringing myself."

"Yeah?"

He nodded. "Before I was shifted to my first foster home," he started, heaving a giant sigh, "I lived with my uncle until I was ten. He…wasn't a good man. Had no interest in raising a kid who'd just lost both parents, not even when one of them was his own fucking brother. He was cranky and walked with a cane that he used to beat me when I didn't do my chores the right way."

I gasped, touching his chest with my free hand. Beneath my palm, his heartbeat was steady, which surprised me for such a wretched memory. "Oh, Gavin."

He squeezed his eyes shut as he continued, almost as though this was something he'd been holding in for so long that he couldn't stop talking.

I could relate. So very much.

"When DCFS came and found out I hadn't been going to school, mainly because he didn't bother to register me and didn't have the money to pay for it, I become a ward of the state."

I sucked in a breath, waiting for him to continue. Part of me wanted him to stop talking. A part that said *If you know him, you won't be able to walk away from him.* But a tiny part of me—okay, a *huge* part of me—did want to hear what made up the mystery that was Gavin St. James. Which is why I didn't interrupt him or make a joke or even try to distract him with sex.

For the first time in a long time, I just listened.

"My first year, I went through six different foster homes. After a couple of months, most of the people who'd taken me in decided they didn't want broken ten-year-old boys. Babies and toddlers were easier."

"More bullshit," I blurted out. "Babies and toddlers are hell." I shuddered, then cringed when I remembered how in eight months, I'd be popping out one of those.

Fingers brushed against my chin, and I reopened my eyes, finding him even closer, our lips nearly touching. "Gotta agree with you there, but I wasn't exactly an easy kid."

My heart skipped as one side of his mouth curved up. An image ran through my mind as he studied me: a baby boy with a grin, his father's green eyes, and my blond hair.

Panic forced my stomach into knots, and I rolled over onto my back, needing distance.

He sighed, the sound filled with disappointment, but resolve at the same time. "The point of the story is, at the last house where I stayed through my high school graduation, I had a pretty good foster family. A foster mom named Heidi, a foster dad named Jake, and an older foster brother, Adam, who was huge on all things sports, including that underground fighting shit." He laughed softly under his breath. "Seventeen years old and he'd sneak out at night, then come back later with a wad of cash and promises to get us to college." Gavin moved onto his back too, but his hand was down, and before I could protest, he laced our fingers together. As much as I knew I should move away, I couldn't.

"He was awesome, always standing up for me.

Introduced me to baseball and football. Pretty much any sport I wanted to learn, he'd teach me about it."

My words were a whisper as I said, "He sounds amazing."

"He was."

And just like that, Gavin's mask went back into place. Only this time, I didn't see it. I heard it, felt it. I waited for him to finish his story. To tell me what he meant by *was*. But by the time I turned my head to ask him, his breaths had evened out and his lips were parted in sleep. His chest rose and fell, up and down. I watched, soothed by another's breaths—soothed by his story, even if it wasn't necessarily happy.

And as I studied him in the dark, I came to the sad conclusion that Gavin was pretty much just like me. Someone with a shitty past but a future full of possibilities—including one currently swimming like a flea in my lower abdomen.

That's when I decided to do what I'd sworn I wouldn't and stay the night in his bed. Because it was apparent the both of us had been alone for too long.

Baby steps. That's what I'd call this.

CHAPTER 14

Gavin

"Good morning." I smiled. Big, wide, real. Because for the first time in a long time, I had something to smile about. McKenna was in my bed.

"Thank you," she whispered, taking me by surprise.

"For...?"

"Last night. For just listening to me. Nobody has done that for a long time."

I reached over and touched her cheek, knowing what that was like. "Feeling's mutual."

Telling her what I had the night before had been a risk. But I'd never expected her to open up to me too—even the small amount that she did.

Slowly, she lowered her lips to my chest, kissing my skin, the spot over my racing heart. My cock jerked to attention. I swallowed hard, watching, curious what would happen next. I could have stopped her. No, I *should* have stopped her. But that would mean letting her go. And after last night, I wasn't ready. Likely not ever now.

"This okay?" she asked, thick lashes batting against her cheeks.

"More than." My voice cracked.

"Good."

Her fingers joined in on the action, but they had a mind of their own, skimming down my stomach and landing at the top of my boxers. There, she hesitated for a second, waiting for my approval.

Hands shaking, I reached down and tugged my boxers to my knees. Her cheeks went pink as she watched, an adorable shade I wasn't used to seeing on her face.

But the second she eyed my cock, her vixen ways were back. She inched her hand closer, wrapping it around the base, lips parting as she pressed them against my stomach.

I hissed through my teeth, watching as McKenna's soft hand began to stroke. One long pull, another shorter one... A dribble of come spilled out of the tip, and that heavenly hand used its thumb to coat the head.

I hadn't been given a hand job in at least five years. And fuck if I wasn't suddenly fifteen again, feeling on top of the world.

Not wanting to disturb the beautiful blond on the giving end, I lay as still as possible, my eyes closed, curling my fists into the blanket. My thighs burned as I flexed them in place, but I refused to move. A low moan sounded from my throat though; I couldn't help it. It felt so good. So tight. So warm. So real.

Jesus. Who was I kidding? This was very, very real.

"Kenna," I finally said, reopening my eyes to look at her. More than anything, I had to know she was with me. This wasn't what I'd intended today. Not that I wasn't

pleasantly surprised, believe me. But she'd been pushing me away for five weeks straight. I figured I'd have
to take what I got.

Still, I hadn't expected a good-morning hand job.

Unfortunately, it'd never be enough for me. Which
is why I reached down to grab her wrist, stopping her.
"No. This isn't right. We shouldn't…" I gritted my teeth,
hating my morals. Hating how badly I wanted to forgo
my need for security and control. To just let myself feel
with this woman. To take what I could get.

"W-what's wrong?" Her blue eyes searched my face
when she leaned back.

I sucked in a breath to speak. "You can't do this to me
and expect me to walk when it's all done. I can't handle
having you leave again."

That bottom lip of hers puffed out into a frown, and
more than anything, I wanted to pull it between my teeth.
Still, I waited as patiently as I could, watching as a battle
seemed to be waging behind her pretty stare. I held my
breath, my chest going tight as I did. I didn't take relationships with women lightly. Hell, I'd only had one
one-night stand in my life, and that was two years ago.

Her hand loosened around my cock, but she didn't
let it go completely. Instead, she looked at me, unsure,
waiting…confused most of all.

"What're you gonna do, McKenna?" I asked, leaning
forward to run one finger down her cheek, down her
chin, down her neck, stopping right above her heart.

"I…"

"Tell me yes or tell me no. It's that easy."

Her lips parted as if she wanted to talk. But before
she could, I sat up, leaned forward, kissed her once, and

made the decision she obviously couldn't—raging hard on be damned.

"Time to get up. I promised you breakfast this morning."

—◆◆◆—

She ate like a woman on a mission, shoving in food left and right. Bacon, eggs, hash browns, pancakes… And I couldn't stop grinning across the table at her because of it. She was not just gorgeous; she was damn near glowing with every bite she took. As though it was the first meal she'd eaten in years, the best food of her life.

"You eat like you're feeding an army." I took a sip of my coffee. "I'm not going to take it from you."

Mid-bite, fork still in the air, she froze, face paling. I leaned closer and pressed my hand against her wrist. She startled at the contact, and her fork fell against the plate with a clatter, eggs splattering all over the table.

"I need to use the restroom." She jumped out of the booth and ran to the back of the restaurant.

It took me thirty seconds before I could take my head out of my ass. And then another thirty seconds to realize it was my job to go after her. I wasn't good at this romance thing.

Just outside the door to the ladies' room, I found her sitting on the floor, leaning back against the wall. Déjà vu hit me full force, only this time she wasn't drunk. Fear had me dropping to my knee in front of her. I cupped her face between my hands.

"What is it?" I asked. Her cheeks were red, her lips quivering. My heart thudded harder in my chest at the sight, the thumping beats reaching my ears. "Talk to me."

"I…" She blinked, and tears slipped over my fingers.

"That was an asshole thing to say at the table. I'm sorry."

"No." She shook her head. "That's not it."

"What is it?"

She pulled her bottom lip between her teeth, holding a breath. Once she let it out, she whispered, "Gavin, I'm pr—"

My phone rang. "Damn. Hold that thought." I reached into my pocket to mute it, but then I got a look at who it was. "I'm sorry. I gotta take this. It's Collin."

She wiped at her tears and nodded, pushing up off the floor. "Yes. Answer." She smiled, but I could see the strain. I knew already which smiles were real and which weren't. She pointed to the bathroom, one finger in the air. I nodded and waited outside as I answered the phone.

"What's up, Colly?"

"At the airport. Got an early flight in. Can you come get me?"

"Yeah, of course. We'll be there in twenty."

"Who's 'we'?" he asked.

"McKenna and me," I answered, no hesitation. From here on out, I'd make it known to the world what my intentions were with this woman. And I didn't care what anyone thought or said. I wanted her, and I'd do anything to make her mine.

"That's real good, Gav. She's a sweet girl. Reminds me of you in a lotta ways."

I smiled at his approval. "Yeah."

Kenna came out of the ladies' room just then, looking a little more composed. I reached for her hand, gave it a squeeze, then told Collin to hold tight. That we'd be there soon.

We walked back to the table and grabbed the bill, taking it to the register. Kenna stayed stuck to my side like glue but didn't speak.

Whatever she'd been about to tell me before Collin called was obviously important. But the moment had passed, and the last thing I wanted to do was upset her again.

I'd told her where we were going, and she'd agreed to ride with me, but she was quiet along the way—not the same girl who'd lain in bed with me last night. She was closed off. And I hated it. I wondered if this was what it was like for people who hung around with me.

"Tomorrow morning, I go back to work, but I was hoping you'd go out with me tonight."

She snorted, the sound loud and abrupt in the space of my SUV. I turned to look at her, frowning.

"You don't need me. I'm pretty much a hot mess of dog shit."

I wouldn't take the bait. She was trying to push me away again. "Maybe I like the smell of dog shit."

"If you liked the smell, you'd get a dog."

"Can't do that. I already have a cat." I chuckled.

She rolled her eyes, which meant her sass was coming back. "Whatever. Take me out. Just know I am not the easiest person to please."

I reached down to grab her hand again, this time pulling it to my mouth for a kiss. "Good thing I like a challenge."

McKenna

I'm not sure when or how it happened, but somewhere along the way from the restaurant to the airport, and back to the hospital, I'd become a part of Gavin's inner circle.

I sat in the passenger seat of his SUV, my hand in his as he drove us down the highway. Collin's feet were kicked up between us on the console, and my elbow and Gavin's were propped up in front of them. It was weird and awkward, but neither Gavin nor Collin made a big deal out of it, so I let it be, pretending I wasn't drowning in a sea of testosterone.

"The doctor said her mom wasn't gonna make it through the day. Addie's handling it okay, but…shit, I wanted so bad to be there for her." Collin sighed, and I immediately dug my phone out of my pocket, the pain for my best friend bringing tears to my eyes.

Addie may not have had the best relationship with her parents, but they *were* her parents. Losing her mom wouldn't be easy, no matter the situation.

I texted her.

Me: You okay?

Addie: Hey. Yeah, I'm as good as I can be.

I swallowed the lump in my throat, wishing like hell I could be there to hug her.

Me: Text me if you need anything. I'm thinking about you.

**Addie: Thx. And BTW? Will you officially be
my maid of honor? =)**

Me: WTH?

"What the hell?" I said it out loud as I typed it, then
looked over my shoulder at Collin.

His eyes were bloodshot red, and there were dark
shadows underneath. He didn't look like a newly
engaged man as he stared out his window. He looked like
a worried father and boyfriend. Or should I say *fiancé*?

Gavin's brows rose. "What's wrong?"

I giggled, then nodded as I typed my reply, thankful
for a little happiness when things were kind of messed
up for both of us.

Me: You're kidding, right?

Addie: Nope.

"Holy shit." I might have been anti-relationship, but
seriously. *Holy. Shit.* My best friend getting engaged
was pretty much the most epic thing ever.

"What is it?" Gavin asked, his gaze bouncing back
and forth between me and the road.

"Oh, I don't know… Why don't you ask *Collin* back
there if he's got any exciting news he'd like to share."

"Damn," Collin groaned, shutting his eyes. "Addie
just couldn't wait, could she?" Still, I saw the smile on
his lips.

"Someone mind filling me in?" Gavin grumbled,
obviously annoyed with the secrecy. His grip on my hand

tightened a little, and I set my phone on my lap before reaching over to brush my fingers along the back of his wrist. He instantly relaxed…and I couldn't help but grin wider, knowing I'd been the one to do that for him.

In a way, I had power over Gavin, like he had power over me. And though I knew my confession could break that off in a heartbeat, I was selfish enough to enjoy that power for as long as I could.

"The question *you* should be asking is who Mr. Collin back there is going to be picking for a best man."

"What the fuck?" Gavin barked.

I laughed so loudly at the noise that I choked.

He swerved the SUV, trying to reach in the back seat to swat at Collin's knee, which made me laugh louder.

"So, she finally said yes?" Gavin got the question out through his wide smile. His eyes were squinted, and the corners turned up just as much as his lips did.

A truly happy Gavin was a stunning Gavin. The sight made my lungs squeeze.

"Yup." Collin smirked, not offering the details a girl needed to know about an engagement. I'd get them from Addie sooner or later, I supposed. This was Gavin and Collin's moment.

After dropping Collin off at the hospital to see Chloe, Gavin couldn't wipe the smile off his face. Still, the last thing I expected was for him to ask if I'd be upset if he took me home.

A tiny part of me didn't want to be left alone, because if I were, the negative thoughts inside my head would start haunting me again. Still, I didn't want to come across as clingy.

"No problem. I'm probably going to take a nap or something."

He winked at me, so incredibly playful for the man I had begun to think ran on only two levels in life: sad or broody. "Good. Because I need the afternoon to get some things in order. But I'll bring your car to pick you up tonight, unless you've got somewhere to be today."

In your arms is what I was stupidly thinking, but I immediately kicked that idea out of my head. God, what was wrong with me? One night in his bed, and it was Pisser Paul syndrome all over again.

Before I could contemplate what he was thinking when he looked at me—what could happen if I let him in the way I had sworn not to let another man in again—I needed to tell him the truth about the baby.

"Kenna." He squeezed my hand again. "You good with this? Because I can come inside for a little while if you want me to."

I nodded, turning away so he wouldn't see the tears forming in my eyes. I had no idea why I was even crying. Hormones? Guilt? Fear?

Letting go of my fingers, he moved his hand to my leg. "Six okay tonight?" he asked, his thumb resting against my inner thigh, stroking.

Again, I nodded, just as he pulled into the lot of my apartment complex.

A few kids were outside, running to the small playground on the back of the grounds. A woman followed behind, hair plastered to her face and a flustered toddler flailing in her arms. I'd never seen her before, but I suddenly wanted to watch her, study her. Learn from her.

"You okay?" Gavin squeezed my thigh and I squeaked, jumping in place.

"Shit, I'm ticklish. Don't do that." I giggled, momentarily forgetting why I was upset.

"Yeah?" One dark eyebrow rose, and a teasing smile tugged up the side of his mouth. "Good to know."

"Um, I *don't like* to be tickled." I pursed my lips. "Why would you need to know that when any further tickling could end with a junk-punch?"

Gavin dropped his head back against the seat. "Trust me, if I tickle you…" He licked his lips. "You'll be begging me to never stop."

I sucked in a breath, my fear of his tickling gone. In its place was curiosity, paired with desire and an undeniable warmth growing between my thighs. My already sensitive nipples tingled against my bra, and I secretly hoped we could start the tickle game right there in his car.

Apparently, pregnancy did weird things to my already active libido.

Gavin's smirk faded into heat when he looked down at my chest. I squeezed my thighs together, trapping his hand in, totally not thinking about what it meant, just needing him to ease the building pressure, the ache that had been in place for weeks now. I'd missed this—missed what he could do for me.

And I was done waiting.

Forgetting all my internal battles, I lost myself to his touch, urging his hand up higher. "Please." I shut my eyes, using the side of his palm to rub against the seam of my shorts.

"I'll take care of you." The edge of his palm slipped to where I craved it most, the calloused base just catching my zipper. "But you have to promise me you won't run." He applied a little pressure, just enough to send a flash of heat through my belly. "I need more than just this from you."

I tipped my head back, refusing to think of the consequences to my answer before it slipped out. His coercion was everything I'd been denying myself.

"Yes, okay, yes. Anything."

He moved his hand away, and I reopened my eyes on a protesting gasp. "What are you…"

The driver's side door opened and shut in a flash. Throat dry, I watched him run around the front of his SUV, bopping the hood of his Suburban just once. He popped up on my side, a wide grin on his face through my window. I shook my head, grinning as my door opened with a bang.

"In a hurry?" I teased, regardless of my own urges.

"Up." He nodded at me with his chin.

"Up?" I squirmed in my seat, needing him to get back in here and finish what he'd started.

"I won't do this in broad daylight with you. The last thing I want is for a few random kids to freak out if they hear a woman screaming from my truck."

"Who says I'll scream?" My lips twitched. "You must have some serious confidence in your skills if that's the—"

He cut me off with his lips, his hand at the nape of my neck, his mouth overpowering mine. As I rose to my feet, our chests were crushed together. Gavin kissed me with the sort of strength that had me sinking into him and all he had to offer.

I curled my fingers in his long hair as the delicious

sting of his beard rubbed my cheeks almost raw. With his tongue, he begged for entrance, pushing aside my lips with a feral growl.

My mind whirled with sensations, needs, wants. Hard and powerful, that's how this man kissed me—as if he could coax the orgasm out of my body with his talented mouth alone. Before I could beg for what I needed again, his hands were on my ass, yanking me hard against his erection with a low groan. "You seem to forget about our night together."

I smiled against his mouth. "I remember everything about that night."

The way he'd felt inside me.

The way he'd pulled at my hair when he fucked me briefly from behind.

And the thing I remembered the most? How sore my throat had been in the morning when I woke. Because yes, I'd screamed *really* loud that night.

And it had everything to do with Gavin's ability to fuck me.

"Hmm" was his only response. Again, the man of few words.

Giggling to myself, I latched my legs around his waist and kissed his cheek, then his ear, only to squeak when he pinched my ass.

"Where are your keys?" he asked as he walked me toward the front of my apartment, not letting me go. Not even pausing to catch his breath, other than when he spoke.

"They're in my pocket." I sighed, then leaned my forehead against his shoulder. One part of me was embarrassed because another person walked by, but the other part wished he'd just given me what I needed in his SUV.

"Well, fuck."

I laughed again, but it fast turned into a moan as he slowly undid my legs from around his body and let me slide down the front of his hardness. My breasts ached from loss of contact with his chest when he nudged me away to dig in my pockets. Thankfully, it lasted only a few seconds.

He quickly unlocked the building's door, only stopping to hike me up around his waist again. "I like you like this."

I shuddered as fingers crept beneath the line of my shorts. "Like what?"

"Against me." He nuzzled his nose against my cheek, then kissed me gently there. Intimate and sweet—nothing like the broody man I'd come to know.

As he carried me down the hall, the cold air from inside the complex brushed against the back of my neck. I shivered, tightening my arms around his neck.

Sensing my discomfort, he stroked a heavy hand up and down my spine. "Apartment number one-seventeen, right?"

I nodded, my body suddenly too heavy and lax for words. I was already sated in his arms, a comfort I hadn't felt from a man—or even another human—in so long.

I counted fifteen steps before we arrived in front of my apartment door. He'd gone quiet again, as had I, neither of us saying a word when he unlocked my door and shoved it open. Five long steps after that, we were in my kitchen—Gavin placing me on the edge of the counter, merciless toward my poor, unsuspecting dishes.

Several plates fell to the floor with a crash, shattering over his shoes. "Shit." He stumbled back a bit, eyes narrowed at the mess. He looked so much like a guilty, little boy, his eyes filled with fear and sadness as they shifted from the floor to my face. "I'm sorry."

I touched his cheek, not giving a damn about a set of garage-sale dishes. "It's fine."

He shut his eyes, blew out a breath, then nodded, moving a step closer again. "I'll buy you new ones."

I shrugged, then reached for the button of my shorts. "Or you can pay me back in other ways."

He grinned, leaning over me, only to reach the button first. "So demanding."

I arched my back, allowing him the access he needed to get the shorts off. "*Needy* is what I am."

His grin was smug as he dropped to his knees between my bare thighs. "As you should be."

With gentle hands, he pressed his palms to my knees, then slipped them up and over my thighs. At the edge of my panties, he stopped, eyes flaring, breaths ragged at the same time. I looked down, frowning.

"Everything…okay?" I gulped, suddenly remembering the truth as I took in the small bulge just above my pubic bone. He couldn't tell that I was pregnant, this I knew, but Jesus, *I* could. My belly wasn't flat anymore. It was like I'd overeaten during a meal.

"Better than okay." His eyes flashed up at me as he slowly slid the panties down my leg. Mischief lit the green, and I shuddered for a different reason all together. Then with a teasing grin still on his face, he whispered, "Now's the time when you say 'please,' beautiful."

CHAPTER 15

Gavin

I KISSED THE INSIDE OF HER KNEE, WONDERING HOW ONE woman could wind me up so tightly. All I wanted was to sink inside her, but Kenna needed to be shown how good a man could be to her first. If we had sex again, there'd be no way for me to get inside her heart. And *that* was my end goal.

"Gavin." She moaned my name as though she was on the verge of breaking, and I'd yet to get to the good stuff. I moved my lips higher and higher, until her legs were propped over my shoulders and my nose was buried against her pussy. I inhaled and shut my eyes. "Tell me yes. Tell me I can taste you."

"God, Gavin, please. Do it now."

The first dip of my tongue had her arching her back. By the time I parted her folds with my fingers, she was scissoring my neck with her knees, both thighs going tight around my head.

I loved every fucking minute of the pain.

She gripped the edges of the counter as though she was scared of falling, her chest rising and falling with heavy pants. Wanting her to feel secure, safe, I lowered one hand under her ass, then squeezed.

"Fuck yes," she whispered, the dirty mouth I remembered from the first night we'd spent together coming back like lighting in a storm.

I groaned. Every time she moved, I went faster. I had a reaction to go along with every one of her actions, so in tune with her body that I didn't ever want to stop. She moved one of her hands to grip my hair, tugging me closer, smothering me against her. I could hardly breathe, but that's exactly what I wanted.

Removing my hand from her ass, I pushed it around front, splaying it over her stomach. For a half second, while my palm settled over her belly button, she froze—locked down, really. Thinking I'd messed up, I pulled my hand away and dropped it to my side, only for her to arch her pussy harder against my mouth.

Just the thought of upsetting her had my nails digging into my palms, my tongue moving faster, my lips sucking harder. I wouldn't hurt her. Physically, emotionally, *anyway*. I wanted her to feel good. I wanted her to remember this. Love this as much as I did.

She cried out my name, just as her legs shook beside my ears. "Oh my God, oh my God, Gavin, yes…" And just like last time, she came hard on a scream.

I nuzzled my nose against her clit, savoring the taste of her on my tongue, just in time for her to finally relax.

She covered her eyes with an arm, head tipped back. "Jesus, St. James."

"You okay?" I smiled when she nodded.

"More than okay." She propped herself up on both elbows and looked up at me when I stood. Thighs parted, pussy bare, she looked the way any gorgeous, sated woman should look after a good orgasm: fucking beautiful.

"Yeah?" I leaned down to grab her panties, helping her slip them up and over her legs. "I must be damn good at getting you off, then."

When I reached for her shorts, she shook her head and stood, wrapping her arms around my waist. "Thank you."

I froze for a second, not used to the affection. Then when I realized she wasn't going to pull away, I shut my eyes, savoring the rare moment. "For what?"

"For…being here."

I hated the hesitation in her voice, needed to see her face, to know what she was thinking, more than anything. McKenna was a hard person to read, which wasn't good for a guy who didn't take cues well.

"Hey." I pulled back and pressed my hands to her cheeks. Her soft eyes met mine, glistening with tears. "What's wrong?"

She quickly shook her head and tugged on her shorts. "Nothing. I'm just tired. Didn't get much sleep last night." She sniffled, and my back stiffened.

"But you're crying."

"Am not."

"Liar."

She shoved at my chest playfully, but I only moved back enough to see her face again. "It's just been a while, is all."

"A while since you last had an orgasm?"

"At least *that* way." Her cheeks turned pink.

"So...you laugh when someone is hurting or in pain, yet you cry when something feels good." I rubbed her chin, holding her face with my other palm. "You are pretty much the weirdest, most wonderful woman I know."

She rolled her eyes and grabbed my hand—the one against her cheek. "And *you* have things to do, remember?" She tugged me to the door behind her, her ass so fucking gorgeous in those shorts that I wanted to fall to my knees and worship it. Hell, I wanted to worship every inch of this woman. But I needed to earn something first: her trust.

I knew I couldn't do that by continually pushing for more when she was obviously scared of commitment. That mean meant I needed to do this her way—*and* mine.

Compromise the best way I knew how.

She turned the handle on the door, and this time, I didn't fight her about leaving. "Six. Be ready." I leaned over and kissed her cheek, lingering for a minute when she reached forward to grab the bottom of my tee. She held me close, her fingers tight on the fabric. It was as though her head was fighting her heart about something.

Before she could decide which part of her body she wanted to side with, I turned and made the decision for her by walking out the door. I knew she was watching me walk away though—could almost feel her eyes burning into the back of my head.

I could only imagine the thoughts running through her mind.

McKenna

Holy crap. I'm falling for my baby's daddy.

Those were the first thoughts that hit me as soon as I shut the door to my apartment and leaned back against the wood. I had either lost my mind or was on the verge of losing it, because there was no way in hell I could possibly be falling for this guy already.

I barely knew him.

Well, that'd be a tiny lie, because I did know him, rather well actually. Not just from firsthand experience, but from Addie too.

Gavin's so quiet.

Gavin's so protective.

Gavin's so smart.

Gavin, Gavin, Gavin.

Blah, blah, blah.

"Ugh." I flopped onto the couch, internally cursing the voice of my best friend. She might have known *Gavin* from a *friend's* point of view. But had she ever stayed up half the night talking to the guy? Had she ever kissed him or held his hand? Had she ever looked into his eyes and realized that she wasn't alone in the world after all?

"Of course not. That'd be me." I covered my face with my palms, wanting to scream or cry or throw something. Yet my dishes were already cracked and on the floor, and I couldn't find the energy to pick them up— let alone toss them.

Thinking maybe I needed a reminder about all things bad relationships, I headed to my room, reaching for the Forbidden Box of Shame at the top of my closet.

If there ever was a time to encourage myself *not* to feel something for a man, this was it. Gavin was a great guy, as far as I could tell. In fact, I knew his perfect woman was somewhere out there. Someone patient and caring. Someone loving, who wouldn't run every time he gave her an extraordinary orgasm. Someone who would make him happy in a way I could not.

Gavin and I were like a bomb waiting to explode.

One that was, again, currently the size of a pea in my stomach.

As I sat on my bed in my room, I fingered the lid of the old shoebox before slowly opening it. This beat-up thing held crap from all my mistaken relationships. Whenever someone broke up with me, or I broke up with them, I saved a memento reaffirming the fact that they were not the man for me.

Breath held, I pulled out the first item. A money clip made of pure silver with his initials engraved on the front. The money clip I'd given him two weeks after he told me he loved me. Two weeks *before* I found him in bed with another woman.

Paul.

The one guy I thought I could trust—the nerd with the cute dimple and the ability to wreck me emotionally. I cried for weeks over Paul. Nearly drank myself into oblivion and broke my iPod with all the depressing music I played on it. Princess Paul is what I'd labeled him at first—a diva inside an Armani suit. He was the final reason I'd sworn off men altogether. But he wasn't the first one to leave me questioning my ability to pick something other than garbage when it came to guys in my life.

Using the limited nails I had left, I picked up the ziplock bag with the money clip inside, disgusted with myself for even keeping it. Shaking my head, I tossed it in the garbage can next to my bed.

"Take that, *Paul*."

Next, I pulled out a napkin from McDonald's for Asshole Abe—the starving artist who turned out to be not so starving after all. Instead, he'd been a trust-fund baby who didn't believe in spending money on his girlfriends— like me. It was on our one-year anniversary, when he said *surprise* and took me to Mickey D's, saying he'd be *splurging* on a dollar hot fudge sundae for me, that I realized I did not, in fact, want to continue our relationship.

Then there was Dickhead Daniel, who called out another woman's name during sex. I'd stolen his mix tape called Cock Rock from his nineteen-whatever Dodge Omni. It really was a good tape—one I'd still listen to if I had something to play it on.

As I went through all my collected goods, I couldn't help but laugh, and yeah, tear up on occasion. I'd done a bang-up job picking boyfriends, but what would happen if Gavin turned out to be different? Did I somehow know this already, and that was the reason for my messed-up, confusing emotions? Or was I just pregnant and looking for a reason to think positively when the negative thoughts were stacking up like Legos?

I sighed, tossing the box onto the floor, just as my cell rang. I wasn't in the mood to talk to anyone, not Addie or Emma. But when I saw my mother's name light up on the screen, my heart jumped into my throat with fear and worry. The lady never called for the hell of it.

Something was wrong.

CHAPTER 16

Gavin

I WAS ALMOST RUNNING LATE—AND I FELT LIKE A JACKASS because of it. All my prepping for our date tonight was nearly ruined by the fact that I'd had to keep my two best friends from killing each other. But if I were Collin and had walked in on Max having sex with my little sister, I probably would've punched him out too.

I wasn't choosing sides this time. Not when Collin was a mess over the fact that Addie's mom had died this afternoon and he couldn't be there with her when it all went down. And not when Max said he'd never back down, that he was in love with Lia.

My buddies had issues to work out, but I was going to steer clear of them. I had my own life to attend to now. And for once, I was gonna be selfish.

Luckily, McKenna was good with me showing up at seven. Supposedly, she'd taken a nap and overslept. I wasn't entirely convinced she hadn't overslept on purpose to avoid spending the evening with me, but I didn't bother pointing it out. If I did, she'd probably use that as another excuse to run from me. And again, I needed to trust her as much as I wanted her to trust me. Especially since I wanted more out of this than just a few good nights of sex.

When I stood to get out of her car, the front door to Kenna's complex flew open. "Jesus Christ," I whispered, a hand clamped like a vise around the top of my door when I caught sight of her.

Wearing high heels and dressed in a flowing, peach-colored dress with one shoulder exposed, Kenna was the most beautiful thing I'd ever seen.

"If you don't plan on feeding me tonight," she grumbled, heels clipping the concrete as she walked toward me, "then we need to head to a drive-through before—"

I jogged to meet her halfway, cutting her off with a kiss. One hand in her hair, the other gripping the nape of her neck tightly… God, I needed her. All of her. Last night and today had only amplified that feeling.

She sagged against me as if she'd been waiting to be held—waiting for my arms. I grabbed her around the waist with one hand, using the other to keep hold of her neck. Our lips moved slowly, a savoring kiss that had my chest going tight. I could kiss this woman forever, and it still wouldn't be enough.

Smiling, I pulled back and rubbed my knuckles down her flushed cheek. "Hi," I whispered, only to say, "What kind of date would this be if I didn't feed you?"

She scrunched up her nose, eyes twinkling. "The worst."

"Come on, then." I motioned my head toward her car and opened the door.

She jumped right in, her hips grazing mine. "What's this?" she asked, leaning over to find the box I'd left on the floorboard.

"Told you I'd replace them."

Turning around with the box pressed against her chest, she looked up at me with the widest, wettest eyes. "You replaced my dishes?"

I scratched at the back of my head, wondering why I'd made her cry. "Are they the wrong color or something? I saved the receipt in case."

"No." She quickly shook her head, then opened the white set I'd picked up from Target earlier. "They're perfect."

"Then what's wrong? Why're you crying?"

She blinked, and a tear fell down her cheek. "It's just that nobody has ever bought me anything like this before."

I cleared my throat, nervous. "Is that a good thing?"

She nodded, a small smile pulling at the side of her mouth. "Very."

"Good." I dropped a kiss onto her forehead and urged her leg inside the truck with my knee, waiting for her to buckle before I shut the door.

It was as if I'd given her the world by replacing those dishes. It made me want to buy her more. Cups and silverware, a new kitchen table... Hell, I'd build her an entire new *kitchen* if I could. McKenna wasn't greedy, but I somehow knew she was a woman who hadn't been treated right. I wanted to do everything I could to make up for that.

"Where are we headed?" she asked as I pulled out of the parking lot.

"It's a secret..." *That I've been keeping from*

everyone. I trusted her, and more than anything else, I wanted her to know that. And because I wasn't good with words, and feelings, shit like that, sharing this part of my life with her, when I hadn't shared it with anyone else, was one of the only ways I could show that trust.

I pulled her hand onto my lap.

"I'm not a fan of secrets." Her voice cracked as she looked out her window.

"I'm not a fan of keeping them either." I kissed her wrist, speaking against her skin. "Which is why I'm going to show you something I've never shown anyone else."

"Why?"

"Why what?"

"Why show me? I'm nothing to you, Gavin."

"*What*?" As I pulled onto the interstate that headed toward Arlo, I glanced at her from the corner of my eye. "How can you say that?"

She shrugged, still not answering. What had happened from the time we'd gotten into the car until now?

"Kenna. Are you trying to push me away again?" My teeth clenched at the thought.

"No." She sighed, squeezing my hand this time. "What I'm asking is, why share this secret with me when you hardly know who I am?"

Because you're everything to me. That's what I wanted to say. Not just by kissing her and touching her, but by showing her pieces of myself that nobody else saw. But expressing myself verbally was like drowning in slow motion. Inevitable, painful. Nothing I'd wish upon anyone.

"Forget it. We're just going to eat dinner, that's all."

Distracted, I set my foot to the accelerator, distancing

my feelings from her as we cruised the road. God, one step forward, fifty steps back. That was my life with this woman, and it killed me.

The tree-covered road was nearly dark when I finally made the turn down my lane twenty minutes later. Fear of a deer running out in front of us had me turning on my brights.

"It's creepy down here," she eventually said.

"Arlo's not a real populated town." With its one convenient store, it barely counted as a place to live. "It's why I like it." I shrugged and turned down my drive, the gravel sending small pings against my wheels.

"You like to be alone, don't you?"

"Yup."

"Why?"

I glanced at her, still agitated, though more at myself than her. I knew it was just a question, her asking why I bothered to care. But damn, if it didn't send my mood down further. I liked this woman. A whole lot. More than any woman I'd been around in a long while—if ever. She got me when I didn't even get myself, made me laugh when I had nothing to laugh about. Most of all, she made my heart feel heavy and desperate for things I'd never wanted before.

"It's just who I am. I was alone without anyone but my uncle until I was ten. He attempted to homeschool me, when he wasn't liquored up or sleeping. But even though I stayed up to date on schooling, I still had no idea how to talk to people."

In high school and college, I didn't have many friends. It was safer that way. Fewer friendships meant less pain if they left me. But as much as I tried to keep that mind-set, everything changed when I met Max and Collin.

"That's really sad."

I pulled into my driveway. "Maybe. But I didn't know any better. It wasn't until I met Max at boot camp, and he wouldn't leave me alone, that I realized having friends was better than being alone." I met Collin that same week, and the three of us had been friends ever since.

"What about your parents?"

My body tensed as I pulled my key from the ignition. The only sound around us was the summer night outside—crickets, an owl, and the rustle of branches. "What about them?"

She fidgeted in her seat, hands flexing and unflexing. "They died, didn't they?"

"Yeah." Frowning, I reached into the back seat, grabbing the blankets I'd brought for our makeshift picnic inside.

"Well, I meant—"

"They're dead. Not sure what else you want to know."

She flinched and stared down at her lap. "I'm sorry. I was just trying to piece things together."

"Can't be sorry when you don't know what you're missing."

That was a lie. Because even though I was little when they died, I could still smell my mom's perfume when she hugged me, and I could still feel the pressure of my father's hand as he patted the top of my head. Yeah, I barely remembered their faces—had a couple of scratched-up pictures to remind me when I wanted to remember—but that was nothing to me. Those people were strangers. Their spirit would always feel real to me.

I went to open the door of my Suburban but stopped short when she grabbed my arm. "Gavin, I…" She sucked in a breath, her face pained as she studied mine.

"What is it?"

"I really am sorry. It's just that I got some not-so-good news about my little sister this afternoon, and I'm kind of on edge about it." She shook her head. "I promise I won't ask again. About them. Or your past. Unless you want to talk about it."

I frowned. "Everything okay with your sister?"

"Yeah. It will be."

I studied her in the near dark, just able to make out her features. Something shifted in her face as she spoke, and the longer I looked, the more I wanted to know the secrets lurking behind her pretty eyes. I wanted to heal her sadness and piece together the broken parts of her that she rarely showed me.

My throat burned when she smiled, because it wasn't a real smile. Not like the one I'd seen when I gave her those stupid dishes, or when she was rambling on about names for my dick in that elevator. And not like the one I'd seen on her lips postorgasm either. This was the smile of a girl who didn't want to smile, and it tore me up.

McKenna

With his hand in mine, Gavin led me inside a tiny house set back from a long driveway. Behind it sat the Mississippi River in all its quiet brilliance, shining silver in the moonlight. I opened my mouth, wanting to ask if we could go stand next to the edge to study the stars and the slight ripple in the water. But I'd messed everything up with my crying, my rudeness, and my fear of opening up to this man, despite how badly I wanted to. At this point, I was nothing more than an unappreciative piece of garbage—an unappreciative piece of shit who held more secrets than a Maury Povich guest.

I was going straight to hell at this point.

Inside the door, Gavin clicked on a number of battery-powered lanterns. About seven in total, from what I could count. On a small table nearby sat two empty glasses and a wine bottle.

Wine.

Pregnant.

Baby.

"Shit," I whispered under my breath, my hand automatically going to my abdomen.

"Thirsty?" he asked, walking to the table and, thankfully, not hearing me. I looked down at his hands when he turned around few minutes later, finding two full glasses there. I gulped, wondering if I could get away with a sip—or at least pretend to.

"McKenna?" He dipped his head to the side.

"Huh?"

He held my glass out. "I asked if you wanted some wine."

My throat grew hot as I swallowed, but I somehow managed to speak. "Um, actually, do you have any water? I've been trying to cut back on my, uh, wine consumption lately." *Lame, K. So lame.*

Gavin placed the full glass down on a piece of plywood set across the top of two sawhorses. "Sure. Water it is."

Through the lights, I watched him, wondering how a man of his stature—so tall, so built—could move as if he had wings attached to his back.

He opened a blue cooler, the sound of ice rustling in front of him. I took the moment to compose myself, eyeing the small, cozy space. The entire place was a work in progress. An open layout, plywood floors, exposed walls with the plumbing still visible. In its own way, though, it was beautiful. Natural. A new beginning.

"Here you go." He stood in front of me and pushed a water bottle my way.

"Thank you." Our fingers grazed as I took it from his hand. Tiny sparks jumped up my arms and I shivered again.

"Welcome to my home away from home." He spread one arm out. The unsure smile on his face was so endearing that I couldn't help but grin back.

"It's really great."

"You don't have to lie. I'll still feed you even if you think this place should be set on fire before I bother fixing it up."

I poked him in the ribs, then uncapped my water, turning to look at other parts of the home. "Once you get it fixed up, it's going to be great." I pointed at the open area to our right. "That will be the family room. I can see a big screen on the wall and a sectional that will take up half the space." I walked to where I pointed, careful to step over the drop cords running across my path.

Footsteps sounded against the floor as he moved to stand at my side again. "That right?"

"Uh-huh." I smiled, imagining him watching a football or baseball game in there—drinking his beer and being all…sporty. "It'll be all…man-ish."

"Man-ish?" He quirked a brow, looking adorably delicious.

"Yep." I grinned and glanced to the left, finding a small area with an exposed toilet. "And obviously there will be walls surrounding the bathroom, but I can picture a Jacuzzi tub inside the bathroom. Then when you're done with the game, you can soak in it."

"Guys don't soak. They shower, wash, shave, and be done with it."

I nudged him with my elbow once more. But before I could pull away, he grabbed my hand and interlocked our fingers, a sweet smile on his gorgeous face.

On instinct, I reached up to tug on his beard, grinning. "Don't shave. I like this too much."

He took a step closer, his face mere inches from mine, our thighs pressed close. "For you, Kenna"—he leaned forward, rubbing his bearded cheek against my cheek—"I'll never shave again."

I shut my eyes, inhaling the scent of his skin, woodsy and warm, perfect. If I could sneak into his shower when he wasn't looking and steal whatever soap he used, my life would be complete.

"Now." He pulled back just enough to kiss the tip of my nose. "Where were we?"

The space between my thighs grew warm with need at his gravelly voice. God, he'd asked me a question, yet I had no damn clue how to answer it without begging for a quickie, right then and there.

But then my stomach growled.

One side of his mouth lifted into a grin. "I promised to feed you."

"Hmm, you did." But for Gavin, I'd forgo food for sex in a heartbeat.

"Come on." He winked as if he knew exactly where my dirty mind had gone.

We moved in front of a set of glass doors, his hand lingering on the intricately designed knob. "*This* is where the magic happens." He waggled his eyebrows. A playful Gavin made for one hell of a gorgeous sight.

I sighed, wondering how I was going to make it through the rest of the evening without tossing my no-sex rule out the window.

Though that rule had already been broken this morning on my kitchen counter.

There again, that was oral sex, not *sex* sex, and I—

Before I could finish my thoughts, he opened the doors, showing a three-season porch to die for.

I gasped. "Oh my *God*."

He flicked on another couple of battery-powered lanterns to our left. "That a good *oh my God* or a bad one?"

"Very good. Did you do this all yourself?"

He nodded. "It's why I was late for dinner the other night. I was just supposed to swing by and drop off some tools, but my new permit was actually up, and I… Shit, I just got carried away."

"You weren't *that* late," I reminded him as I stepped farther into the room. To my right sat a chocolate-brown leather sofa that looked well loved. In front of it was a coffee table made with the same ceramic tile that covered the floors. I wondered if the table was homemade.

The walls to our left and right were lined with pine,

while the wall in front of us was nothing but windows. The steepled ceiling held a long fan that probably was not hooked up if he didn't have electricity yet. In the corner of the room, I saw the makings of a wood-burning fireplace, unlit, unfinished, and detached from the wall. A chimney drew down from the ceiling, unattached as well.

"This is extraordinary." I looked back at him, watching as his cheeks turned pink. It was adorable. *Gavin* was adorable.

I walked toward the window, pressing a palm to the glass. The dark backyard was alive with lightning bugs, and beyond a few trees, I could barely make out the river.

"Sit," he ordered from behind.

"Bossy much?" I smiled and turned anyway, finding the blanket he'd been carrying over his shoulder spread out over the sofa.

"Sorry. I don't mean to be a dick. I just—"

"Hey." I grabbed his hand and gave it a squeeze. "I'm kidding."

The tension in his shoulders eased with my words. Then he nodded, exhaling, making me feel a little guilty for teasing him.

Wordlessly, he began pulling things out of a picnic basket and placing them on top of the table. I took off my heels and settled them at the end of the couch before easing down on it.

"I've got cold chicken, homemade bread, courtesy of Max, and some other stuff I picked up at the store today." The last things he pulled out were strawberries and pickles.

My eyes widened a little at the view. It was a pregnant woman's dream.

"This is amazing, Gavin."

"Hmm," he mumbled his familiar response, sitting beside me to dish up our plates. It didn't matter that the thought of cold chicken made my stomach want to turn in on itself. I'd eat this, and I'd eat it all—then I'd ask for seconds, because nobody had ever done something like this for me before. This was almost as romantic as the dishes.

"Thank you for bringing me here," I added.

He shrugged. "I don't really go out a lot. Hate being around crowds. So, this is how I roll when it comes to dating."

Dating.

The simple thought of him bringing another woman here had my blood running hot with jealousy. I turned my face and pretended to focus on something outside. "But you go to O'Paddy's. And you went to Jimney's too."

"On occasion. But I usually have to be pretty fucked up to deal with it, or it has to be a weeknight."

I frowned. "Because of the noise."

"A little. But it's mostly because of the crowds and tight spaces. I've always had issues with being around people."

"What about being a marine?" I turned, reaching for something to eat as my stomach growled again. "Didn't that, you know, set you off even more?"

I brought a drumstick to my mouth, taking a small bite. It was greasy, salty, and everything I'd loved pre-pregnancy.

"In some ways. The death, destruction, war in general messes up a man." He brought his bottle of water to his lips and took a sip, only to stare out the back wall of windows as I'd done. I loved how he'd passed on the wine too. "But other shit happened during my childhood that sent me over the edge before that."

I swallowed hard. "Like…?"

"It's not something worth sharing." He looked to the floor.

"How would you know what I want to hear and what I don't, hmm?"

"Wouldn't that be too *personal*?" He glanced up at me again, a tiny grin on his lips.

I knew he was only teasing, but his comment hit too close to home. The truth I needed to tell sooner rather than later was sitting there on the tip of my tongue. Yet getting it out was like pulling teeth.

"How about we do a comparison?" I asked.

Setting his chicken down on the paper plate, he leaned back against the couch, pulling me with him, an arm around my shoulder. The move was so natural that I didn't even think twice. "What do you mean?"

"*Meaning*, I tell you something crappy that happened to me, and you try to one-up me with something even crappier."

"This sounds like fucking torture." He groaned.

I laid my head on his shoulder, wondering if the time would ever be right to tell him the truth. "Maybe."

Warm breath cascaded over the top of my head as he set his chin on top. Strands of hair scattered across my forehead with each of his exhales. Honestly, I didn't think he'd follow through with it. Digging deep would mean exposing himself to vulnerability, something I tended to avoid myself. But he was the father of my child, and soon he'd know. I just… I needed to know the man who'd be my second half. Even if he could never be mine.

"How about I go first?" I traced my finger over the V in his shirt. The gesture wasn't meant to be sexual, but a small shiver ricocheted throughout his body, regardless. Whether he was aware of it or not didn't matter; it soothed me to know I made him as uneasy as he always did me. Not in the uncomfortable sense, but in the sense that every second longer we were together, new feelings and sensations were beginning to ignite.

"Go for it."

"Okay. Hmm." I paused for dramatic effect. "When I was eleven, my mother called me an unappreciative bitch because I told her I didn't feel like eating the dinner she cooked."

Gavin's arm tightened around my shoulder, but he didn't respond. I was thankful for it; otherwise, I might not have been able to finish.

"I'd told her my stomach hurt, but she said I was faking." Among other unmentionable words... "I was up all night, crying in pain. It wasn't until I started throwing up blood that she decided maybe she should take me to the hospital after all." I scoffed, pulling my thumbnail to my mouth. Around it, I mumbled, "Turns out I had appendicitis."

"Jesus," he whispered, kissing the top of my head, only to rub the back of his hand down my cheek.

"Jesus obviously had nothing to do with me." I laughed and shook my head, hating the bitterness in my voice.

"I'm sorry, McKenna. You deserved better."

I shut my eyes at his simple words. People had

apologized to me countless of times, but coming from Gavin? It felt different.

"Your turn." I poked him in the stomach, lifting my leg over his.

A beat passed before he spoke. When he did, the sound of his voice was hoarse. "Wanna know the real reason I can't stand small, tight spaces?"

My throat closed off. Suddenly, the idea of this game scared me for reasons that had nothing to do with me. "You don't have to tell me. We can talk about something else. This is kind of depressing, actually."

"I do want to tell you… That's the thing." He blew out a shuddering breath, a humorless chuckle leaving his mouth. "You're the first person I've ever wanted to tell."

I nodded slowly, taking in his admission. I didn't deserve his secrets, but selfishly, I wanted to know them all. "Okay. Then tell me."

He paused before letting his hand fall to his lap. "When I was nine years old, about a week after my parents died, I came to live with my uncle. It was the middle of winter and…"

I reached over and grabbed the ends of his fingers, no second thoughts as I settled them over my heart. They shook, but the rest of his body relaxed as though the movement soothed him.

"The guy… Christ, Kenna. He used to lock me in a tiny storage shed at night."

I squeezed his hand in reassurance. "Take your time."

He dropped his head back against the couch and shut his eyes as I lifted my chin to look up at him. I watched as his Adam's apple bobbed, wishing I could reach inside him and wrap myself around his heart just to protect it.

"For nine to ten hours a night, I would be forced to stay inside that thing because he said he couldn't stand all my crying. I didn't know this dude. I'd just lost my fucking parents, yet he was pissed at me, saying I ruined his fucking buzz with all my bawling."

"Oh, Gavin." I snuggled closer, tucking an arm through his. My lips began to tremble, and several tears escaped my eyes.

"It was too much for him, you know?"

There was absolutely no excuse for what the man did. He was certifiable. And had I known where he was, I would've gotten in the car and driven to his house and… and… God, I would've *killed* him. And I didn't even know the whole story yet. But I'd keep that inside for now, wait for Gavin to finish. He obviously wanted to get this out, and I *would* be the ears he needed, no matter how badly my emotions raged.

"He said I was a sissy, that he never wanted me in the first place. Told me every fucking night before locking me out there that he'd hoped I'd freeze to death, so he didn't have to deal with me anymore."

My tears grew thick. Ugly and angry for the boy who'd deserved the world. "Why did he keep you?" I managed.

"Money. Life insurance. I don't fucking know…"

I bit my lip to curb the noises in my throat.

"Every morning, for three months, he'd wake up and find me alive. I'd cover myself in anything I could find just to keep warm. Used garbage bags, boxes, shop towels, shit like that." He laughed, but the sound was ominous. "I used to hide inside an old gardening wagon.

Then I'd cover my hands in the worn-out gloves, waking up every hour just to switch them to my feet, or back to my hands. I never showered. I never got clean clothes…"

"Gavin." I muffled my cries in his shirtsleeve, hating how I couldn't be strong for him. But even as I cried, he kept going, letting it out like a nest of bees escaping from a hive.

"During the day, he'd let me come in. Feed me even. He always fucking apologized. Promised not to do it again. And then he'd go to work. But after work, it would all just…start over. A fucking endless loop."

I sniffled, wiping my face on my bare shoulder. "Did you ever try to run away?"

A nod. "Once. Around the last week of the third month. Just so happened that he was sick that day and came home from work early." Gavin snorted under his breath, laying his cheek on my head. "He was so pissed that he stopped letting me inside the house during the day. Then at night, he'd shine this huge fucking spotlight into the shed and blare heavy metal music at me. Called it my punishment."

Unable to take another second, I sat up and straddled his lap. I snuggled as close as I could against his chest, wrapping both arms around his waist. With my ear against his chest, I could just make out his racing heart.

One of his hands came up around me to stroke my spine as he finished. "The music was so loud one night that someone a mile up the road heard it and called the police. My uncle was passed out drunk inside, and when the cops came to turn off the music, they found me."

Minutes passed, but neither of us bothered to move—other than the occasional stroke of Gavin's hand down my spine. We were wrapped in each other, emotionally spent. Physically worn. Beaten, yeah, but not broken. Never in my life had I had such an urge to kill and comfort at the same time.

"What happened?" I asked.

"What do you mean?"

"To you. To your uncle…"

His warm breath blew against my forehead as he sighed. "Guy went to jail. I went into the system." He shrugged. "That wasn't even the worst part of my life growing up. I mean, it was shitty. Pretty much scarred me. But the thing that sits with me the most is the fact that I saw my foster brother put a gun to his head and kill himself."

"No," I cried, pressing my forehead against his. He squeezed his eyes, yet hugged me even closer, as if the thought of letting me go was painful.

And truthfully, I couldn't stand the thought of him doing it either.

"It was my last foster home. I lived with the Andersons from the time I was fourteen until I graduated from high school. The ones I told you about the other night."

I nodded.

"They were an older couple. Could never have kids of their own."

"Were they good to you?"

"Yeah." He smiled, but it didn't reach his eyes. "Mr. Anderson and my foster brother introduced me to Little League. I caught right on, and by the time I was fifteen, I was playing varsity."

At the thought of Gavin playing ball, of being happy with something as a teenager, I couldn't help but smile through my remaining tears. Even knowing how this story ended, I liked the thought of him finding one thing in life that made him happy, even if it hadn't lasted long. "Anyway, I got really close to Adam. My foster brother. But…he was a cutter. Always ripping up his skin. Said it helped him feel better."

I flinched, remembering a time in my life when I'd contemplated self-harm. I had nobody as a teen, and my parents were like dictators who rarely spoke to me, other than to punish or insult me. So, cutting myself seemed like it might be a way to gain some control in my life. In the end, I chose another route. One that stuck with me until adulthood. I picked the worst kind of men there were and pushed them in my parents' faces any chance I got.

Now, neither of them cared if I was dead or alive.

But I didn't tell Gavin that. This was his moment, not mine.

"Anyway, the Andersons tried to get him help, but nothing worked." He pressed his lips to the top of my head, releasing a shuddering breath as he continued. "A few weeks after he died, I had to go play at some tournament because the college scouts were there. Only I was so fucked in the head that I blew the game on purpose. And after that, I quit. Baseball wasn't worth it without him to share it with, ya know?"

"I'm so sorry," I whispered against his chest, my fingers tightening in his shirt.

"Don't be sorry." He dropped his lips against my forehead this time.

Squeezing my eyes shut, I decided that I'd tell him about my own demons to help ease his a little. "My sob story isn't quite as bad." I stroked a hand over his chest, breathing deeply.

"Anything bad that happened to you is too much."

I kissed his lips, just once in thanks, then laid my head on his shoulder, my lips close to his throat as I spoke. "When I was sixteen and living with my father, he left me home to go to some sort of illegal street fight. The neighbor guy, who'd always been friendly to us, snuck into our apartment that night and tried to hurt me." My fingers gripped the neckline of Gavin's shirt, my voice shaking. His arms tightened around me, and I could hear the low growl in his chest as I continued. "Luckily, the older lady across the hall heard me scream and called the police before anything happened." I swallowed hard. "The worst part was, the cops held me at the station until four the next morning, when my father finally figured out I was there and came to get me. He hadn't known. And they had no way to get in touch with him."

"Where's your father now?" Gavin asked, anger evident in the scratch of his voice.

I shrugged. "Not sure. I lost touch with him after high school. I went to college, met Addie, and she's been my only family since." Sure, I had my stepbrother and stepsister, and we kept in touch as much as possible, but it was never the same.

"Family has never been more than one or two people. Even when I lived with my mother, it never felt real. More…reality TV-ish, if that makes sense."

"Hmm." Gavin lifted a hand, and instead of stroking my spine, he rubbed the back of my head. "I get it," he said.

"Guess what I'm saying is, I don't know what it's like to have a big, tight-knit group of people around me to love. Not like you do with Collin and Max. I've been alone for so long that it's easier for me to live that way."

"I was the same way until I met them, believe me." He chuckled. "Probably would've been fine with it too, until we got back from our last tour of duty and I met Chloe."

I held my breath, not wanting to ask the question. But what else could I do? I needed to know the answer now more than I needed air to breathe. "Do you think maybe you want to, I don't know, have a family of your own someday?"

A second passed, then two. I felt him hold his breath, heard the unsteady shudder as he let it go. And it wasn't until he said the words that I relaxed for the first time since I'd found out I was pregnant.

"Yeah. I think I do want that."

Gavin

We didn't talk much after that. I was still ready to rage on the world over the fact that someone had tried to hurt her, and even more pissed at her parents for treating her the way they did. If I ever saw or met them, I'd let it be known that they'd messed with the wrong woman.

With McKenna on my lap, straddled and quiet, I took the moment to think about the could-have-beens in my own life. I'd grown up under pretty shitty circumstances, yeah, but what would've happened if my parents hadn't died? No doubt I wouldn't be where I was now. Not just with Collin and Max and Chloe, but it might have meant a life without ever knowing and feeling things for the woman I was holding. Fate had a way of fucking with your head when it came to life, that's for sure. But I knew things happened for a reason. And I swear my reason was McKenna.

My eyes grew heavy, but my hold on her never faltered. I had a feeling I'd be fighting to hang on to her for as long as I could. The thought of her not in my lap, by my side, in my life, was torture. Especially now that I knew she and I had similar backgrounds.

Her breath was warm on my neck, while her wet eyelashes batted against my skin, letting me know she was awake. I wanted to talk to her again, tell her that this thing we had wasn't going to end. But then she moved just right, and her hips rubbed against me in that agonizing way my cock craved, and all other thoughts fled my mind.

I wanted her, here and now. I wanted to make love to this woman. Show her the right way it was done. Not just in the heat of the moment, not after a night of drinking either. I wanted to show her how right we were together. Emotionally and physically.

I started to kiss her temple, her cheek after that, and soon her sleepy body awakened. I pressed my lips to her neck, down her throat, going to the other side to repeat the same process all over again.

"Gavin, what are you doing?" Her fingers tightened in my hair, but her hips moved against me.

"Kissing you." I smiled against her skin, inhaling the scent of her body.

"D-do you think that's a good idea?"

Slowly pulling back, I met her stare, my hands on

her thighs and running up and under her soft dress. "I think it's a damn good idea, actually. But if you don't want to—"

Her lips crashed into mine, ten fingers going painfully tight against my scalp. I welcomed the sensation, answering her pace by pushing my hands further beneath her dress. With a groan, I squeezed her ass, rocking her pussy up and over my jeans.

"Gotta see you." I started tugging her dress up, but she froze, gripping my wrists, holding me in place.

"Wait," she whispered. "Let me." She reached down and slipped the dress up and over her head on her own, shaking out her hair when she finished.

"Jesus, Kenna." Met with the cream, see-through lace of her bra, I took in the pale skin of her curves and the peachy-pink nipples that called to my mouth. "You're perfect."

She grinned and kissed me again, this time tugging at my clothes until I was shirtless and her nearly naked flesh was flush against mine. Needing to touch her all over, I reached back and quickly unsnapped her bra, never breaking away from her mouth as I tugged the straps down her shoulders and exposed her gorgeous breasts.

She hissed as though in pain, and I leaned back, looking at their fullness, her pert pink nipples, worried I'd done something wrong. "Did I hurt you?"

She shook her head slowly, a soft smile on her mouth that hinted at shyness I wasn't used to seeing on her face. "They're...sensitive." She tugged her bottom lip between her teeth and looked away, went distant on me again.

"Don't look away." Fearing I was losing her, I

cupped her cheeks, urging her gaze back on me, only for her eyes to stay closed. "McKenna, open your eyes, please…" My throat burned as I swallowed and waited. Eventually, she did as I asked, looking at me with the full power of her baby blues. But the tears I saw there had me fearing the worst.

"What is it?"

She licked her lips and shook her head. "Nothing. I'm just sensitive, is all. I'll be okay." She leaned forward to try to kiss me again, but I wasn't having it.

"Talk to me."

She opened her mouth, then shut it once more. Just when I was thinking she was going to flip a switch on me, become another version of herself, she said the last two words I'd ever expected to hear.

"I'm pregnant."

CHAPTER 17

Gavin

"Pregnant." I frowned, unable to comprehend what that word met.

As in, pregnant with another man's child? Or…

"It's not…" I put a hand on my chest, patting once.

She nodded slowly, looking down at her own hands settled between our stomachs. "It's yours. I haven't been with another man since that night."

That night, six weeks ago. That night I decided I wanted something for the first time, something that might hurt me in the end. The first time I made a decision that wasn't careful and calculated.

"No…" I shook my head, refusing to believe it. "I used a condom that night."

"The condom didn't work, Gavin." Her lips began to tremble. She was either fighting her tears or fighting a laugh.

Jesus Christ. McKenna was… "Gonna be the mother of my child?"

She stiffened, eyes welling with tears.

I hadn't meant to say the words out loud. Hell, I should have been shoving her away, fighting this with all I had, because I wasn't father material, damn it. I couldn't even take care of Chloe when she was a baby, for fuck's sake. I was a useless son of a bitch when it came to children, yet somehow *I* was going to be a dad. Me.

"That'd be me." She pulled her leg from over my lap, reaching for her dress on the floor.

For a split second, I almost let her go, thinking maybe I needed more time to think this through. Plan what to do next and figure shit out.

Yet the thought of doing so was like a razor to the throat—and the last thing I wanted.

Not thinking twice, I wrapped my arms around her waist and pulled her closer. "No."

She met my stare and whispered, "No?"

I shook my head, then I kissed her, harder this time. I expected her to fight me. Push me away and run, but her body instantly relaxed against mine, and we were right back where we'd been. Only this time, things moved faster.

"Need you," I all but begged. "So much."

Slowly, I pulled back remembering her comment about her breasts. It made sense now why she'd said they were sensitive, but that didn't stop me from wanting them in my mouth. Wanting to taste them. So, I lowered my head, taking my time as I held one of them in my hand. Then with the gentlest of licks, I sucked one of her nipples in between my lips, gentle laps of my tongue across the tips. She shivered so hard goose bumps danced across her skin and a soft gasp of pleasure escaped her mouth. I teased and toyed, using my lips to kiss the peak, my tongue to taste the edges. I gave her gentle, because she deserved it.

"That feels so good," she moaned, encouraging me to pull a little harder, not too hard, but enough to drag out the low noise in her throat.

Slow, steady kisses led me to the other breast, and I used my finger to trail around the same wet tip I'd just teased. Her hips worked harder over my jeans, and I could feel the change in her body with every touch of my tongue, every lick, every kiss.

This was the stuff of movies, the way I held her close. I didn't know it could be this way, feel this good, and we hadn't even gotten to the good stuff yet. Whether that had to do with her being pregnant with my baby, or the simple thought of her not running away, I didn't know. What I did know was that I was falling hard for the first time in my life, and it didn't scare me like I'd thought it would.

That thought spurred me into action, and soon I had her flat on her back on the couch. Big, blue eyes blinked up at me, lips parted, breaths panting, cheeks flushed. "You're so beautiful," I murmured, having no idea where to start when it came to her body—to *her*. More than anything, I wanted to take my time, savor the moment, but I couldn't wait either.

Decision made, I stood and pulled my jeans and boxers off. My cock sprang free, ready, and those eyes of hers shimmered with heat as she took me in from head to toe, back up and down again.

"I want you, McKenna. All of you. No running. No more fighting this thing between us. Just…" I sighed, dropping to my knees next to her, desperate and pleading like a man on the edge of death begging for one more minute of life. "Just…tell me you want this too." I gripped the edges of her panties, the lace and silk doing little to steady my shaking hands. I was ready to pull them down, give her everything she'd ever desired. But I needed her consent, that one word. Her yes.

And then it happened.

One smile.

One nod.

Three words I never expected.

"Yes. I'm yours."

The tightening in my chest released, and I smiled too. I smiled so fucking wide that it hurt. But I didn't care. Because McKenna *actually* wanted to be with me.

With *me*.

That was the best fucking moment of my life so far.

I lowered my mouth to her pussy, not wasting another second. With my tongue, I lapped at her wetness before clamping my lips down and sucking. She cried out my name and bucked her hips, but I settled her, held her knees in place with the flat of my palms.

I flicked her once more with my tongue and added a finger.

"Gavin, yes…" Her hands were in my hair, pulling at the scalp once more. The feeling was unlike any other. A pain that led to pleasure. Hers and mine. Ours.

I reached down with my other hand to stroke myself, needing to ease the ache. More than anything, I wanted her to come against my lips and tongue again, but I also wanted her to come while I was buried deep inside her.

Soon, she solved my dilemma, urging me up the length of her body with her hands. I moved until my cock was centered between her thighs, ready to find its home.

"I need more," she moaned.

"What about a condom?"

She grinned, the look playful, happy. "That's kind of a moot point now, don't you think?"

I cringed. "Shit." I hadn't forgotten what she'd just told me. Fuck no, how could I? I'd asked because I was nervous. Hadn't had sober sex in a long-ass time.

"I'm clean, just so you know." Her face went pink, embarrassment shadowing her blues as she spoke.

I cupped her face, urging her to look at me, one arm propped along the couch so I wouldn't squish her. "Me too. I make it a habit to get checked since I work as an EMT."

"Okay."

"So…" It was my turn to be unsure, my face going hot, my stomach tight. Just when I thought I had myself under control, one little emotional setback had me questioning my sanity. But then she whispered a few game-changing words.

And I was done for.

"Make love to me, Gavin?"

That word: *love*.

I knew she didn't mean it the way I secretly might have been thinking. It was too soon, even though the thought of it building toward love made me want to jump for fucking joy. Still, I managed to keep my cool… That is, until I met her stare.

The sincerity in her gorgeous gaze immediately caught me off guard. I swallowed so hard I swear my throat shriveled to nothing. But it was her hand on my face that led me to where I needed to be. With her and only her.

Slowly and steadily, I lowered my mouth, letting her taste herself on my lips. Then I slipped my cock inside her, only to be pushed in deeper when her legs wrapped around my waist.

"Ah, Kenna. You don't know what you do to me." The erratic beat inside my chest proved how wild she made me feel. How reckless I was when it came to my heart meshing with hers.

"I do know." She kissed me on the chin, the cheek, finishing by my ear. "Because you make me feel the same way."

Eyes squeezed shut in pleasure, and with one foot balanced on the floor, I pushed inside her completely, sweat already dripping down between my shoulder blades.

"Gavin." She whispered my name with so much reverence that I had to look at her again to make sure it was real. And when I saw that fire in her eyes, I let myself go. Completely.

She cried out my name and clawed at my back, the pain so perfect I wanted to roar. Our stares never wavered as I pushed in deeper, then pulled back, the love I didn't know how to give coming forward in my movements. Over and over, I thrust my hips against hers, our skin slapping in the room like lightning, our bodies melting against each other as if this was where we were always meant to be. Glued together, her and me. A perfect, raging storm.

She moaned, rolling her hips, crying out in pleasure. I reached down, gripping her thigh, moving my body higher, groaning. And soon she was screaming my name once more.

Seconds later, I cried out too, saying the only words I had on my tongue as I filled her body with my own release.

"Forever. Need you...forever."

CHAPTER 18

McKenna

SATED AND SATISFIED, I LAY ON HIS COUCH, ARMS WRAPPED around his waist as I contemplated his words.

Forever. Was that possible with this man? Was I capable of it too? I wanted to be. More than anything else in my life, I wanted that chance with him.

Hot breath covered my neck like a blanket, and I found my fingers stroking his spine of their own accord.

"That should've been our first time," he finally said, pulling back to kiss me softly on the lips. Afterward, he trailed his nose up and down my cheek in a move that went beyond sexy, running straight toward intimate.

"But it wasn't." I rolled out from under him and onto my side, facing him, contentment so warm in my chest that I almost believed it wasn't real.

Until he smiled at me. Lips wet and pink from mine.

"You know what they say though." He winked.

"What's that?" I reached forward, tracing a drop of sweat that ran between his pecs. He had the most incredible body: sculpted and handcrafted by the gods, it would seem.

"First the worst, second the best." He smiled so widely that I couldn't help but kiss his lips again.

Out of my element, but no longer able to stop myself, I pulled back and reached up to stroke his cheek with the back of my knuckles. Beneath my fingers, his beard tickled my skin, and I swear my heart burst inside my chest when he nuzzled against my hand.

Part of me should have been disgusted that we were still lying there, his release trickling down my thigh, our bodies covered with the stench of sweat and sex. But instead, I was lost in a world of postorgasmic bliss, something I rarely let myself experience.

"We need to talk though." He pressed his finger along my naked hip, stroking a circle around the bone. This was the part where I should have gotten up and run. Yet now all I wanted was to fall asleep in his arms.

I yawned, as if on cue. "I know."

"You're pregnant with my baby."

I nodded, squirming at the low rumble of his words. The familiar tug of fear I'd been living with for a week started to burn my chest, and I pulled my hand away from his face to cover my heart, willing the pain away. "I am."

"That's a pretty big deal, don't you think?" He frowned.

Shrugging, I looked down at his chest, trying to keep my body from stiffening. I told him I'd try, that I'd give us a chance. And I wanted that. Truly. But I wasn't sure how. And now that the intimacy had passed and the postorgasmic bliss was waning, reality was pushing me into flight mode again.

Forever, he'd said. *Need you forever.*

God, what had I done?

Sex more than once with a man?

And my feelings? I felt them inside like unwanted gifts on holidays. Gifts I wouldn't dare give back but wasn't sure I wanted to keep. Yet things were different now. And though the idea of pursuing a relationship with this man scared me, I knew I couldn't walk. Not anymore. Because no matter what happened, Gavin was now a permanent fixture in my life.

"It is a big deal," I finally said as I sat up. When I reached for my dress on the floor, he didn't stop me. Instead, he sat up too, grabbing his shirt and pulling up his boxers and jeans.

My nipples ached from his lips and mouth, and the thought of putting my bra back on was not appealing in the least. Instead, I settled my dress over my body, sans coverage, thankful it was dark enough outside that nobody would see what I had stashed beneath.

I cleared my throat, stuffing my bra into my purse. "Which is why I think adoption is probably the best road. That way we don't have to worry and all."

Gavin grew quiet, his body dangerously still.

"Adoption," he finally said, lowering his chin to his chest.

I touched his shoulder, my skin now ice cold. "Gavin?"

He nodded once, then stood, looking everywhere but my face. "Sounds to me like you've got this all figured out." His voice was soft. Not mean in the least. But hearing him say that was like a punch to the chest. A kick in the gut. Why was he giving up so easily? And why did I care, when this was supposed to be what I wanted?

"Well, no. Not exactly. I mean, I know this is your baby too, but—"

"But it's your body, McKenna." He sighed, running a hand through his shaggy hair. "In the end, you should get to decide what you want, not me."

"But *you're* the father." I frowned, not understanding where this was coming from. Why I was arguing, when I knew adoption was for the best.

"I am." He rubbed the back of his neck, clearly uncomfortable, though when we'd made love just minutes before, he'd looked like the happiest man alive. "But, like I said, this should be your decision."

I licked my lips as I gathered words. "Gavin, I-I really like you, okay? I'm just not sure if a baby is right for me. But if for some reason, you wanted to keep it…"

His gaze flickered to mine, a light shining back on inside. Right then and there, I knew the truth. Gavin did want this baby. But he wanted me more.

I loved kids. Truly. That wasn't the problem. I just didn't have it in me to mother one. Had never really had a desire to either. I was never taught compassion growing up, and I was always making terrible, rash decisions. Having a baby meant making responsible choices for a tiny human who would rely on me for everything.

What if I made a mistake? What if I messed him or her up because of that?

"The timing sucks, yeah. And neither of us is in a place for kids, but…" A glimmer of a smile touched his lips.

That smile that settled it for me once and for all.

If Gavin wanted this baby—our baby—he could have it.

Unfortunately, in that moment, the baby and I were not a package deal.

CHAPTER 19

Gavin

"To the women in our lives who fuck with our hearts but make them better at the same time." Max lifted his cup into the air, then took a long sip of his beer. His eyes were already glassy, but I knew that had nothing to do with the fact that he was drinking. The guy was in a hell of a lotta pain—the heart-aching kind.

Collin and I were sitting across from him at O'Paddy's, trying to help him through the shittiest time of his life. Lia had moved to Springfield, and he'd just gotten home from dropping her off. Seeing him like this, so torn up inside, left me questioning my own thoughts more than ever: *Is the pain of being in love worth it?*

I'd been back to work for almost three weeks now, and as much as I wanted to be fucking ecstatic about it, I wasn't. Instead, I was a mess, constantly worried about Kenna. Contemplating the offer she'd put on the table before we left my house that night.

She'd let me keep the baby.

And in the end, she would likely walk away.

On our way home that night, we had barely spoken a word—other than me telling her that this wasn't over before she got out of the car. That we had *months* to figure things out. She'd smiled sadly at me, grabbed her dishes, and told me she'd call me soon.

That was twenty-two days ago. Twenty-one days without a phone call. Twenty-one days of her avoiding me. And it fucking sucked.

"It's not forever, Max." Collin rubbed his hand over his chin. "Don't play it off like it is. Lia'd kill you if she knew you were here feeling sorry for yourself."

The fact that Collin had accepted his sister and Max's relationship wasn't surprising, even though he'd not been happy about finding them in bed together. Max might have been the biggest playboy to ever hit Carinthia, but he was also a good person who'd do anything for the people he loved. And it was more than obvious that he loved Lia Montgomery.

"No. Not forever. I wouldn't let that happen. And I get why she had to do it. That's not the problem." Max sighed. "I just didn't expect for it to hurt this bad."

I leaned forward on my elbows, hating that I couldn't fully be there for him when my mind was spinning with its own shit storm. Still, I had to say something. "You're going to visit her next weekend, right?" He nodded. "And when you can't make it home to her, she can come back here?" He nodded again, shoulders slumping.

I leaned back in my seat, unable to sit still. I was antsier than usual, my skin crawling. O'Paddy's was packed for a Sunday night, not to mention loud as fuck. Any other night, I would've gone home, but I had to get over my shit and stick it out. For Max. "Like Collin said, it's not forever."

"But it's still fucking torture." He groaned, then took another drink.

"She needs this to prove to herself that she's over all that shit that happened to her in college. That she can handle herself." Collin jammed his finger in the air at Max. "So don't be the type of ass that holds her down."

Lia had been attacked at a frat party in college, the night before we were to be shipped off to boot camp. Of all the people to find her, it'd been Max, and none of us had ever—would ever—be able to forget that time in our lives.

"I know that better than either of you guys." Max's lip curled in annoyance. "And that's not me, and you know it, Colly." He scrubbed his fists against his temples. "All I'm saying is it hurts."

"Like someone ripped your heart out?" I frowned, stirring the ice in my water.

"No, it's worse. More like someone beat me upside the head with a fucking mallet, then dumped my heart in a pile of lava while it was still attached to my body."

I grinned, trying not to laugh at the analogy. When Max felt something, he felt it hard.

Collin didn't fight his reaction like I did. "You"—he slapped the table with his palm and leaned back, hooting toward the light—"are a big, fucking baby."

"Fuck you all." Maxwell stood, ready to move, but Collin grabbed his wrist.

"Whoa, whoa. Calm down." Collin laughed, earning another glare from Max. "Sorry. It's just weird seeing you torn up like this." He sobered and shook his head.

"And to know it's over my little sister makes it even weirder. But we're here for you." Collin looked at me.

I nodded. "He's right. You're a whole lotta messed up right now, Max. And honestly, it's pretty fucking cool to see you so...so in love and shit. We're just not used to it, is all."

I cleared my throat as both of my best friends shot their gazes in my direction.

"What?" I frowned down at the table, not liking the sudden attention.

It's true. Most of the time I sat back and took shit in, rarely saying what was on my mind. But things had changed for me over the course of the last few months. More so in the last few weeks.

Clearing my throat again, I continued. "You and Lia have been into each other for years. It's just taken you a while to both finally realize it."

"Wow." Max's grin was slow, knowing, and pretty damn frustrating. "You sure you're not referring to yourself there, Gav?" Like always, he'd flipped his sob story off himself and onto me. I knew it was his way of diverting the bad shit, but I wasn't in the mood.

"The hell's that supposed to mean?" I asked.

"I didn't realize it before. But I do now." Collin leaned back in his seat and grinned. "*You're* the reason Kenna's been coming over more."

"Again, what the hell's that supposed to mean?"

"First, I thought nothing of it, until two nights ago when I found McKenna cuddled on my couch with Beaner reading books."

I rubbed my sweaty hands on my shorts, eyes narrowed in confusion.

"The woman was crying and emotional. Said it was the book's fault."

Damn her. If Kenna wasn't so stubborn, this could all be different. She and I could be happy, together, we could even raise the baby together. I mean, we didn't have to get married. We could just…co-parent while exploring where this thing went between us.

"She good now?" I asked, voice cracking.

Collin smirked. "Just about as good as any pregnant woman can be."

I lowered my face to my hands and groaned. "Shit." He knew.

"*Pregnant?*" Max screeched like a damn owl, then slapped the table. I lifted my head to glare at him. "You got her pregnant? Stuck a bat in her cave? Joined the pudding club?"

"Shut the fu—"

"Sure did." Collin set his elbows on the table, smirking. "Then he blew her off."

"I…*what?*" I blinked, trying to process what Collin had just said.

"Now *that's* low for you, Gavvy." Max shook his head.

"I thought so too." Collin frowned at me.

"That's not true. She's…" I leaned back, arms over my chest. The room spun as I gritted my teeth. The ache of my nails digging into my palms didn't help. "She told me I could *keep* it. Raise the baby on my own. That she didn't think she was ready to be a mom yet." Why was she twisting this all around?

The table grew quiet. Neither of my buddies was ever known to just shut up. Which is how I knew I'd shocked them.

Collin was the first to speak. "You wanna know what I think?"

"What?" I frowned.

"I think she loves you. Or she's falling for you, at least. She's just been burned in the past."

I froze, hand tight around my water glass.

Collin continued. "I also think you'd do anything to have a family, unlike her. She obviously knows this and cares about you enough that she'd be willing to give up on her own happiness just to make you happy."

I shut my eyes and sucked in a breath. How the fuck had I not seen that before?

"For the record." Max was suddenly at my side, his hand on my shoulder. "You'd make one hell of a good father."

But without the love of a woman by my side, how could I truly be a good father?

CHAPTER

McKenna

I COULDN'T REMEMBER THE LAST TIME I'D BEEN HOME early from work. Maybe when I first started out as a nurse? Either way, I was exhausted—beyond belief—and in no way ready to deal with my new roommate: my little sister.

My apartment door clicked shut behind me. I kicked off my shoes, moaning in relief as I stretched out my feet. After setting my keys on the counter in the kitchen, I made my way into the living room, finding her on my sofa. I could almost bet she'd been there all day.

"Hey. Got off a little early tonight. Thought maybe you'd want to go grab some pizza or something."

"No thank you. I'm not hungry."

Even with my new aversion to all things greasy, I'd do anything to get Hanna out of my house for at least an hour. But the fact that she wasn't in the mood for her favorite food? It left me feeling as helpless as ever.

I sat down on the couch and lifted her feet onto my

thighs. She winced but managed a smile, still in loads of pain from her broken ribs. She'd already been here a few weeks, yet she looked no better than the day I'd picked her up at the airport—the day *after* Gavin's and my night together at the cabin. The bruises on her face were fading from black and blue to yellow, but she was far from healed. Inside or out.

"You feeling okay today?" I asked.

"I'm fine." She smiled shyly, but it didn't reach her eyes. Hanna was incredibly sweet. The word *kind* should have been her middle name. It's one of the reasons why I loved her dearly. Yet at the same time, I knew how weak she was, how skittish she'd become too. I blamed it not only on her stupid, abusive ex, but also on my mother for not seeing the signs.

"Have you heard from him?" I asked, praying she wasn't stupid enough to try to get in contact with the guy.

She shook her head and stared down at the book she was reading. "No. Since Mom took my phone before I got on the plane, he doesn't know where I am."

"Okay. I'll run and get you a new phone tomorrow and put you on my plan."

"Thanks." She met my gaze but quickly looked away, as though holding eye contact with *me* would land her in the hospital again.

I knew she was safe here, away from the trouble she'd face at home. But I was still worried about her. Her first and only boyfriend had been messing with her head for a long while before he started messing with her body. Nobody had known, not even her father or my mother, and especially not me. My guilt over not keeping in touch with her over the past year had doubled. So when my mother asked me to let Hanna stay with me for a month or so, until things calmed down at home, I had no choice but to agree.

The timing couldn't have been worse. But at least having her there distracted me from my own problems for a little while.

"Have you eaten anything today?" I asked.

She shook her head.

I sighed, feet aching as I stood. "I'll make us some sandwiches."

A nod—that's all I got.

Defeat accompanied exhaustion as I stood and headed toward the kitchen. My shoulders sagged with the weight of the evening, and my heart was in my throat with the thought of my sister so broken.

It was odd to make food for another person when most of my life I'd done stuff on my own—for myself. Which was another reason the thought of keeping this baby freaked me out. No doubt I could do it if I had to. Be a mom, care and love for something. Yet the thought of not being any *good* at it was the main reason I didn't want to commit to being a mother.

But Gavin was a good man. And though he might have been a little broken and inexperienced when it came to kids, I had no doubt that he'd be an excellent father.

I handed Hanna her PB&J, then sat down on the couch. She managed to sit up, her breathing labored as she moved. I didn't offer to help her, not when she'd inevitably push me away. From what I'd relearned about my sister, she was as stubborn as she was closed off. Still, she never complained about the pain. Never did she mention needing anything to help with it. But I managed to give it to her in my own way, silently placing her pain medication on her plate as I'd just done.

Out of the corner of my eye, I watched as she lifted the pills to her lips and drank them down with a glass of milk. The more she ate and drank, the more alive she became. I stared down at her wrists, then her arms, followed by her legs. She was tinier than I remembered, almost malnourished. Brittle, even. All I wanted to do was make her happy and care for her. Give life to her lifeless eyes, her lifeless way of living most of all.

"Will you be up to getting out this weekend?" I asked, hopeful she'd say yes. If she didn't, there's no way I'd go where Addie had begged me to. A rugby game, the first seven-on-seven tournament of the season. I wasn't a huge fan of the sport, but I might have had another reason for wanting to attend. *Gavin*, to be more precise.

I knew I was being stupid in avoiding him. We did need to talk—a lot, actually. He could also meet my sister. I knew I shouldn't use her as an excuse for why I hadn't called him, but I'd never claimed to be a good girl.

"Maybe."

That wasn't a no. I'd take it.

"Okay. It's just to a rugby game, nothing big."

She looked at me in surprise. "You like rugby?"

I shrugged and took a bite of my sandwich. "I like rugby *players*."

A grin took over her lips, a hint of the old sister coming through. At fifteen, she'd been more boy crazy than I was at eighteen.

"Plus, I want you to meet Addie." And Gavin too, but that wasn't going to be mentioned outright until I could tell her exactly why. She talked to my mother almost every day. I could hear her in the bathroom or outside on my deck. The lady had Hanna under her lock and key, even all these states away. For the first time in my life, I was thankful the woman had sent me away, because if she hadn't, I could've been in Hanna's shoes.

"Okay. I'll go."

My eyes widened. "Really?"

She nodded, never lifting her gaze from her plate. Dark-brown hair covered her face and hung down to the middle of her back. It was thin and straight and always combed, something I expected had been ingrained in her from a young age.

"We can go shopping Friday afternoon. I have a four-day weekend. You don't have any shorts, and it's supposed to be really hot on Saturday."

"I don't wear shorts."

I frowned. "Why not?"

"My legs…" She cleared her throat. "They're too skinny. Mom told me I looked better with pants."

"That bitch," I grumbled, leaning back on the couch.

"She was just—"

"Hey." I touched her arm, lightly so as not to scare her. "I think you have great legs. And if you want to wear shorts, you should totally do it." I'd buy her shorts and a tank, maybe even some dresses. If she didn't want to wear them now, so be it, but I wasn't about to let my mother tear her down.

"Thanks, Kenna," she whispered, and I'm pretty sure she was crying when she said it. But I didn't call her out on it. Instead, I wrapped my arm around her shoulder and hugged her close, thankful she didn't flinch like she usually did.

We relaxed against the couch a while later, bellies full of comfort food as a black-and-white Western played in the background.

This was the family I'd never had growing up, and there was no way I'd let it go now.

Gavin

I scooped up Chloe and pulled her onto my lap, willing her to stop crying. She'd fallen, gotten carpet burn from what I could tell, and other than putting a Band-Aid on the barely there mark, I was struggling to find ways to calm her.

She was almost sixteen months, and bouncing her in my arms didn't work anymore. Walking the carpet with her wasn't an option either, when she'd just cry and squirm to get down. I knew I was screwed when not even her favorite bunny on the TV could do the job.

Addie had gone to get her hair cut. Collin was out getting groceries. And Max was taking a nap—too many drinks out the night before. And because I felt bad about not babysitting more lately, I'd agreed to do it, thanking God it was only for a half hour.

"Hey, Beaner, it's okay. You're okay." I rubbed her back and her boo-boo, then cringed when she cried louder. "Don't cry, baby girl, please." I stood with her and walked us to the kitchen. In the back of the freezer was the leftover ice cream from when McKenna was here.

Not thinking twice, I pulled it out and yanked off the cover. There was a layer of ice on top—no doubt the shit was freezer burned—but one look at it and Chloe stopped crying, already reaching for it.

"This make you feel better?"

She bounced up and down in my arms, still hiccupping from her sobs. Regardless of the tears on her face, she waved her little arms excitedly in the air at the misshapen carton.

I chuckled, hitching her up higher on my waist. "You are some… Shit."

She stuck her casted arm into the tub before I could stop her. Her big, blue eyes wide, she looked at me while bringing a thumb full of the old, coffee-flavored stuff to her mouth.

"Bite?" she asked, offering me some from her fingers.

I shook my head and chuckled to myself. "Your daddy's gonna kill me."

But she'd stopped crying. And fuck, that's all that mattered to me.

Footsteps sounded from behind. I looked over my shoulder, finding Max. He rubbed his eyes, then let his arms fall to his sides.

"Jesus, what's wrong?" He glared at me, face going soft when he stared at Beaner.

"She fell. Scraped her knee." I shrugged, praying he wouldn't look in the carton. No doubt he'd be on my ass like Collin would about feeding her caffeinated ice cream that was at least a couple months old.

He glanced at his cell phone and frowned, obviously distracted. "Shit. Lee-Lee called when I was sleeping."

"She called me too," Collin grumbled as he walked into the kitchen. He slapped a couple of bags on the counter, then reached for Chloe. Luckily, I'd wiped her off, hiding the evidence back in the freezer. He frowned at her leg. "What happened?"

I opened my mouth to say what happened, only for Chloe to say, "Boo-boo."

Collin leaned over and kissed the mark, something I hadn't even thought of. "All better, baby girl."

Her pretty face began to glow, and I wanted to smack myself in the head for forgetting the kiss thing. That'd been the key all along, damn it.

Max leaned against the fridge, watching Beaner but talking to us. "I'm leaving Saturday night. After the game, I'm gonna take some time off. Go stay with her."

I frowned. "With Lia?"

"Yeah."

"What about your job?" Collin asked, folding his arms.

"I can't fucking take it. I'll go there, stay during the week, then drive home on the weekends for my gigs I've got set up." Max had opened his own catering business, earning a lot of customer interest. Cooking was basically his life now. Other than Lia.

Max walked toward Chloe and poked her stomach. She giggled and leaned forward into her dad's arms, curls falling over her cheeks.

"For how long?" I propped my elbows against the counter, studying his dark face. He looked like shit. I could relate.

"Does it matter?" He looked back and forth between Collin and me, red eyes narrowing. "I can't stand the thought of being apart when all I want is to be with her."

It made sense now—the power of his emotions, the meaning behind them. It's something I hadn't understood until McKenna came along. If you wanted someone, you needed to be with them. Still, I'd miss the hell out of this guy.

"Besides, me going with her, staying there, would be the perfect time for us to get to know each other better."

"You already know each other." I tapped my fingers along my arm.

Max rubbed the back of his neck. "Not in all the ways I'd like to."

"Ah, hell. I'm done." Collin rammed into Max as he walked out of the room, but called over his shoulder once more to say, "Just don't make me an uncle yet. Already gotta deal with Gavin bringing a kid into this world. I only have enough guidance for one right now."

I followed Collin, watching as he set Chloe on the floor. "I don't need guidance. I can handle myself."

"Yeah?" Collin laughed as he turned to face me. "Then why are you here and not with Kenna?"

"Because she doesn't want me." Anger had my hands balling into fists. "Plus, I'm not a huge asshole like you who can't take no for an answer."

Collin shrugged, not denying it.

Max, on the other hand, sat on the chair, kicking his feet out, relaxed now that the conversation was directed at me again. "And you believe that?" he asked.

"Believe what?"

He frowned. "That she doesn't want you."

"I do. She's been pushing me away for weeks." It hurt, admitting it out loud. And though she told me at my river house that she *liked* me, that obviously wasn't enough to try to explore things further between us before the baby arrived.

Chloe moved to the couch and started jumping on the

cushions, giggling loudly. I moved to grab her. The last thing I wanted was another broken arm. She pushed me away and did it again. I gave up after three times and wound up sitting on the couch next to her, my arm out to keep her from falling onto the floor.

"You'd be a good dad." Collin pointed at my arm, then Chloe, then me.

"Yeah, but *she* doesn't want to be a mom."

Max cleared his throat and leaned forward onto his knees. "My mom didn't want to be a mom at eighteen. Almost gave me up for adoption. Ended up changing her mind and told me constantly I was the best mistake she'd ever made."

My lips pursed. Chloe jumped onto her butt and started bouncing that way. "That doesn't mean Kenna would do the same. She didn't even want kids." I knew why that was: her issues with her family and her fear of turning into her parents. But her parents didn't define her. Nobody did but her.

Chloe flapped her arms, squealing at the top of her lungs. She jumped off the couch and started to run around the coffee table. "La, la, la, la," she sang on a loop. It put the hugest fucking smile on my face, even with the conversation looming around us.

I stood to keep an eye on her—make sure she didn't run into the corners of the table. Yeah, I'd put that edging stuff on when she'd first started to walk, but that didn't mean she might not fall now. It's why I'd told Collin and Max to leave it on.

"Avvy," she screeched, the chase all a game. Damn, this kid was quick.

I picked up speed, chasing her into the dining room.

She ran under the table and landed on her back, kicking her feet in the air until she started lashing out at the legs of the chairs next.

Ignoring his daughter's behavior, Collin kept talking over her screeches. "You want this baby, right?"

Sweat ran down between my shoulders as I reached for Chloe. She jerked back and giggled louder.

"Yeah, I do. I want it a lot."

As scary as it was to admit, I knew there wasn't another answer. I may not be the best candidate for the job, but I'd love that child to death. And after what I'd been through, I didn't take that emotion lightly. Especially when it came to something that was going to be my flesh and blood.

No doubt McKenna would be the same way if she let herself. Maybe she just needed me to prove that to her. It wasn't like I had much to lose by trying—she'd walk away in the end anyway. No matter what she decided for herself, though, I knew this baby would be with me.

"Then there you go." Max stood up and fumbled his way into the dining room, pulling back the chairs. Beaner squealed louder but didn't go to Max when he reached for her.

"Then tell her the truth. Tell her how you feel. Go from there. One big *take it or leave it* gesture," Collin finished.

My answer was a grunt as I struggled to grab Chloe's ankle, a thought racing through my head at the same time.

I had a messed-up mind, but did that mean I wouldn't know how to raise a baby? Or even love it? No. If anything, it meant I'd probably try harder at everything, just to make sure I didn't screw it all up. Would it be hard? Fuck yeah, no doubt in my mind. But with the support system I had around me with my friends, I knew this was one choice I wouldn't hide from.

"Beaner, what is your issue?" Collin groaned, just missing her as she darted to the corner under a bench by the wall.

"It's like she's hyped up on something." Max snorted. "Kind of wish I was there with her." He cringed, rubbing at his temples.

I froze when I finally realized what was wrong with her. "Fuck."

"Fuck!" Chloe repeated, pointing at me.

I looked at Collin, who glared at me, a knowing look in his squinted eyes.

Goddamn ice cream.

CHAPTER 21

McKenna

THE WEATHER WAS CRAZY WARM FOR EARLY JUNE. NINETY degrees, with humidity levels through the roof. I wore a pair of shorts and a tank that flowed over my swelling abdomen, but even that was doing little to help me stay cool. I might have been only ten or so weeks along, but my stomach was already showing a tiny bulge beneath the baggy clothes I wore.

Sitting next to me on the sidelines of the grassy rugby pitch was my sister—knees pulled to her chest and a look of awe on her face. I smiled at her when she glanced my way. She smiled back. Hanna looked better today than she had all week, and I wanted to say it was our shopping trip that had done her good, but I knew better. She was seeing the world outside our mother's lair—and away from the dangers of her ex-boyfriend—for the first time in months. Maybe even longer than that.

It was kind of miraculous, the strides she'd made since she'd arrived.

I wished I could say the same about myself.

I blinked and focused on my best friend. Addie sat to my right, her hands over her mouth as she hollered at the guys on the field—more at Collin than anyone else.

Despite her cheery voice, her brown eyes had dark circles beneath them. I could tell the week had taken its toll on her. The loss of her mother, completely breaking ties with her father for good... She did at least seem to be able to breathe a little easier. I attributed that to the fact that she'd been able to make peace with her mom before she passed. Knowing that eased my guilt over not being there for her the way I should have been the past few weeks. Plus, she had her fiancé now, and I'm pretty sure he'd been taking better care of her than I ever could.

"Get 'em, baby!" she screamed, clapping fast as Collin ran down the field and touched the ball to the ground. His hands shot up in the air, and he ran around the goalpost, scoring the first try of the match. According to Addie, there were two more matches to go, but I could barely sit through one. This sport bored me to tears...though the scenery—the male thighs, more so—was definitely nice.

"This is kind of intense." Hanna's brown eyes were bright as she watched the guys run. "You were right about the players though." She giggled, then nudged my shoulder with her own. It was the first time I'd glimpsed the girl I remembered since she'd arrived.

I reached down and squeezed her fingers. "I'm glad you decided to come."

She looked down at our interlocked hands and grinned. "Me too."

"Are you ladies up for going out tonight? Collin's parents are watching Chloe, so he and I are free to do whatever." Addie tucked her arm through mine and snuggled close, smelling like sunscreen.

I started to shake my head no, but Hanna jumped in, surprising me. "Go where?"

"The after-party. Since it's a home game and we're hosting the tournament, we'll head to O'Paddy's after it's all said and done here."

"O'Paddy's is the team's bar," I clarified. "But we don't have to go. I'm fine with just hanging out with you at home."

Hanna smiled shyly, and one of her dimples appeared. "I'll be okay if you want to go out tonight, Kens."

"You should come too," Addie jumped in.

My sister shook her head. "No thanks. I don't really do bars."

"Oh. Well, we can do something just us ladies." Addie brushed her long hair away from her face and scrunched up her nose. "We don't need to hang out with the guys to have fun."

I looked at my sister, secretly praying she'd say yes. I needed her to stay with me, but I'd missed spending time with Addie.

"Where would we go?" Hanna twisted the string around the waist of her dress with a finger.

"Hmm, let's see." Addie paused. "We can have dinner and then go to the drive-in, watch a late movie and whatnot."

Addie's eagerness was infectious, and I couldn't help but grin.

"That sounds fun." Hanna nodded.

I pumped my fist at her acceptance. "Yay! I want you two to get to know each other better." I pulled them both close to my neck, hugging tightly. "My two favorite girls with me. What more could a woman ask for?" Besides daily orgasms and a non-pregnant belly, that is.

Addie laughed and pressed her palm to my stomach over my loose-fitting tee. "Well, since I'm totally going to need a drinking partner now that Kenna here got herself knocked up, I am happy to have us together too."

The air around me shifted, my breath catching in my throat at the same time.

Hanna was the first to pull away from our group hug, yet I caught her stare as it narrowed quickly down at Addie's hand. "Yeah, definitely."

I shut my eyes.

Crap. More than anything, I'd wanted to tell her. But with everything that had been happening over the last month, I couldn't find a good time to bring it up. Not to mention I wasn't exactly thrilled with the possibility of her running to my mom and spilling the beans. I was supposed to be the older sister with her head in the game, her life in gear, her world pieced together, not the unmarried, preggo sister.

A role model, I was not—according to my mother, at least.

Oblivious to the sudden tension, Addie continued, "Do you want to swing by the house and pick me up around seven?"

My throat went dry as I tried to speak, so I nodded instead, pulling my arms out from around Addie's neck. She kissed my temple and stood, the excitement over a night out evident in her appearance as she marched toward Collin, who stood alongside the pitch.

A good two minutes passed as I waited for Hanna

to speak. And when she did, the girl did not disappoint with her question.

"You're pregnant?"

I cringed, my gaze zooming across the field, instantly landing on Gavin's back from across the pitch. He was bent over, tying his shoes, but I couldn't even take the time to appreciate the curve of his ass in those tiny, black shorts.

"Yes." No point in lying now. "Can you just…not tell Mom, please?"

"I would never," she whispered so softly, so quickly, that I barely heard the words.

Frowning, I faced her, trying to get a good read on her emotions. But like always, she was blank and empty—a million miles away from the world.

"Are you going to keep it?" she eventually asked.

I shrugged, hating how complicated this all was. "That's the million-dollar question at the moment."

She frowned. "Oh."

"I'm really not motherly material." I laughed, though nothing about what I'd said was funny. Being a mother meant sacrifice, love, discipline—three things I wasn't the best at.

"What do you mean by that?" Confusion laced her question.

"*Meaning*, I wasn't given the best parental role models growing up, so as a mother, I would be nothing short of disastrous. I've never even changed a diaper, for God's sake." *But you've assisted someone in changing a diaper.* I scowled at my internal voice, willing it to shut up. Now wasn't a good time.

Hanna laid her head on my shoulder, surprising me. In turn, I lowered my head on top of hers and blinked away my tears, unsure why I was getting emotional in the first place.

"You'd be a wonderful mother. You take care of me."

I smiled at her compliment, regardless of the fact that I knew she was wrong. "Thanks for the vote of confidence."

She didn't speak again for a while. I'm not sure what she was thinking, but I knew what I was. Would I be brave enough to just walk away in the end? Hand over this life I helped create to a man who was nothing short of amazing just because I was scared of screwing it up?

"Who's the father?"

I frowned, wondering if my sister had turned into a mind reader. "You don't know him."

"I don't know anything about *you* either." She stood abruptly and brushed her hand down the front of her dress, her mood shifting. Before I could apologize, a commotion exploded from the field ahead.

Standing to see what was going on, I swallowed hard, torn as my gaze flitted from the guys circling someone on the grass to my sister. "Hanna, I'm sorry I didn't—"

"It's fine." She gave me a tight-lipped smile, nothing about it real. "I won't tell Mom, and as long as you're happy, I'm happy too."

But she wasn't happy. Her eyes were glassy, as if she was on the verge of crying. It hurt my heart terribly, but I didn't have a clue what to say to her.

With a weary heart, I watched as she made her way to the brick bathrooms. I had every intention of going after her, but a familiar figure caught my eye from the side-lines. More so three figures, with Addie not far behind. Gavin was on one side of Max, while Collin stood on the other. They had him supported by the legs and waist, carrying him to Collin's truck.

"Damn it," I mumbled under my breath, dying to find out what was happening, but knowing Hanna would get flustered if I left. So, I waited from a distance, lip pulled between my teeth from nerves as they placed Max in the passenger seat of Collin's truck.

Words were spoken between the three men. Gavin looked on edge and grumpy, as if he was seconds from kicking someone's ass. The sight had goose bumps forming on my arms.

Once Max was settled inside, Gavin jogged toward his Suburban but stopped short of getting inside. I held my breath—waiting, wondering, worried—as he dropped his forehead against the window. The urge to comfort him was incredibly strong, my fingers trembling in turn. A hand on his spine is all I would need to do. Gavin wasn't one for pity, but he thrived on simple touches.

Yet, we hadn't spoken in almost three weeks.

Regardless, I found my feet moving seconds later, as though I was no longer in control of my body. No force, strong or not, could keep me away when he might need me.

Before I could make my way over completely though, he jerked his head back and turned my way, as though sensing me there.

I froze, waiting for him to see me, even more terrified of what his reaction might be.

But then I saw him smile. That's also the moment when my heart decided that this man was going to be *my* man, baby or not.

"McKenna!" he called, jumping over rugby bags,

racing around people, nearly frantic, as though time was running out.

Unable to hide my grin, I watched as he ran my way, his body lithe with every movement, yet strong and brave and everything I'd always wanted in my life. Seconds later, he was there in front of me, panting, and my knees... they nearly buckled with relief.

"Hi," I whispered, breathless myself.

As though knowing the effect he had on me, Gavin shot his arm around my waist in a quick save, our chests suddenly pressed together. Flush.

This man was my real-life superhero.

And my new home.

"McKenna." Fingers pressed to the base of my chin. He urged my gaze up, then searched my face, suddenly mute.

I nodded, having no idea what was going on in his head. "What happened to Max?" I clutched the front of his shirt, righting myself enough that he no longer had to hold me upright—not that I wanted him to stop.

"Someone from the other team was wearing illegal cleats. Fucked Max's hand up. Colly's taking him to the hospital. I'm gonna meet them there." Gorgeous green eyes held mine as he spoke. This was the controlled version of Gavin I was seeing. The worried friend, the fierce protector, the lover I'd never get enough of.

"Okay. Well, let me know what happens?"

He nodded, eyes glancing back at the outhouse. It was so quick I barely noticed. "Who was that girl with you and Addie?"

"My sister."

He nodded.

"Remember when I told you I had some family drama?" I winced, hating how that sounded.

"Yeah."

I cleared my throat. "Well, Hanna had some problems back at home and is staying with me for a few weeks."

A look of understanding passed through his gaze. "Is that why…"

"Why I haven't called you?" I cringed.

He nodded, then said, "I'm sorry."

"For what?"

"Being distant that night at my river house. Not… talking. Sometimes, you know, I just can't."

"Oh, Gavin…" I said his name like a prayer, willing him to be my savior for all of eternity. My knight in black rugby shorts with a beard that rivaled Jesus's. "Don't say 'sorry' when you have nothing to apologize for. I was a bitch that night."

Gavin leaned over and kissed my forehead, staying there while he said, "No. You were scared." He took a small step back, distancing himself from me. Already, I felt cold without him close.

"Not a good excuse. I told you I suck at this kind of stuff."

He smiled but didn't press the issue. "I miss you, Kenna. Every day we're apart…it kills me." My eyes welled with tears at his words, and I watched his throat work as he spoke a truth I could never deny. "Can we just, I don't know, start over or something? See what happens? We have time."

My heart leaped into my throat. Seven or so months wasn't long, but details didn't matter when it came to affairs of the heart, right?

"Really?"

He nodded, taking another step back, adding more space between us. Space I hated it, even knowing why he had to go. "Yes."

"Okay." My cheeks ached from smiling, but Gavin's face stayed serious. He rarely showed emotion, unless we were alone.

"You're in my dreams at night, Kenna."

I blinked, losing my smile as I watched him bend over to pick up his abandoned rugby bag. He hitched it up onto his shoulder as he continued. It was then that I saw a tiny quirk of his lips.

"I am?" Drawn to him like always, I found myself moving closer, even as he took another step back.

He nodded again, pieces of his light-brown hair falling over his cheek from out of his rubber band. "You're also the first thing I think of in the morning when I wake. It's been that way since that night we first met last November." His voice grew louder over the surrounding crowd. "And you're also the last thing I think about before I go to sleep at night."

In spite of the heat, the crowd, and the noise surrounding us, I wanted nothing more than to pull him close to me again. Leap into his arms. Hold him with no end. No second thoughts, just Gavin and me together, seeing where this went.

"Go out with me again tonight," he hollered a little louder, putting more distance between us.

A small shiver rocketed through me, the need to say yes on the tip of my tongue. I held his eyes across the distance a moment longer, seeing an exposed version of this man I'd never seen before. But I couldn't say yes…

At least not tonight.

"Can we do tomorrow instead?" I yelled, both hands now cupping my mouth. The commotion of players·and spectators, though not too terribly many, still held a high volume in the open field.

His smile grew wider. Then I saw his nod, the excitement in it so young and boyish and—

"McKenna." I jerked my head back at the sound of Hanna's voice, the moment over as the soft voice played a sad tune in my ear. "I want to go home now."

"Are you okay?" I asked, turning to face her. Gravel hit tires and the side of cars as Gavin's Suburban tore away from the lot.

Nervousness flickered across my sister's face as she peeked down at the grass. "Yes. Just tired is all." Tired was her code for *I'm done with people for the day.*

"Sure, hon. Anything you need."

We found Addie a minute later. She immediately called off our girls' night out. Her worry for Max and the guys was the reason. She loved Max and Gavin like brothers. And I could see why. They may have had their crass moments, but their unit as a whole was unbreakable.

As Hanna and I settled into my car and buckled a few minutes later, she broke me out of my thoughts with a question. "The man who you were talking to… Is he the baby's father?" Her voice was thick with emotion. But I didn't know what kind.

"Yes."

A beat passed before she said, "He's kind of…bushy."

At that, I laughed, relaxing a little as I pulled us out of the lot. "He hasn't always been like that. Gavin is just…" Complicated. Broken. A lover. A fighter. A man

I could see myself falling for, if I hadn't already been on the verge. There was no denying he and I were a match in a lot of ways. But was it enough? I wasn't sure.

"All that facial hair and the man-bun thing he has going on? It's kind of intense, don't you think?" She clasped her hands on her lap.

Which is why it fit him so perfectly. "I prefer to think of him as lumber-sexual."

Her smile pulled up one side of her mouth, giving her a look of ease that I hadn't seen since she'd arrived. "Try unshaven and motorcycle badass."

"Motorcycle badass, eh?" I snorted. "That's pretty accurate, I suppose, except that he drives a huge-ass Suburban and he's more a big softie than a rough biker."

A few seconds passed before she spoke up again. "Mom would hate him, you know."

I shrugged, knowing that already. "Mom hates all men, except for your father and brother. And even with them, she can be a royal bitch."

"True." Hanna sighed. "He seems nice though. I'd… like to meet him."

Nice wasn't the adjective I'd have used to describe Gavin St. James. It felt too mundane and overused. And while Gavin was a complicated creature, he was also a whole lot more than that. Sweet, charming, the quiet to my loud—a perfect counterpoint to my messed-up self in general. In fact, the longer I thought about it, the more I realized how true that was.

Gavin was the best thing that had ever happened to me.

CHAPTER 22

Gavin

I MADE IT INTO MY HOUSE BY ELEVEN FIFTY-FIVE ON the dot, just five minutes to spare. After spending the day at the hospital with Max and dealing with all the drama that came with the illegal cleats and the rugby club in general, I was more than ready to be done with this day.

Once I was inside my place, I rushed to get showered, changed, and in bed. At exactly 12:31 a.m., I dialed Kenna's number. My plan was to leave her a voicemail. Tell her how Max was—though I was pretty sure she knew already from Addie—then tell her I couldn't wait until I saw her again.

But that plan didn't work because she answered on the third ring, voice heavy with sleep.

"Did I wake you?" I switched off the light next to my bed and lay back on my pillow.

"Hmm, yeah, but it's fine."

I sighed, imagining her sleepy eyes looking up at me. "Sorry."

"Everything okay?" Kenna asked, yawning.

"Yeah. Max made it through surgery fine. Lia's there with him now." I cleared my throat. "Lot of bullshit politics going on about the leagues after today."

"How do you mean?"

I ran my fingers through my hair, taking out the rubber band I'd pulled it back with. More than a few times, I'd been made fun of tonight for my hair—even got called Jesus's twin by some asshole from the Macomb team during an earlier match today.

"The game, the competition. The younger guys doing shit like they did today. There's talk of other leagues in the Midwest playing by a different set of rules and whatnot, which means people think all normal rules are bullshit now."

"That sucks," she said on another yawn.

I shrugged. "It is what it is, you know?"

"I do."

Silence lingered between us, and at the same time, Cat jumped on the foot of my bed. His purring sounded like a motor, and he rubbed his nose and chin against my head and the hand holding the phone.

"Is that Cat?" she asked. I could hear the smile in her voice.

"Yeah, he's a needy little shit." I rubbed the top of his head. My hand dwarfed his face and ears, but he liked it. I was glad I'd decided to keep him. Having him there made me feel less alone.

"Poor guy. I bet he's missing me."

I squeezed my eyes shut, the words *He's not the*

only one right there in my mouth. "Yeah, you can stop by anytime and see him now that you know where my extra key is."

"You know it's totally cliché of you to leave it under the doormat," she huffed.

I rolled onto my side. "I'm a simple cliché man. What can I say?"

She laughed, the easy sound making my cock twitch. Eyes squeezed shut, I thought of anything that would get my mind off sex and Kenna—*having* sex with Kenna.

Cleaning Cat's litter box, dirty laundry, dirty diapers… But it wasn't enough. I missed this woman. The feel of her hands on my body, the smell of her skin when I inhaled. The taste of her lips when I kissed them, and the way her lips parted when I sunk my cock inside her.

Christ, get it together, St. James.

"Can you hold on a sec?" Without waiting for an answer, I dropped my cell on the bed and stood, rubbing my hand over my face with quick passes. I paced the room, even stubbed my toe, but nothing could contain the hardening in my shorts.

Guess I hadn't realized how tough this would be, talking to her so late at night, listening to her sleepy voice on the other end. So close, yet so far away.

Once I'd inhaled enough breaths to fill a balloon, I got back on the phone. "Sorry."

"You okay?" Her voice cracked with sleep.

My eyes shut again, imagining her settled in bed, covers up to her chin. I'd slept next to her all night twice before, and both times I'd woken up before her, studying her face, her beautiful lips parted in sleep.

Screw the hard-on. When it came to Kenna, I couldn't

control it. "I'm good now that I'm talking to you again. I've missed you, Brewer."

She snorted. "You flatter me, St. James."

"Good." My cheeks hurt from smiling so damn much. I felt like a kid. "You need to be flattered all the time."

She giggled. "God, I feel like I'm sixteen again: staying up late, talking with boys on the phone, trying not to be heard…"

"Hmm." I cleared my throat, still grinning.

"Bet you were quite the lady's man back in the day, huh?" she asked. "The quiet, baseball-playing hottie and all."

I rubbed my forehead. "Not really. I only had one girlfriend in high school. But I didn't have a phone to talk to her with."

It was the summer after my junior year when I met Lacey—six months *after* my foster brother killed himself. Regardless of what I'd been through, I was still a decent enough kid. Smart. Studied, kept my grades high, never got in trouble.

Lacey became my world—the only person in my life who seemed to give two shits about me. Her father was a minister who treated me like a son, and her mother, a homemaker, had been the same. I'd struck gold when it came to that girl. To this day, I had no idea what she'd seen in me back then. Had no idea why she fell in love with a bum foster kid who barely spoke.

Still, we spent a year together. Then she left to go to college in New York, and me to the University of Illinois. Neither of us looked back.

"You mean to tell me you're twenty-seven years old and—"

"I just turned twenty-eight last month."

She gasped. "I missed your birthday?"

"I don't celebrate it. It's no big deal. Collin and Max didn't even know."

"*Gavin.*"

"Again. Not a big deal." I rolled over to my other side and threw an arm over my eyes.

"It *is* a big deal. And *we* are going to celebrate it by staying up on the phone together all night. Complete the rite of passage you never got to experience in high school. *If* we fall asleep, then we still can't hang up, so like, make sure you don't roll over onto your phone and accidentally mess this up, okay?"

My lips twitched. I loved it when she rambled.

"We're going to talk about all the *good* things you've experienced in your twenty-eight years of life this time, and I'm going to give you what you never had as a teen-age boy."

"Oh yeah?" She left herself wide open with that one.

"Oh yeah. And if you're really good…" Her voice lowered. The husky sound was filled with promises and secrets. "We can maybe check off another thing you probably haven't done before."

"What's that?" I dropped my arm and sat up a little, leaning back against the wall, shoulders rigid, gut tight, cock so hard I couldn't control it if I tried.

She was quiet, but I could hear her breathing, almost as though she was shifting in the bed. If I listened hard enough, maybe I could hear her legs sliding against her sheets. In my mind, she'd inhale heavily, her moans soft as her hand crept up underneath her shirt. She'd stroke her breasts until her panties were wet, then she'd reach between her thighs, slide a finger under the seam…

My cock twitched, growing even harder, reminding me how alone I was, how much I *wanted* this woman too.

"Gavin?"

"Hmm?" I shut my eyes, freezing like I'd been caught, but imagining her eyes on me at the same time.

"Let's play a game," she said.

"What kind of game?" I yanked my hand through my hair and sighed.

"How about Never Have I Ever?"

"Not sure I've ever played that one before."

"Really? Not even in high school or college?"

"Nope."

She sighed. "Oh. That's sad."

"Not to me. I preferred it that way. Hated talking to people. Still do."

"But you talk to me."

I grinned. "You're easy to talk to."

"Aww, Gav…"

My heart twisted when she used my nickname like that. Whether she knew it or not, this woman had me so wrapped around her finger it wasn't even funny.

She cleared her throat. "I'll go first."

"You going to tell me how to play, or should I just pretend to know what the hell I'm doing?"

"It's pretty easy. Just follow my lead. I'll say *never have I ever* and you say *yes, I have* or *no, I haven't*. Then we'll switch."

I shifted around, annoying Cat. He mewed low, then ran from the room. "Sounds good."

"Okay, I'll go first. Never have I ever been on a blind date."

"Me neither."

"Now *your* turn."

I scratched at my beard. "Feels like there should be some sort of compensation that goes along with this game. A win-lose scenario." I sat up in bed and kicked the covers off, restless.

"There *is* compensation. We get to know each other better."

I laughed. "I was thinking we know each other pretty well already, don't you?"

And in more ways than just sex. I knew she talked a lot. I knew she loved to have fun and hang out with our friends. She liked her job when she was *working* at her job, but off the job, she hated it. She had crappy parents, an equally crappy childhood as mine, but came out on top as a survivor and strong. Did I know her favorite color? Her favorite food? No. Those things would come later. All that mattered was that I knew the important stuff. The stuff that counted.

"Oh. Well, do you not want to do it?"

"No, I do. But, like I said, we should make this interesting." I cleared my throat. "You have FaceTime on your phone?"

"I do."

I grinned. "FaceTime me, then."

"On it," she said, only for the line to go dead a second later.

I fought a smile when my phone began to ring again. Just the thought of seeing her had my heart racing.

"Hey." She waved.

"Hi." I studied her face, the light on her phone highlighting it. Pale cheeks and blue eyes, that wide, addicting smile, a white T-shirt hanging off one shoulder… God, I'd be a lucky bastard if I could get her to agree to be mine.

"So, it's your turn." She pointed at the screen.

"Fine." I twisted my free hand into the sheets. "Never have I ever been skydiving."

"I have."

"No shit?" I grinned and rested the phone on my stomach, holding it at the base.

She nodded. "Yep. Spring break in college. Me, Addie, and a couple of girls went down to Jamaica. It was scary as hell, and I'd never do it again. But it was a bucket-list thing. Plus, it pissed my mom off when she saw I'd charged her credit card to do it."

"Jesus, you're trouble."

She winked. "I'm surprised you never did anything like that in the marines. Like, jump from a helicopter."

"That's not skydiving; it's called fast roping. We didn't wear parachutes, and we climbed down ropes. It wasn't fun." My stomach dropped as one of those memories came barreling back at me. A dust storm. Enemy fire coming from all directions. Blindly making my way to safety and not having a goddamn clue where anyone was…

It was a fucked-up time, something I didn't wanna think about, though I knew I'd never forget it either.

Movement caught my eye. Her phone shifted. I could see her adjusting, but I couldn't see her face. Seconds later, she popped up into the view, her head buried under her blanket.

"What're you doing?" I laughed, thankful for the distraction.

"I'm cold. Hanna likes the temperature to stay around sixty-seven during the nights when she actually sleeps, and I feel like I'm living in an igloo." She scrunched her nose up like a rabbit.

"I'd like to meet her."

Kenna grinned brightly. "She said the same thing about you today."

A few seconds later, I asked the stupidest question I could. Not thinking, just…going with my gut. "How's the baby…? Everything still good?"

She lost her smile but nodded, her eyes sad. "Yes. Everything is good."

Still, she wasn't hanging up on me. That had to be a good sign. "And you're feeling okay? Sick at all anymore?"

"A little." She shrugged, and a strand of her hair fell over her forehead. She blew it away, but it came back down over her eye again. "I'm also exhausted all the time."

I wanted to know everything about this pregnancy, yeah, but at the same time, even though I had adjusted to the idea of fatherhood, I knew Kenna wasn't there yet. Which is why I said what I did. "I'm here whenever you want to talk about it." I bit the inside of my cheek, nervous.

She smiled. "Thank you."

"For?"

"Not pushing me yet. I just… I'm scared."

"Me too." I ran my fingers through my hair, frustrated with my inability to comfort her.

"What are you scared of the most?" she asked, chewing on her thumbnail.

That was a loaded question. "I've got nothing to offer a kid except a little bit of money and a roof over its head. No family, just our friends—people who I have no doubt would be there for us if we needed them. I worry I'm not enough, even though I want to be."

She sighed. "It's not about what you have to offer, right? It's about what you want."

"What do *you* want?" I asked, hoping I wasn't pushing too hard.

"Well, I can tell you what I *don't* want." She thought for a second, her eyes narrowing slightly. "I don't want to be a messed-up mom like mine was. And I sure as hell don't want to abandon a child when things get tough."

"How do you know you'd be that kind of parent?"

"Because it's in my blood to screw things up." She sighed. "To walk away. To push stuff away. To not care…"

"Not true." I shook my head. "Did you walk away from Addie when she needed you?"

"No, but I walked away from my sister. Plus, my mom sent Hanna here so she didn't have to deal with her issues. I had no idea she was going through the hell she was, Gavin." She told me about Hanna's ex, about what had happened. To think a guy could ever be like that with a woman fucking disgusted me.

"Did your sister call you? Keep in touch with *you*?"

Her shoulders dropped. "No, not exactly, but I don't think she was in the right frame of mind to call me. All I'm saying is I could've done better."

"I get that. But you're not her mother."

"I would be to this child…" She paused. "My own mother didn't have a clue what was going on with Hanna. What if we have a daughter and the same thing happens, and I miss the signs, then can't deal with them in the end?"

"Fuck your mom, Kenna. You are not her. At all." I grumbled, angry that we even had to have this conversation. McKenna did not give herself enough credit. "And you seem to be missing the fact that I'm not your dad either. We are two different people who have learned from the mistakes of others."

"But what about you?" she continued, not really listening to me. "I walked away from *you* after our night together in your river house. I run. I don't follow through with things. I make stupid, impulsive decisions that will no doubt affect everyone I care about in my life. And that includes you and this baby."

"For one, you had a damn good reason for running." If anything, I think we both needed the space apart to work through this. "I wasn't exactly running in to save the day either, was I?"

She cringed and looked down at the bed. I wished I were there, holding her face between my hands. But this would have to be enough for now.

"Look where we are though," I said.

She bit her bottom lip. "I've been dicked over so many times in my life. Not just by my family, but by men in general." She laughed humorlessly but was losing the excuses. "I've got a shoebox to prove it, actually."

"Let me show you what it's like to *not* to be dicked over then." I touched the phone screen and trailed my finger down over her face. She looked up, as if knowing what I was doing. "Let me show you what it's like to be loved."

Tears dripped down her cheek, but her eyes widened. "Loved?"

I nodded, not ready to admit something I wasn't even sure I could do. But ready to try, at least.

"I don't know…"

"Don't make a decision yet." My throat burned when I swallowed. "Let's just be together. See where it goes."

"Like…a relationship?"

"Yeah." I grinned at the idea of being able to take her out, kiss her, hold her hand. I may not have had a lot of experience when it came to women, but I knew I'd be a damn good scholar.

"But the baby, Gavin. I don't know if I even want it."

"What if we pretend you're not pregnant?"

She snorted. "Yeah. Not gonna happen."

"Fine. So how do we do this? You tell me."

She wiped at her face and sniffed. "I-I don't know."

"We could pick up where we left off," I suggested. "How does that sound?"

Her nose scrunched up. I loved it when she did that. "Is it really that easy, do you think?"

I nodded fast, not a doubt in my mind. "Yeah. I think it is."

CHAPTER 23

McKenna

IT WAS FIVE IN THE MORNING BEFORE I FINALLY FELL asleep—the head-to-the-pillow, deep kind of sleep. Talking with Gavin for a straight four hours on FaceTime had pretty much worn me down and picked me up at the same time.

The guy wasn't just charming and sweet, but incredibly funny too. Not the kind of funny that had me laughing out loud, but the kind that was abrupt and so unexpected that when I did laugh, it was genuine and hard to contain. The last remaining walls around me were being stripped away every second we spoke. In their place were feelings I wasn't quite sure what to do with but knew I didn't want to ignore anymore either.

We didn't discuss the baby again. But I knew the truth—saw it in his eyes. Gavin wanted a happily ever after, and he wanted it with me. But how could that happen when I didn't believe in fairy tales?

With a sigh, I rolled over and glanced at the clock.

It was three in the afternoon, a glorious time to behold. I had nowhere important to be today other than right where I was. My sister and I could hang out the rest of the afternoon, watch a little TV, and order some takeout. It would be nice to just be.

Then tonight, Gav and I could do it all over again.

"Sweet Jesus, am I screwed." I tossed an arm over my eyes and groaned.

Even though I should've been slamming my head against the wall, that sense of real happiness I had always tried to avoid was gripping its claws in deep. Thoughts of Penis-Head Paul, and all the idiots before him were there in the back of my head as always, but the memory of Gavin's words from last night—*Let me show you what it's like to be loved*—had grown in place of all the bad crap from the exes.

A knock sounded at my door. Followed by a very unexpected voice.

"Kenna?"

I jerked up in bed at the noise, scrambling for my pants on the floor. "Uh, just a minute."

Oh my God.

Oh. My. God.

Gavin? He was here? In my *house*?

Just outside my freaking bedroom door, at that.

"Breathe, Kenna," I reminded myself as I looked in the mirror to check for possible drool lines.

Once assured that my condition was, well, *semi*-presentable, I inhaled through my nose once more and opened the door, blinking quickly at what I saw.

Gavin, just like I thought, but with Stargazer lilies in hand.

"Hi," he said shyly, those dark lashes of his batting lazily against his cheeks.

"You…me…flowers?" I'm pretty sure I was speaking gibberish. Apparently, swoon-sucker me didn't have the ability to say coherent sentences. Never had I been incapable of words to the point where I stuttered like an idiot. But, there again, never had I been wooed by Gavin St. James.

"They're lilies."

He cleared his throat, his green eyes as bright as the leaves with the flowers. I died a little inside at the sight. And believe me when I say, it was the best way to go.

"They're beautiful."

"The, um, florist said they mean I missed you. I asked her."

Heart? Meet belly.

I smiled widely at the gesture and urged him inside. When it came to romance, a man asking for the meaning of flowers before purchasing them was pretty much a woman's dream. Or at least mine.

The door clicked shut behind me as I turned to face my new guest. There was something incredibly intimate about having him in my room. A step in a direction I wasn't sure I was meant to take…until that moment.

"Did I wake you?" he asked. "Your sister let me in. Said you were in here."

Hand in his shorts pockets, chin to his chest, Gavin looked downright adorable. His cheeks were pink, barely visible under his beard, and beneath his dark lashes, he stared back at me as though I was a certified goddess.

"No, I, um… I've been awake for a while." I ran my hand over the front of my shirt, then winced at the tiny bulge there. When I looked up, I found him at my dresser, his eyes flitting over the framed pictures of me and my sister, and me and Addie.

"Um, so, wanna do a late lunch or early dinner?" He turned to face me, his back to my mirror and dresser. One of his hands was on the nape of his neck, rubbing feverishly, the other still held the flowers.

Feeling like an idiot for not taking them earlier, I stepped forward and pulled the bouquet from his hands. He smiled as I settled them against my chest, and I heard him chuckle when I pressed them to my nose and inhaled.

"Lunch, huh?" I tipped my head back to look up at him when I was done, licking my lips.

He nodded, eyes twinkling as he stared at my mouth. For a big, bearded, muscular marine, this guy had a secret, softy heart when you got to know him.

"I'm pretty tired." I teased, setting the bouquet on the dresser. "Kind of had a long night."

"Someone keep you up late?" His brows lifted in suspicion, but I saw the twitch of his lips all the same.

"Maybe I kept *that* person up late instead." I closed the distance between us, our chests just a foot apart.

His lips pulled up in an easy grin. Gavin had the type of presence that always managed to suck me in, no matter what kind of mood he displayed. It was engaging, the way he spoke to others. Short, brief, to the point. And it turned me on in more ways than I could count. I'm pretty sure his lack of communication bothered him more than it did anyone else. But the fact of the matter was, I liked how he was. How he acted. Gavin knew what he wanted, though it took him some time to *get* what he wanted. In a way, he reminded me of a tiger: slow to pounce, but all claws and bite once he took his prey. That occasional shyness he exhibited only complemented—not to mention complicated—his ways, making him more intriguing.

I'm not sure if I'd ever figure him out completely, but I was going to have a damn good time trying.

"Where do you want to go eat?" I asked, pressing my palms to his chest, loving how his heart picked up speed under my hands.

"I, uh…" He cleared his throat, blushing even more.

"I'll give you a moment to think about it." With a wink, I walked to my dresser, keeping my movements slow and deliberate. I pulled a new bra and panty set out of my drawer to take a shower, nonchalant as I turned to face him again.

Gavin didn't need to know that having him here in my space like this, asking to take me out, was pretty much a seal-the-deal thing when it came to getting laid. I might not have been completely sold on giving him my heart, but my body? Yeah, that was all his.

"I was thinking the bar and grill along the river. Spencer's. Then we could take a Channel Cat boat ride after." He cleared his throat. "I gotta work the night shift tonight, so I can't be out late."

A public boat ride with Gavin on my arm? I liked the sound of that more than I had a right to. "Sure." I smiled widely, ignoring my bitchy inner voice that said I didn't deserve so much happiness.

My throat grew dry as I watched him move closer. His hands were balled against his sides as though maybe, just maybe, he was fighting against the same urge I was.

To reach out. To touch me. Kiss me. Maybe more…

Please let there be more.

"I've always wanted to do that boat ride with some-one," he said, voice cracking a little.

"Like, a girl someone?"

He nodded, his body inches from mine.

My chest rose quickly with my breaths. I tipped my head back to meet his gaze once again, hating to think of myself as someone who just happened to come along and fill his to-do list. Yet at the same time, there I stood, praying I was the only girl he'd ever want to ask again. Those were dangerous thoughts with a possible danger-ous outcome. Yet did that deter me?

"Then I guess it's your lucky day."

Absolutely not.

Gone were his pink cheeks and unsure gaze. In their place was a sure, confident man who needed something from me—something I was suddenly ready to give. Gavin said he was an inexperienced lover. But I didn't see that in his stature. Didn't feel that when his hands were on my body, when he was driving inside me.

"You better get in the shower, then." He nodded toward the hall.

My face grew hot. Suddenly, the last thing I wanted to do was leave this room.

"I better…" The words trailed off, my heart racing at the possibility of him joining me.

He nodded slowly, moving in even closer, until his chest was flush with mine. "Unless you don't want to." He licked his lips.

I licked mine.

"I do want to. Really, really bad."

He lifted his brows in question.

"Wanna shower, I mean." I cleared my throat, knees shaking now.

Warm, calloused hands brushed against my waistline and my shirt slid upward beneath. I shivered, automatically leaning closer. Fingers grasped tenderly at my bare flesh, and I sucked in a breath as he drew circles with his thumbs.

Screw the damn shower. There were at *least* half a dozen things I wanted to do in that moment other than getting clean. And every one of them required Gavin and me naked in the bed.

"Stop making those noises." He shut his eyes, looking pained as he lowered his forehead to mine.

"What noises?" I asked, drunk on his touches.

"Noises that have me thinking you want me to touch you more. Like you don't care what happens, as long as you're touching me too."

Fingertips grazed my spine as he wrapped his hands around my back. My skin erupted in goose bumps, the need for pleasure the reason. The air-conditioning flipped on at the same time and a low hum filled the room, acting as noise deflection.

My sister was down the hall. She wouldn't be able to hear us…

I licked my lips again, shutting my eyes at the same time. "Maybe I do want to."

A low growl erupted in his throat. "You've gotta be more specific with me than that. I need your words, Kenna."

I opened my eyes, slowly, as if I was taking in a new world, needing to savor it in case it all disappeared— which I knew it could, but no longer seemed to care.

In a way, Gavin was that new world, filling me with all things peace and man, breathing life into me when I didn't know I was so desperate for it. As ridiculous as it sounded, I'd been lost before I knew Gavin, and now, standing there, I knew without a doubt in my mind that I'd been found. Who knew "Amazing Grace" was going to become my new theme song?

Wordless, I dropped to my knees, my hands trailing down his hard thighs, running up beneath his shorts in the back. "I need you…"

Tortured eyes met mine from above. Lips pressed together, throat bobbing, he whispered back, "You have me, beautiful. You've always had me."

Gavin

Kenna down on her knees, unbuttoning my shorts, was the stuff of fantasies, something I'd never known existed. Twenty-eight years old, and I'd never felt the way I did for McKenna with any other woman. Seeing her so unleashed before me only emphasized that.

"I want to touch you," she whispered and tugged down the zipper of my shorts. Confident. Beautiful. Perfect.

Hands shaking, she reached inside my boxers until she had my cock in her hands.

I sucked in a breath. "You're doing a pretty fucking fantastic job of that, I'd say." My voice sounded garbled, and my knees began to shake. I lowered my hands on the dresser for support, scared I'd fall on top of her.

She pulled me free of my zipper, her long fingers wrapped tightly around the base. I swallowed so hard I could feel it in my balls, but I didn't move, afraid she'd change her mind. Afraid I'd change my mind too.

Did I want her hands on me? Fuck yes, I did. Did I want her pretty mouth wrapped around the head of my cock? More than anything else. But I hadn't come here expecting this, especially since last night was the first time we'd spoken in almost a month. Still, Kenna worked in unusual ways. She didn't need to be wooed, but she did need to be put up a pedestal—something I'd always do if she'd let me. She deserved everything she never thought she'd get, and I'd be the guy to try to give that to her.

Wordless, she dropped a kiss on the head of my cock. Her tongue slipped over the slit seconds later, then circled around the head. I jerked my hips forward, and she lapped at the pre-come already slipping out. I shuddered, my spine going so rigid I thought I'd break. Her eyes met mine when I dropped my chin to my chest. That blond hair of hers fell over her cheeks, and I swore I'd never seen anything so beautiful in my life.

Needing to touch her, to make sure she was real, I reached down and ran my knuckles over her cheek. She shut her eyes, taking me in deeper.

"Fuck…" I hissed, struggling to keep from jamming myself down her throat. I'd been given head only twice in my life—and that was when I was fucking seventeen and twenty-four. My experience was limited when it came to women. Not that I didn't have a lot of opportunities—I just never felt like taking anyone up on it. Still, I knew what felt good, and her mouth wrapped around me was fucking amazing.

Slowly, she slid her free hand around to my ass and used the other to squeeze the base of my balls. Then her mouth slipped down further, and her tongue slid across the base, and I was so damn done for.

I gripped her hair with the hand that'd been on her cheek, still using the other to hold myself up against the dresser. In and out, I guided her slowly, setting the pace as the sound of her sucks filled the small bedroom. I licked my lips, watching her. More than anything else, I wanted to kiss her, taste her, feel her body against mine, around mine.

"You're damn good at that." I groaned, teeth gritted. I held my breath as the base of my balls started to tingle.

I was close. Too close.

Kenna smiled around my cock, and her eyes turned into seductive blue slits. She looked like the devil's temptress, and damn if that didn't make me want to sin.

She sucked harder, speeding up, then slowing down. My fingers clenched tighter in her hair, and with every pull of my hand, she went faster. Harder. *Deeper.*

"Damn it, no." I finally hissed, not ready for this to end so soon. I pulled her off me, not caring about the pout on her lips as she stood, only needing to make her feel as fucking wanted as she made me.

I turned her so her back faced the dresser, then I slid my sweaty palms around her hips. With no second thoughts, I walked backward, urging her with me, until the back of my knees grazed her mattress. She giggled as I stumbled, then moaned as I pulled her down on top of me. When I tugged her head close to press my lips to hers, her laughter was soon replaced with a low moan.

Back arched, she rode my bare cock through her wet panties, panting, her skin damp with sweat. I gripped her ass harder, encouraging her to move faster, wishing she'd take the lead, strip those silky things away, and fuck me right.

"Gavin," she whispered, pulling her face back to look down at me, her arms along both sides of my head. Our eyes met, holding, an unspoken question in her stare that faded only when she lowered her forehead to mine.

I shuddered, that image forever ingrained in my head. McKenna was hurting, and the only one who could fix her in that moment was me.

"Need you," I whispered between slow kisses, my throat twisted in knots.

"I'm yours," she whispered, panting. "Always yours."

The words were like angels singing in my ears, only reaffirming what I already knew.

McKenna was the final missing piece to my heart.

Desperate to please her, I reached down and tugged her thin panties aside. Seconds later, she lowered her pussy over my cock, moaning so loudly I had to press her mouth back to mine to silence her. Not that I minded. Kissing Kenna was like performing magic. Something I wanted to master, even if I knew it could all be an illusion in the end.

"Gavin," she managed, pulling away as she rode me. "You feel so good."

I groaned, hands on her hips as I guided her over me. Slow, hard, deep.

Minutes later, she moved to sit up, her hands going flat against my chest as she rocked her hips. She bit down on her lip this time, stifling her moans. And I hated that she had to be quiet, when all I wanted was to hear her scream my name.

Seconds passed, maybe minutes—fuck, it could've been

hours for all I know. I didn't ever want to stop. I wanted her to fuck me until I couldn't think. Couldn't breathe.

She dropped her head back, her movements taking me so deep I had to grit my teeth to keep from yelling.

"Yes, Gavin, yes," she whispered, rocking even faster. The headboard clanked against the wall, and I reached back, holding it steady with one hand, while I used the other to palm her breast over her bra.

"Jesus, Kenna."

Her body trembled at my words, her hands shaking on my chest too. Then she came like a storm in the night, her lips parted but silent. Fast as lightning, impossible to contain, and so fucking beautiful I didn't ever want it to stop. I palmed her ass and squeezed it hard with my release, more than positive I'd probably just left bruises on her beautiful skin.

She collapsed face-first against my chest, panting and unable to catch her breath. I rested my lips over the pulse point in her neck, feeling it race. Peace filled my chest, surrounding my heart, as one solitary word flashed through my mind: *love.*

It was a concept foreign to me, yet something I wanted so badly—with *her.* With our baby. If I were a crying man, I'd have been sobbing at the thought. Instead, all I could do was hold her to me. Promise to never let her go.

"That was…" She sighed.

"Perfect." I shut my eyes, grinning against her skin.

Didn't matter that my pants were still at my ankles, or that I was still half-hard and seated inside her. I loved this woman.

I loved McKenna.

CHAPTER 24

McKenna

PREGNANCY SUCKED, AND I HAD THE NEWLY MESSED-UP brain to prove it. After an amazing bout of sex with Gavin, I remembered that I could not, in fact, go out with him as he'd asked.

Mainly because I didn't want to leave my sister.

So, what did I do? I showered, begged Gavin to hide out in my room for a little while longer, so as not to freak Hanna out, then pulled her aside in the kitchen.

"Hey, are you okay?" I asked, rubbing my damp hair with a towel.

Hanna was leaning against the sink, clutching a full glass of water. "I'm fine." She smiled a little. "So, that's him, huh?"

"It is." My cheeks heated, worried now more than ever that she'd heard us. I'd been disrespectful by not checking on her when he got here. No doubt showing up like he did freaked her out.

She nodded and looked at the floor. "He's nice."

"Yeah?" I grinned and leaned back against the sink next to her.

"Uh-huh. He said he was your friend though. I thought…"

This time I was the one to look at the floor. "It's complicated." God, though. What was so complicated about it? I liked him. I liked the idea of him being the father to the baby we'd made. And I liked even more that he was open to the possibility of being with someone like me.

Someone who, sadly, couldn't figure out what she wanted.

"What's so complicated about it?"

I shrugged, twisting my hands at my waist. "He wants to keep the baby."

"And you don't?"

"That's complicated too."

"Everything is complicated with you, isn't it?"

I flinched, hating that she could so easily point out my flaws right there in front of me. Deciding now wasn't the time to get into it, I asked if it was okay for him to hang out with us.

"Sure." This time when she looked up, her dark eyes were lighter. Proof, again, that she was getting better every day with being around men and healing emotionally. I would never push her, but I was glad she'd been pushing herself.

Fifteen minutes later, though, Hanna sat on the floor by my feet, clutching my right leg as if it were her literal lifeline, while to my left sat Gavin, stiff as a bean pole, only harder because of the muscles. Muscles I wanted run my hand over again, and again, and again…

I swallowed, shutting my eyes, ignoring the cries of

the woman on the TV. Normally, watching rom-coms and romantic dramas was my thing—one way to obtain that temporary happiness I craved—but today, it was the last thing I wanted. On one side, I had a sexy, yet uncomfortable man, and on the other, a woman who screamed, terrified, with each of the sexy, yet uncomfortable man's movements. Hanna may have agreed to let Gavin hang with us, but that didn't mean she was doing well with it.

On my lap sat a plate of spaghetti and garlic bread from my favorite takeout restaurant, but I couldn't eat it because I'd forgotten my fork. Normal circumstances would mean pausing the movie, walking toward the kitchen, and grabbing said utensil, but this was not a normal circumstance.

"Hanna." I cleared my throat. "I need a fork. Would you mind grabbing one for me?"

Like a toddler, she clung harder to my leg, her nails digging into my calf. Her eyes stayed locked on the TV, but I knew her attention was anywhere but. I sucked in a breath, earning a look from Gavin, who stared down at my sister, then me again, brows furrowed.

He nodded a second later, likely sensing the situation—God bless his sweet ways. "I'll grab one," he said.

"Thank you." I watched him stand, loving how perfect his ass looked in his cargo khakis. I wanted a quarter, because bouncing it off his backside would no doubt be the highlight of my life.

Once he was out of the room, my sister relaxed. But when I pressed my hand to her shoulder, she jumped like I'd slapped her. "Hey. You're okay," I soothed.

Slowly, as though it hurt to move, she turned to look up at me, her eyes going to the spot where Gavin had been, then back to me. She opened her mouth as if she wanted to speak but shut it the second he walked back into the room.

"Here you go." He sat on the edge of the couch and set a fork on my plate and a napkin on my knee.

Tears blurred my eyes. *Jesus.* What was wrong with me? A man brings me a napkin and a fork, and I swoon? Die a million emotional deaths?

"Thank you." I zeroed in on the TV again, fearing he'd see how warped I was.

I felt my sister's stare on my face and the question in her eyes at the same time. I didn't look at her. No doubt if I did, she'd freak out over the fact that I was on the edge of tears because of a simple gesture by a man.

Gavin cleared his throat and sat back against the couch cushions. Hanna's grip loosened a bit on my leg, but throughout the movie, she never once stopped touching me. Gavin, on the other hand, kept his distance— didn't even try to hold my hand once I'd finished my food. Part of me worried that he was second-guessing everything, but the saner side of my brain convinced me he was just being respectful because of Hanna.

Once the credits started rolling, I glanced out the window. It was already dusk, the sunlight barely sneaking through my curtains.

The three of us were silent. And other than the credits on the TV, everything was still. Eventually, I had to wipe my eyes, because nothing said depressingly romantic like an old couple dying on a bed within each other's arms.

Hanna, on the other hand, didn't move. I half

wondered if she was asleep. When I leaned forward to check, I found tears on her face and a glazed-over look in her eyes.

I settled my hand on her shoulder and squeezed lightly, but before I could open my mouth to ask her if she was okay, she broke in first. "I've always wondered, why the birds?"

I frowned. "What do you mean?"

She pulled her bottom lip between her teeth as she peered up at me from over her shoulder. "I mean, why the birds at the end? Do they signify something?"

"Umm…" *Well, hell.*

Gavin cleared his throat. "I'm guessing they signify freedom. Going home. Finding peace. Hope."

I swiveled around to look at him, finding his eyes still on the screen. Philosophical Gavin made my insides flip-flop.

Hanna cleared her throat and started in again. "So, like…peace after death?"

I looked back and forth between the pair, wondering if I should intervene.

"In a way, yes," Gavin said.

"So, let me get this straight. The birds fly away, and all is okay? Because I'm not feeling okay after that movie." Hanna scowled harder at the screen, still not looking at us.

I narrowed my eyes at my sister, confused by her sudden ability to communicate with Gavin, when she'd been scared to death of him the entire movie.

He leaned forward, his forearms on his knees, and dropped his head as he spoke. Or should I say *recited freaking poetry.*

> *"'Hope' is the thing with feathers—*
> *That perches in the soul—*
> *And sings the tune without the*
> *words—*
> *And never stops—at all—"*

Boom. Crash. Sputter. Those were the remaining bits of my heart fluttering to a free fall into my toes.

"Y-you know Emily Dickinson's poetry?" Hanna questioned, eyes widening.

I looked at him too. Confidence oozed off his body like sweat from skin, but not purposeful confidence. Natural. A man with a hidden heart that was moments from bursting alive.

My fingers itched to grab him, pull him to me, hold him close. He didn't know that my little sister had been a history major, with a minor in English lit at Tulane University, studying artifacts and…stuff like that. Stuff I wasn't into, that bored me to tears, that she related to on a level I never could.

Hanna relaxed more than she had all night, turning just enough to see Gavin completely. A smile split my lips as I listened to the two of them converse.

"I do." He rubbed the back of his neck, suddenly shy once more.

My eyes were the ones to widen in surprise at his confession. But I didn't question him, too afraid I'd break the spell between him and my sister.

"Really?" Hanna asked. "That's…incredible."

Inch by inch, her body relaxed, and warmth filled her eyes in a way I hadn't seen in a very long time. Hanna had always been a smart girl, but she'd never had anyone to have intelligent conversations with. I was the compulsive, distracted sister who came around every once in a blue moon, the one who failed to concentrate on anything longer than two seconds at a time. Her brother—my stepbrother—was ten years older than she was, so by the time she was ready to have deep, stimulating conversations, he was out of the house and married. Mom was a wicked bitch who discussed fashion and traveled in more social circles than any normal parent should. And her father? My stepdad? He was never home, always away on some random adventure across the world, mostly of the leisure variety because he couldn't stand my mother either.

Gavin nodded and looked at the floor. "When I was younger, I did a lot of reading, mostly old poetry books and whatnot. That's not the kind of stuff I can forget." He cleared his throat, definitely uncomfortable. I snuck my hand close to his and grabbed his pinkie, squeezing. It was the only way I could get across to him how thankful I was for what he was doing, even though he probably didn't have a clue.

"Color me impressed, St. James." I smiled.

His gaze flittered down to our joined fingers, and his face seemed to brighten with his grin.

"Do you ever, I don't know, maybe go to the museums around here?" Hanna met his stare, then quickly looked at the floor again.

His brows furrowed. "Like, history museums?"

She nodded slowly.

"Not really. History wasn't my thing." He stroked his beard, a sign he was thinking. "But there is a historical writers' museum in downtown Chicago that

I wouldn't mind going to. They showcase different authors from the nation's past. F. Scott Fitzgerald to Maya Angelou."

Hanna gasped, her brown eyes twinkling with excitement when they met mine. "Oh my God, can we go? I mean, I'm not into literary history much, but I'm a sucker for new museums."

"Absolutely." I smiled. At this point, I'd do anything to see that kind of excitement light up her face again.

"Do you, um, think you'd want to go too, Gavin?" She bit down on her bottom lip.

My insides warmed, and pride radiated through my chest. She was taking a new step—a positive one.

"Sure." He nodded once. "If it's okay with you."

"Yes. That would be great." Both dimples filled her cheeks this time. My insides went to total mush too. It had taken *me* weeks to find that smile, yet one conversation with Gavin and he'd pulled it right out of her. If that didn't cement my feelings for this man, I didn't know what would.

—∿∿—

Gavin

Whether I'd done more damage or curbed it, I wasn't sure. But from the good-night kiss I got outside Kenna's door, I knew I'd done something right.

Her hands slid under the front of my shirt, my stomach tightening at her touch. "Thank you for today." She kissed my chin, on the only spot where my beard didn't cover it. Maybe shaving would have its benefits if I could feel her lips in new places. Yeah, she'd asked me to keep it once, but fuck if I wasn't a selfish man. "You have no idea what it meant to me that you just hung out with us like you did."

My own hands skated down her back, tightening along her hips. "No problem." I kissed her forehead and shut my eyes. "She's sweet."

"Yeah, she is…"

I heard the unease in her words and frowned, pulling back to look at her. "What's up?"

Her eyes met mine. "I just worry about her. She got out of an abusive relationship and has pretty much shut herself off from the world."

"She seems like she's getting along better," I said.

"Could be that you're just really awesome. Next thing I know, she'll be falling in love with you."

"That so?" I grinned.

A nod. "Yeah, because you make feeling things pretty easy." She lowered her head, her gaze going to my neck.

I lifted her chin, needing to meet her eyes again. "And how do I make *you* feel, Kenna?"

"Alive."

I brushed my knuckles down her neck, then her cheek. That word was running through me like a fire. "You make me feel that way too."

"Do I?" She whispered the question, disbelief in her gaze.

"Yes."

Her face transformed, her eyes narrowing into slits. One step, then two, and she had me pressed against her apartment door. Her hands were under my shirt again, long fingers tracing lines over my abs. I shuddered, then sucked in a heavy breath. Jesus, she could be wild. And I liked it a whole fucking lot.

"I know how to make you feel even more alive." She kissed my neck, then my chin once more.

My eyes shut. "I should go…"

"Call into work. Stay with me tonight."

I'll stay with you forever, I wanted to say. I *needed* to say. Every second longer that this woman was in my life, the more I knew, without a doubt, she was my end game. She was Collin's Addie and Max's Lia rolled into one even more amazing woman—for me.

Fucking job. For the first time, I didn't want to work or have the distraction that went along with it. Didn't want to do anything *but* be with her.

I kissed her again, and her hips grew restless as she ground them against my cock. I could feel her heat through the tiny shorts she wore, and nothing teased me more. I lifted my hand, toying with the button on her shorts, only to slip my fingers inside and cup her through her panties.

"Gavin," she whispered, slowly dropping her head back against the wall. I took the free opportunity, pressing my lips to her pulse point, loving the sound of her warm pants against my ear.

"Gotta be quick." I slipped her panties aside, pressing one finger to her clit. On contact, she gripped my shoulders and squeezed, a loud moan filling the hall. Her eyes were shut, head still tipped back. "Fucking beautiful," I whispered, sliding my middle and pointer fingers deep inside.

"I'm gonna…"

"Let it go." I bit down on her neck, mainly to keep

myself from cussing, but her cries soon filled the hallway, no doubt giving her neighbors an earful. I didn't
care. She said I made her feel things, and I didn't want
to stop with just emotions. For the rest of my fucking
life, I wanted to make her come. Several times a day if
it was possible.

She laid her forehead against my shoulder, and words
I'd never used sat on the tip of my tongue. Saying them
would no doubt make her run, but not saying them
would kill me.

"I'm falling for you." Slowly, I slid my fingers out,
clenching them at my sides.

She froze, her hands now on the button of her shorts.

"Kenna…" I took a small step back, lifting her face
with a thumb and forefinger. "Did you hear what I said?"
Her eyes were wide with panic, her cheeks red too. Was
it the orgasm I'd just given her or my admission? Either
way, I'd done what I feared: effectively freaked her the
hell out.

She folded her arms over her chest, stepping out of
my hold. "Will you, um, be at dinner tomorrow night
with Addie and the gang?"

My eyes narrowed. "Don't pretend I didn't just say
what I did."

She looked at her door, then down at the floor, avoiding my gaze. "Max and Lia will be there too, won't
they?" Her body trembled. First her arms, then her
shoulders… "I'd like to get to know Lia a little better. I
used to judge her, but Addie loves her, so I want to give
her the benefit of the doubt. Plus, she—"

"Talk. To. Me." I cupped her cheeks with both hands,
cutting her off.

"I *am* talking to you." She squeezed her eyes shut. "You have to work soon. And I need to go be with my sister."

"Kenna." I pressed my forehead to hers. "Please."

She leaned into me too, her body relaxing. "I'm pretty tired…"

"I'm *falling* for you."

"You shouldn't."

I grinned, kissing her cheek. "Can't help myself."

"What if I run? What if I decide I still don't want this baby? What will you do then?" She took a breath, leaning back, her hands gripping my upper arms for dear life.

"We'll take it slow. No rush."

"I'm scared."

I tucked some of her hair behind her ear, letting my fingers linger against her cheek. "Me too."

"I'm a mess."

I leaned forward, dropping a kiss to her lips. "Then let's be a mess together."

McKenna

TWENTY-THREE IS HOW MANY TIMES I CHECKED MY PHONE the next night at the restaurant. Gavin was a half hour late and had yet to answer my calls or texts. Addie assured me it was normal for him to just go missing for a while, but I figured maybe he was working on his house and had lost track of time.

Still, I didn't like not knowing where he was. If he wanted to make this work between us, he needed to change his ways as much as I did. And that meant not disappearing for an entire day and ignoring my phone calls.

"Earth to McKenna." Addie snapped her fingers in front of my face.

I shook my head and pasted on a smile. "What was that?"

"You zoned out on me for a minute there. Everything okay?" She tipped her head to the side.

"She's in love."

I jerked my head up and narrowed my eyes at Max. "*What?*"

"I said *she*, meaning *you*, have been struck by that love shit." He leaned forward on the table, bringing Lia's hand with him. Since having surgery on his hand, he'd moved to Springfield to be with her. Devoted and in love, that's what the two of them were. It was sickening…and I hated how jealous I was.

"I'd recognize the look anywhere because I see it every time I look in the mirror now," Max finished with a wink.

"Aww." Addie pressed her hands together beneath her chin in a prayer-like manner. "You two are so freaking sweet."

"Gimme a break." Collin wrapped his arm around Addie's shoulder, kissing her temple. "Max is half the man I am." Addie snorted out a laugh but moved closer to his body.

I frowned, feeling like the fifth wheel as I checked the clock on my cell phone once more.

"Yeah, right." Max chuckled, bringing Lia's hand to his mouth. He kissed her knuckles. "I am all man, plus one. And I've got this sexy thing to prove it." He kissed Lia's cheek, and I watched how he smelled her hair. It was a very non-Max thing to do, very intimate, and it also made me itchy inside and out. All this affection, all these thoughts of love and happiness and finding it when it's the most unexpected…

I'm falling for you. Since last night, Gavin's voice had echoed in my mind on an endless loop. *God, why me?* What did he see that none of my other boyfriends had? Or maybe we'd end up together, only for him to realize, too late, that I wasn't what he thought I was. Then I'd lose him. Forever.

Lia rested her head on Max's shoulder. "No need to lay it on so thick when you know you're still gonna be taking me home tonight."

"I'm gonna be doing more to you than just taking you home tonight." Max grinned.

"And that shit's not coming back to my place." Collin pointed a finger at Max.

"Aww, Colly. You know you've been missing me. Don't lie."

Collin grunted, curling his lip at Max.

I shook my head at their weirdness, deciding it was time for me to break in with my thoughts on love. "Hate to break it to you, Maxwell, but I am not—nor am I likely to ever be—in love." The words felt thick on my tongue, like the biggest, ugliest lie I'd ever told.

"That's news to me," Gavin said, his voice a whisper for my ears alone.

I stiffened as he sat down next to me, a soft hand grazing my neck in hello.

"Sorry I'm late." He looked around the table, greeting the group, yet avoiding my eyes. Nobody saw it but me—the hard flex of his bearded jaw, the twitch in his right eye when he looked down at the menu. I'd screwed up. Again. "Got hung up at work."

"Didn't know you worked today," Collin said, moving back in his chair. Addie went right along with him, completely in tune with his movements.

Gavin *didn't* work today. Last night, on the other hand… It was obvious he'd been *working* at his river house instead.

"Yeah, kind of need something to keep me occupied right now."

Guilt had me chewing the inside of my cheek. I cared a lot about Gavin, but was I ready to break down with a confession of love when I wasn't sure I even believed in it?

"…need you all to take a weekend off next month." I blinked, focusing on Collin. He nodded at Gavin, Max, Lia, then me, a bright, happy smile on his normally grumpy face.

I looked at Addie. "For what, exactly?"

"We're eloping." My best friend clapped her hands excitedly, her dark hair bouncing on her shoulders like a cheerleader's.

"What?" I asked, Gavin's issues momentarily forgotten. I jumped up from my seat and ran around the table to hug her. She shot out of her chair too, arms ready. "Oh my God, Addie. I'm so happy for you." We rocked back and forth in a dance.

"You'll be there, right?" Pulling back, she held me at arm's length, eyes filled with tears.

"Absolutely." I sniffled, twice as emotional as I'd been just moments before. "I mean, who's gonna be there to hold your hair when you puke from nerves? Or when you decide, last minute, that you're too good for the douche canoe?"

I winked at Collin, all in good fun, of course. It earned me the middle finger, which wasn't exactly a new thing. He and I had a funny sort of friendship. Knowing he'd put a ring on my best friend's finger helped with the murderous, angry thoughts I'd had about him in the past, but still… I wasn't sold on forever, which meant I didn't trust anyone else to find a forever either.

Lia laughed and stood. "Ah! Make room for me, ladies!" She squealed and wrapped her arms around us. The three of us soon jumped around in a circle, heads pressed together.

"Ladies, ladies, ladies…" Max stood, arms stretched out at his sides, a goofy grin on his face. "You wanna celebrate something, then how about celebrating the fact that I'd *love* to be the stripper at Short Stuff's bachelorette party." He jerked his chin at Addie.

"Fuck no." Collin groaned, taking a drink of his beer, while Addie sat on his lap and wrapped her arms around his neck, kissing him. "I don't want her blinded."

The whole scene was sickening, really. Something out of a romantic comedy. All happy flowers and rainbows and butterflies. Something I didn't normally feel. I glanced at Gavin from the corner of my eyes, watching as he set his elbows on the table. He was quiet, stiff, contemplative as he watched his friends… It made my chest tighten in unease. This was what he wanted as well, no doubt in my mind. Yet next to him sat a woman who held no real promise of forever, other than the fact that she was pregnant with his child.

"The ceremony will be in Galena, at an inn." Addie grinned excitedly as she spoke. "We've already spoken to Collin and Lia's parents about it, and since I obviously don't have parents, his family's all that matters to me besides you guys." Addie said, turning to face us. Her cheeks were rosy, her eyes sparkling with pure and utter joy.

Lia's lips turned into a pout. "I don't have vacation time yet, so I won't be able to come until the Saturday of the wedding."

"That's okay. Just as long as you can be there for the ceremony." Addie grinned, always the optimist.

"You'll be able to make it, right, Gav?" Collin pointed his stare at Gavin.

"Of course." He nodded, shoulders stiff. "Wouldn't miss it for anything."

The rest of the dinner was spent talking about wedding plans and dresses and all things Galena, Illinois—at least among us girls. The guys, on the other hand, headed to the restaurant bar, refusing to let us rub off on them. Well, at least that's what Collin and Max said. Gavin, on the other hand, had barely spoken two words to me since he'd arrived.

"So, I've reserved a room for your parents at the inn where the wedding will be," Addie said to Lia. "And a room for you and Max too."

Lia rubbed her hands together. "Looking forward to it."

"That just leaves us with the situation that is you and Gavin." With her eyebrow arched, Addie looked at me from across the table. "So...what'll it be? One room or two?"

I looked down at the table, opening and closing my mouth. In the back of my mind, I already knew the answer. *Yes. Absolutely, no doubt in my mind, one room.* Gavin and I were two consenting adults who enjoyed each other's company and genuinely had an amazing connection—both in *and* out of bed. Yes, we had the obstacle of this baby between us, but I was trying my hardest to work through it. Figure out how it fit into our lives. But when I opened my mouth to tell her my final decision, she cut me off with, "Two rooms. Got it."

"Two rooms for what?" Collin asked, sitting back down at the table, Max in tow. They were like magnets to their women, forcing me to hold back on my answer, question my mind-set, and wonder out loud to myself…

"What the hell is wrong with me?"

"Kenna?" I could hear Addie's voice somewhere in the distance, calling my name, questioning my zone-out. But all I could focus on was the man walking back from the bar. Dressed in a blue tee, sporting a sexy-as-hell beard and hair that was prettier than mine. Gavin was the light I'd turned off for months, only to flick on again when my life was at its darkest.

"No, not two rooms…" I shook my head, words trailing off as I stood.

"One, then?" Addie squinted.

I didn't answer. Instead, I watched the gorgeousness of Gavin stride across the room toward us.

His eyebrows were pushed together, his lips pursed in thought. He looked so…broken. Angry. Confused. And I knew it was all my fault. Which was exactly why I ignored Addie and decided I wasn't about to think more. Impulsive or not, this decision had to be made before I screwed my life up entirely.

"Hold that thought." I barely got the words out before darting around the table and meeting Gavin head-on.

"Hey." My throat was filled with unease and fear, the lump nearly choking me as I stared up at him. I'd been such a bitch for so long that being pro-relationship was going to be a challenge. Still, it was time I cut the indecision and grew up.

"What's wrong?" Some of his anger slipped away, replaced with concern. Gavin lifted his hand, as though to press it against my cheek, then dropped it to his side at the last minute.

"I'm sorry." I wrapped my arms around his waist, hugging him close. Life filled me whenever I was in his arms, and the last thing I wanted was for it to be sucked away again.

Against my ear, I could hear his heart thudding, a gentle *pitter-patter* that soothed me. "What are you sorry for?"

"For dragging you along like I've been. For not letting you know how I feel." I closed my eyes and sucked in a breath, willing the last of my unease away. "And for not doing this the second I saw you tonight." Then I leaned back, opened my eyes, and let him know just how sorry I was with my lips as I pressed them firmly to his.

~~~

Gavin

Spread out naked on my bed, her body pink and well loved, Kenna looked like something straight out of heaven—but ten times more beautiful than that. Her lower belly was swollen, not a lot, but enough that I could see the change. And her breasts were fuller than before. Her body was a work of art that made my cock continuously hard and ready—even after being inside her just minutes before.

"Say it again." I grinned, kissing my way up her body until I reached her neck, then her lips.

She sighed against my cheek, absently stroking her

fingers around my shoulder blades. "I'm sorry I was stupid tonight. I—"

I cut off her unnecessary apology with a kiss. "Not that."

"What, then?"

"That you want me for as long as I'll keep you around."

She grinned against my lips, then pressed both hands against my cheeks. "You're a monster. Coercer at his worst."

"Or at his best." I rolled over, pulling her on top of me. She straddled my thighs with a giggle, that gorgeous pussy of hers still wet with our releases.

She settled her head against my chest, right where I wanted it to be and the best feeling in the world. I played with the ends of her hair.

"It's the truth," she whispered against my skin, drawing her hand up and down my sternum.

"Is it?"

She nodded. "But there's still the matter of the... thing."

The *thing* being our child, I guessed. "We've got six months left."

"Yeah..." She drew out a long breath. I could feel her heart against mine. Somewhere in that mind of hers, she had something more to say, but I wasn't gonna be the one to pull it out of her. And she wasn't one to be pushed either. It's how we worked.

A beat past, our breaths matching in pace. For a minute, I thought she'd fallen asleep, until I felt her sigh against me. "We should talk about it."

"And?" I shut my eyes, waiting for the worst.

"I'm still not sure if I can be a mom, Gavin. But I'm willing to try with *you*, no matter what."

Air spilled out of my mouth, blowing against her long bangs. Hearing that was like the best kind of pain. Yet I wouldn't say that. In the end, it was her decision to make, not mine. "One step at a time."

Slowly, she propped her chin on my chest, staring back at me with haunted blue eyes. Tears filled the corners, as if she was terrified I'd turn her away. But I wouldn't. No matter what. How could I be mad at her for being unsure of something she'd never planned for?

The possibility of raising this kid on my own scared the hell out of me, yeah. But if she decided she wanted it that way—walking away from us, no questions asked—I couldn't, in good conscience, stop her, even if it killed me to let her go.

"The whole thing with my sister being here puts a lot of things in a weird perspective for me. If I wind up giving you this baby, letting you raise it alone, I'll feel like I failed worse than my own parents did. And that's not what I want."

"Jesus, Kenna. Don't say that. Please." With my heart nearly in my throat, I stroked a thumb over her cheek. She meant so much to so many people. Me, Addie, her sister, her friends from work… "You are not your parents." I kept going, not willing to stop until she believed it. "You are good and brave, already a far better parent than they ever were because you're making the decision for the baby's sake, not your own."

Tears covered her red cheeks, her words breaking my heart. "How can you say that? I'm so selfish, Gavin. I want to do things in life, like travel, maybe go back to school…get a better degree. And part of me wants to willingly abandon this kid for my own selfishness."

"You can do all that. No matter what choice you make. Nobody will look at you any differently, Kenna. I promise."

She sniffed and buried her face into my neck, sobbing and shaking. And instead of telling her to calm down, to not cry, I let her get it all out. Then, when she was done, I let her lie on my chest and catch her breath while I thought about things myself. McKenna things, baby things, *life* things…things beyond my house on the river and my job. I thought about how a future was possible for the first time in my life, whether that included Kenna or not.

When I'd lived with my uncle, I didn't know whether I'd have a blanket to cover up with at night or a drop of food on my plate to eat. Futures were never set in stone when I was growing up. But the thought of this baby, and this woman, whether we were all together or not, was everything, even though nothing about it was ordinary.

"I'm capable of taking care of a baby financially, just so you know," McKenna mumbled.

I kissed the top of her head. "I know you are."

"And I'm not a bad person either."

"Far from." I squeezed her even closer, willing her to feel my affection. My love.

She sighed. "Giving you our baby would be me being responsible. Proving that I'm not my mother or my father after all."

"You're you, Kenna." I stroked some hair off her face. "You're the woman I'm falling for. The woman who makes me laugh and smile. The only person in my life who makes me feel worthy. I want what *you* want. That's all." Even if it meant her walking away.

Minutes later, in that slow, getting-to-know-your-lips way, McKenna pressed her mouth over mine. We kissed for what could have been minutes or hours. It was the type of kissing that made me drunk with need, with love.

I dug my fingers into her hair, and it fell over our faces even more, a curtain cutting us off from the rest of the world. She moaned against my lips, using her tongue to do all the talking. With her kisses, I felt acceptance, I just didn't know what she was accepting.

She pulled back, kissing my nose, each of my eyes, my cheeks, then my lips. I lifted a hand, holding it to her cheek, and the back of her hair tickled my knuckles.

"You're not who I expected, St. James."

I smiled. "Who were you expecting?"

"The guy with more issues than me." She bit her lip and winced. "Sorry, that came out wrong."

"That's who I am." I shrugged, unashamed.

She shook her head. "You don't show it though. I've only seen you lose it once…in that elevator."

"Everyone handles their issues differently. Maybe I'm just real good at hiding things." Lately, though, I didn't have much to hide.

For a good three months now, things in my world had been calmer. Steadier. I still had the nightmares about seeing my dead brother, about shit going down in Afghanistan, and the feeling of waking up in that tiny shed, shaking. I couldn't get the memories out, no matter how hard I tried.

My doctor had attempted to help me, even when I'd given her hell. I took meds—something nobody knew but me. I wasn't embarrassed that I had issues with anxiety and depression. What I *was* ashamed of was the fact that I hadn't gotten my shit taken care of earlier.

"What happens if you take this baby and decide you can't handle it?" Kenna asked.

"Wouldn't happen." I was sure of that.

"Haven't you had issues in the past? With Chloe, I mean? Addie told me about that time you babysat for Collin and got freaked out because she had a fever." She rolled over to lie next to me, her naked body pressed close, her hand on my face when I turned to look at her. She reached up and ran her finger across the scar by my eyebrow. The one I'd gotten when I'd knocked my head into the wall repeatedly at sixteen, after Adam died, to try to escape the image of seeing him bleeding out in the bathtub.

"I was pretty fucked up back then." I swallowed at the memory, leaning into her hand. "But at the time, I didn't think I had issues anymore. Thought it was just me not being used to kids. When really, I was just overwhelmed with life."

Cat jumped up, nuzzling between us on top of the blanket. Kenna pulled her hand from my face and reached down to stroke the top of his head.

When she didn't question what had happened, what had made me the way I was, I took the quiet moment to keep talking—give her my truth. I told her about my uncle's river house going up for auction. "I knew nothing about remodeling and construction. But I was damn glad I took the chance. Being there…it made me feel like I was taking that part of my life and breaking it apart, just so I could start over." I didn't tell Kenna what happened after I first went inside though. How I'd sat there in that old, empty kitchen, fucking crying like a baby because I knew I was never going to forget that time in my life, no matter what happened. But I was willing to try to make it right again.

She smiled. "That's a pretty amazing story."

"And you're a pretty amazing woman."

"Puh-lease." She shooed me away with her hand, eyes rolling. But I grabbed her wrist, pulled it to my mouth, and kissed it.

"No matter what you decide, I'm gonna stick by you, McKenna. I just want you to know that."

She understood what I meant. I could see it in the thick tears filling her eyes. But she didn't talk anymore. And neither did I. Instead, I pulled her into my arms and fell asleep with her there.

Then in the morning, when I rolled over and found her body still sprawled across mine, I knew I'd made strides with her. Big ones.

CHAPTER 26

McKenna

LEAVING MY SISTER TO GO TO GALENA HAD BEEN ONE OF THE hardest things I'd ever done. No matter how many times I offered to pay for her to come with, she refused, saying she wanted to try to be alone for once. In a way, I think she didn't want to be around my friends. Not because she didn't like them, but because she didn't know them well enough to want to be with them like I did.

"She's fine." Gavin squeezed my hand as we walked along the small sidewalk toward our cozy, little cottage near the back of the inn's property.

I'd put my cell phone in my purse after texting Hanna for the fifth time in the three hours we'd been there, trying to grab hold of the optimism Gavin seemed to be filled with.

"Yeah, I feel better knowing that she's staying with Emma for the weekend, but it's still hard, ya know?"

"You're a good sister." Gavin reached behind his head, tying his hair into a bun. He'd been wearing it down all day, and it only made him that much sexier. Heck, everything about this man was epically sexy. Not to mention he had a heart made of softness that rivaled the clouds and heaven above. I'd never been a fuzzy, unicorns-and-rainbows kind of lady, but one month of dating Gavin, and I was pretty sure I'd morphed into a classic romance heroine.

"Thanks for the vote of confidence, St. James, but there's no need to lay it on so thick." I hip-checked him. "I'm a guaranteed lay."

His green eyes sparkled with amusement, but his words were serious. "I'm not kidding. Hanna's lucky to have you. Don't pretend that you're not amazing."

I grinned and poked him in the ribs. He grunted, reaching for my hand as we came to the door of the cottage.

"Come on, now. What's a guy gotta do to compliment his girl and have her believe him?"

"Absolutely nothing." I stepped forward and kissed him once on the cheek. Like a teenage schoolgirl, I couldn't help but wonder if the next step in my infatuation with him would be doodling *Gavin*, *Gav*, or *Gavvy* all over my file folders and charts at work.

He pulled out the key, but before he opened the door, he turned to me full on, eyes suddenly narrowed with concern. "If you're really worried about your sister, we can leave right after the ceremony tomorrow."

"And miss out on more sex with the hottest guy who's ever been inside me?" I licked my lips, scoping him out from head to toe. I tugged the tail of his button-down shirt, the one he'd bought *after* I'd gone down on him in a dressing room at the mall last week. He called it his *lucky shirt*, and I couldn't agree more. "Hell no."

"You like this, don't you?" He chuckled under his breath as I moved in to kiss his chin. The sun was setting, reflecting off the Mississippi River that sat at our backs in the distance. It warmed my forehead almost as much as Gavin warmed my insides with his words, his hands, his body.

"What exactly do I like, hmm?" I grinned, moving to his throat, his beard tickling my nose. Slowly, I lowered my hands to his elbows. "Because if you mean spending nights with you, then yes, I like that a lot."

"Not what I meant."

"Then what did you mean?" I frowned, pulling back to look up at him.

One side of his mouth curled higher than the other in that Gavin way I adored. "You like what we've been doing this past month."

"What, having sex any time we want and then waking up to do it all over again in the morning?"

"No." He pressed his forehead against mine, his face stoic, his breathing suddenly unsteady. "Being *mine*."

My insides melted, dropping to puddles at my feet. Yet the heart inside my chest kept beating, increasing its speed with every breath he exhaled against my lips.

Is that what I was?

His?

And did I want to be his?

"I…do." *Yeah. I did.*

With my toes curled inside my shoes at my admission, I lifted my hands and dipped them into the neck of his shirt. A growl rumbled from his chest as he gripped my hips and tugged them against his. "I've waited a long time to hear that, Brewer."

As his hands grazed the top of my backside, I tipped my head to the side and said, "Take me inside." I needed him more now than ever.

Until Max called his name from behind.

"Fucking Max," he groaned, pulling back so our noses touched. "Sorry. I gotta go." But Gavin's hands said otherwise, trailing over my hips, squeezing tighter.

"Not yet. Max can wait," I mumbled against his lips. Screw the fact that we were about to have an audience. I needed this man. Needed *my* man.

"Hmm," I moaned as he kissed me deeper, pulled me closer, and pushed me back against the door. He hitched my leg up. The skirt I'd been wearing all afternoon slipped so high that the wind brushed against the lace of my panties underneath the hem.

One kiss, two, three. But then he was pulling away, wiping at his mouth with his arm, his hands going in his hair and his eyes squeezing shut as though he was in pain. "I can't stay. I'm already late."

"I know." My shoulders dropped, and I couldn't help but pout. Screw a bachelor's night. *I* needed a *Gavin* night instead.

Max laughed behind him. "Wow. Okay, then. I'm gonna go grab some popcorn and pull up a seat to watch the show."

I glared at him from over Gavin's shoulder, watching as he hopped and jumped down the sidewalk steps like a little kid.

"Go away," I grumbled.

"You two tryin' for twins or what?" Max laughed, hip bumping me as he moved in from my right. He mock-punched scowling Gavin in the shoulder, not taking the hint.

As he shook his head, Gavin looked down at me, heat still in his eyes, accompanied by a silent promise that said *soon*.

"Just so the two of you know, Colly's likely to chop off your nuts if you're late, so you better make 'em useful while you can." Max whistled the theme song from *Jaws*, slapped Gavin's shoulder, then took off up the sidewalk again.

With a growl buried deep in his chest, Gavin turned and unlocked the cottage door.

I laughed, shaking my head, as he scooped me into his arms. "You're a glutton for punishment, you know that, right?"

He smirked and turned the handle with his free hand, carrying me inside. "Totally fucking worth it."

And I couldn't have agreed more.

"Collin may have been a huge dipshit as a kid, but I'm ninety-nine percent sure you made him a better man as an adult." Lia winked at Addie, who was hunkered down on one of the couches that sat in the main lobby of the Goldmoor Inn. Three other couches surrounded a big coffee table that was piled high with chocolates and wine—wine I sadly could not drink. Addie sat on one couch, Lia and her mom on another, and me on the biggest one of all, with Chloe sleeping at my side, her head on my lap.

We'd been there since the guys left around seven, conversing about life and love and all things in between. It was amazing—the first time I'd ever felt like I was part of a family. Even though none of these people was biologically related to me, I wondered whether this was what I'd missed out on for so long. And if that was the case, I cursed the world for robbing me of the happiness it gave me. Cursed myself for not finding it sooner. Temporary happiness had nothing on this.

I stroked Chloe's hair, marveling at all the curls on her head, just as Lia piped in with, "You're going to make a good mom, Kenna."

I blinked, meeting the stares of the three women around me. Mrs. Montgomery stared the hardest. Not with disdain, but with wonder and curiosity. It was a look that both confused and terrified me.

She tapped her chin and leaned forward. Brown hair fell over her cheeks in a menacing way, though she looked like the least menacing person I'd ever seen. "I've known Gavin for a while now," she began, "and have never seen him as happy as he is with you."

My face heated at her words. Embarrassment hit me worse than any nausea I'd felt during the first trimester thus far. I cleared my throat. "Oh?"

"Yes. It's completely mesmerizing, really. That boy"—she *tsk*ed—"was a hot mess when I first met him all those years ago."

"Right?" Lia nodded quickly. "I mean, I thought it was just me." She turned toward her mother, wrapping her black, lacy, fingerless gloves around the woman's wrist. They were so close, always looking as though they held special secrets only best friends shared. A pulse of jealousy passed through me at the thought, and I glanced quickly at Addie, who wore a smile on her face—one only I could see through. No doubt she wished her mom were here for this too. They may not have been close toward the end, but once upon a time, they'd shared what only a mom and daughter could.

"It's pretty amazing, isn't it?" Addie yawned and rubbed her eyes. "I'm really happy for you two, Kenna. Seriously. Not sure if I've mentioned it enough."

"We're *all* happy for you. Especially since Gavin has been through so much," Lia added.

The thing of it was, the three of them only knew the half of it about Gavin and what he'd been through. And as selfish as it sounded, I liked knowing I held his deepest secrets, just as he held some of mine.

Lia raised her glass in the air, words slurring ever so slightly. "And let me tell you what… That baby you're carrying?" She pointed to my stomach. "It's going to be extremely lucky to have two amazing parents."

My shoulders stiffened at her words, thoughts plaguing me in unfamiliar and insecure ways. If I hadn't become pregnant, would Gavin and I be where we were now? Likely not, which had me thinking a million different thoughts. I wasn't even sure if I wanted this baby. But if I gave this baby up, I'd not only lose Gavin, but all the new and wonderful feelings he'd inspired in me over the last couple of months.

The hand that wasn't on Chloe's head trembled against my thigh. I squeezed my nails into my palms, willing my head to shape up or ship out, because I couldn't fathom the thought of Gavin not being in my life.

Conversation between the three women surrounded me, happy giggles and talk of the wedding. I sighed, wishing I could join in the celebration. But doing so only hurt my heart more. So I looked down at Chloe in my lap instead, eyes blurring with unshed tears.

She'd barely moved in her sleep, other than the slow rise and fall of her chest. The little girl seemed so at ease with me, her fickle self only wanting to sit on my lap, not her grandma's or her aunt's, not her dad's or her Mama Addie's, a name she'd only just recently started saying. It felt natural having her there, which was something I hadn't expected.

Is that what it'd be like with my own child? One with Gavin's smile or green eyes? Sandy-brown hair or curled, bow lips? Was that excitement brewing inside me at the simple thought of imagining myself with Gavin, raising a child that was one part him, one part me, one part all his or her own?

His boy. A son? His girl. A daughter?

The couch indented as Addie sat on my other side. "You okay?" she asked, her hand on my shoulder.

When I looked up, I spotted Mrs. Montgomery smothering Lia against her, rocking back and forth in a monstrous hug, oblivious to me, thank goodness. It was bad enough that I was concerning Addie with my quiet mood. She was set to get married tomorrow, yet there I was, worrying her with my crap.

"I'm fine." The truth was too big to keep from my best friend, but for tonight, I had to try.

Addie tucked her arm through my elbow, and I laid my head on her shoulder. There the two of us sat, quiet and contemplative, our minds likely worlds apart from each other.

As if sensing the tension in me, Chloe rolled onto her back, her gaze locking with mine. I held my breath as she studied my face. She blinked a few times, likely attempting to remember where she was, maybe even who I was. Just when I was sure she was seconds from bursting into tears, she smiled softly, curled herself closer to my stomach, and touched a hand over the small bump just showing through the middle of my sundress.

I shut my eyes and inhaled shakily through my nose, fighting back the tears.

God, talk about a sucker punch.

Footsteps sounded from behind my couch. I blinked opened my eyes just in time for Lia and Mrs. Montgomery to stand and greet our visitor.

"Hey, Dad," Lia said first, waving. Mrs. Montgomery smiled fondly at her husband, stepping closer to kiss his cheek. They shared a look, one of contentment and love. It pulled the chain a little harder around my heart, seeing a married couple of their age so incredibly in love.

Mr. Montgomery's resemblance to his son was uncanny. Same eyes, same hair, same bone structure in the face. But he was much softer than Collin was. He wrapped an arm around Lia's shoulders and hugged her to his side. "You ladies need me to take her?" He glanced down at his granddaughter.

Addie nodded. "Sure. She's exhausted."

He looked at me, his brows furrowed a little. It was unnerving to be under his scrutinizing stare, even as kind as he was. The man radiated silent power, probably from years of protecting his family. "I've got an observation, if you will. One that my gorgeous wife can assure you is based on good intentions."

My shoulders grew stiff. I looked to Mrs. Montgomery, whose eyes held an expression that was soft and sincere.

"Oh?" I'd never talked to this man, other than a *hi* or *bye* in passing. So what *observation* did he have that was suddenly so important? And why did this feel like an intervention?

He cleared his throat, looking uncomfortable as he rubbed a hand over the back of his neck. "Well, see, I've learned about your dilemma. And..." He looked at Addie, then Lia, then back at his wife, who nodded him on. "Gavin was telling me how you're not sure you want to be a mom."

My jaw locked.

Just. Fucking. Great. Did *everyone* need to know about my life choices?

"Dad." Lia touched his arm, her voice a warning. "If you even *try* to mansplain this, I'm gonna—"

"What? No. I don't *mansplain*." Lines formed between his eyes as he scowled at his daughter. "Your mom and I just want her to know that we weren't prepared for children when we got pregnant with Collin."

"So? What does that have to do with Kenna here?" Lia propped her free hand on her hip.

Mr. Montgomery smiled at me, his face suddenly warm and welcoming. I didn't look away, mainly because I wasn't one to back down with the unexpected. "Children are a blessing, but you know what? Not wanting them doesn't make you any less of a person. That's my two cents." He winked at me, then motioned for Chloe, hands wiggling. Had he been talking to Gavin about this? Obviously. The thought warmed my chest that Gavin could count on this man, even if things looked grim.

A strange sense of approval washed over me just then. These people I barely knew, they'd come together in reassurance...for me.

Mr. Montgomery pulled Chloe close against him. She stirred again, her eyes popping wide against his chest. "Papa," she whispered, giving him a sleepy smile, only to snuggle against him as though he was her own version of a superhero.

I waved at him and Mrs. Montgomery both, contemplating his words, wondering if under different circumstances, my own dad would have said something similar.

"You should listen to my daddy. He's a smart man." Lia grabbed the wine bottle off the table, sticking it under her arm. "Now, if you'll excuse me, I'm gonna go wait for my Maxwell in the hot tub."

"Night, Lia," Addie said, laughing under her breath.

With a smile, I curled my feet up onto the couch. Addie did the same, still tucked close to my side. We didn't get to do this much anymore—be just me and her, no men.

"You ready for tomorrow?" I asked.

"More than my next breath." There wasn't a doubt in her words.

A large, picturesque window sat over the fireplace. We couldn't see anything but a few random stars, but it was peaceful, nonetheless—and the exact opposite of my current emotional state.

"Is it scary knowing he'll be it for you?"

She shook her head. "It's almost as if I've found something I didn't know I was missing."

I bit down on the inside of my cheek, comparing my thoughts to hers. "No regrets? No thoughts of running away?"

Addie didn't answer right away. I wondered if she was asleep and leaned forward to find her eyes starry, her smile wide. "Sorry. I was just thinking of that night in O'Paddy's when we first met Collin and Gavin."

"You mean the night you pulled a *me* and left them both in the parking lot like a little kid?"

"Yeah. Not one of my finer moments. I know." She rolled her eyes, pausing for a moment. "Do you remember what you said to Gav at all?"

"In my inebriated state, there's no telling what I said." Sadly, that night was basically a blur.

"Yeah…" She grinned widely. "So you *kind of* told him that he was going to be your future baby daddy."

My mouth dropped open. "You're shitting me."

She giggled. "Nope. Irony is a total bitch, huh?"

I pressed my hands over my face and groaned as she started singing *the song*.

"Seriously, Addison? *Ironic?*" I snorted. The wackiness of my bestie never failed, even on the night before she was to get married.

"Come here, you." She reached for my hand and yanked me up.

"You're nuts."

"I know." Eyes twinkling, Addie whipped out her iPhone, found that ridiculous Alanis Morissette song about irony, and banged her head to the beat as she sang along.

Because I was an impromptu karaoke addict, I started singing too. We danced and sang so loud that I was sure the owner of the inn would be coming down to ream us out at any second. But the longer we sang and the louder we got, the less I cared. And the less I cared, the more I realized that fate and irony went hand in hand, giving you things you wanted, even if you didn't realize that you needed them. Like Addie needed Collin and Chloe. Like Lia needed Max. And I needed Gavin.

I'd been scared for so long about decisions and screwing up that I'd forgotten what it was like just to live. The impulsivity my mother had warned me away from had given me something that made me happier than anything else in my life, and I wasn't just talking about dancing in the middle of a fancy inn.

Talk about irony.

Once the music ended, we hugged each other tight. Addie was the one to speak first, and what she said was a doozy. "He loves you so much, Kenna."

I pulled away to look at her, my smile slipping away. "Gavin?"

She nodded. "Yeah. He looks at you as though you hung that moon in a world of endless stars." She flung her hands into the air and tossed her head back.

"Oh, poetic Addie." I laughed and patted her back. "It's a good thing you've found your Prince Charming."

She hip-bumped me, and my pregnant ass nearly wobbled to the floor. She wrapped her arm around my shoulder, steadying me. "I'm not the only one, you know."

I scoffed. "Yeah, Lia and Max *are* quite the pair, huh?"

"Don't be dumb. I'm talking about you, goofy."

Wrapping my arm around her back too, I guided her to the hallway silently as she continued to chat about us being able to *live the dream*. And even as we laughed our way into what she called the Mississippi Suite, I couldn't help but believe her words. She might have been tipsy, but she was right. Addie was *always* right.

"I'm getting married tomorrow." She turned to me in the nearly darkened room and smiled widely. "Can you believe it?"

I leaned against the doorframe with my arms folded. "Yes, you are, beautiful. Yes, you are."

She sighed, spread her arms out to the sides, and fell flat on her back against the mattress. Minutes later, she was asleep. And as I crawled onto the bed beside her and tossed the blankets over our bodies, I realized just how lucky I was to call her my best friend.

CHAPTER 27

Gavin

"Gavvy, Gavvy." Chloe was running down the sidewalk outside the cottage when I closed the door behind me.

"Hey, Beaner." I got down on my knees to greet her and wrapped my arms around her waist in a hug. Tiny hands grabbed the ends of my hair as she snuggled close. I tickled her cheeks with my beard, loving her giggles. "Where are Auntie Lia and Max?" I asked, standing.

A sensational pair of legs caught my eye from ahead, belonging to the woman I hadn't been able to hold in my arms since late yesterday afternoon.

"She's too fast." McKenna wiped a hand across her forehead, nearly tripping over the last step. "Damn little thing."

"Enna!" Chloe squealed. Just like that, I was dust when Chloe reached back for her new favorite of the week.

"Oh, no, you little booger." Eyes narrowed, Kenna poked Beaner in the stomach. Chloe giggled, curling forward in my arms. "I tried to hold you, and all you wanted was *Gavvy, Gavvy*."

"Because I'm awesome, right?"

"Mmm, sexy as hell in a suit is more like it." Kenna leaned forward and kissed me, lingering a while, until Chloe yanked my hair back.

"Ouch." I winced. "Cock blocked by a toddler. Never thought I'd see the day."

"Not blocked." Kenna reached for my hand, a sly grin on her mouth. "Just delayed for a few hours."

I loved that she'd taken the initiative for once with PDA. Throughout the last month, she shied away from touching me in public. Didn't mean she was second-guessing us, just that she still had something else on her mind. Today, though, as we walked up the sidewalk and around the building toward the gazebo, it felt like something had changed.

"Did you enjoy your boy time last night?" she asked me.

I pulled her hand to my mouth and kissed the back of it. "Not when all I was thinking about was you."

"A bachelor party with booze and card playing, yet all you do is think of me? You're not normal, St. James."

"Nope." Never would be either. And for once, I was okay with it.

"Then it's a good thing I have a soft spot for you." She dropped my hand and grabbed the side of my pants, digging her fingers into my pockets.

Goddamn, she was dangerous. "Nothing about what's inside there is ever soft."

Chloe's head popped up from my shoulder. She said my name around the thumb in her mouth and blinked.

"Go find Aunt Lia and Uncle Max," I said, motioning my head toward the chairs.

She grinned as I set her down on the grass, and then her chubby toddler legs ran up the rest of the hill. She was dressed in a little white dress and wore flowers in her hair that fell out every time she moved.

Once she was in Max's arms, I focused fully on my woman. "You missed me last night too. Admit it." I pressed my palms on both sides of her neck, dragging my thumb over her pulse. I felt her swallow against my hand, could see her chest rise and fall under the pale-pink dress that barely covered the curve of her swollen breasts. She looked so damn beautiful I struggled to breathe.

She licked her lips. "I missed you…a lot, actually."

I smiled. The breath from her words warm on my mouth, and the admission burying itself deep inside my chest. Yeah, I wasn't losing my mind. Something *had* changed with her.

"Kiss me again." I lowered my forehead to hers. "Show me how much you missed—"

She did, not even letting me finish.

Desperate hands clung to the front of my suit coat, nails digging into my chest. When she finally pulled away first, I couldn't catch my breath.

"That enough for you?" And she couldn't catch hers either.

I stared down at her damp lips and flushed cheeks, then her fluttering blue eyes. My heart tripped over itself in my chest at what I saw. What I'd wanted to see for months.

McKenna Brewer had fallen for me.

"Hey," Lia yelled from the top of the grassy hill,

doing nothing to break apart our stares. "You guys gonna come be part of this shindig, or what?"

I was the first to smile, but Kenna didn't budge, other than pressing her hand to her throat, her eyes wide with emotion at the same time.

"Let's go. Mrs. Maxwell is calling." Confidence had me wrapping my arm around Kenna's waist, pulling her toward the chairs set up along the top of the hill by the gazebo. She didn't hesitate this time. If anything, she moved closer to me, as if the pull between us had only grown stronger.

Collin nodded from the front of the altar, the grin on his face widening when he looked down at my hand along the curve of Kenna's waist. With a nod back, I sat us down next to Max, who held Chloe in his arms. Lia was on his other side, while Kenna snuggled up to me from the right. Mrs. Montgomery was at the end of the chairs, a handkerchief in her hand as she looked up at her son.

Collin and Addison had decided they didn't want anyone to stand with them, and we were all okay with it, especially me now that I had my hands on my Kenna.

"You look beautiful, by the way." I leaned over and pulled her hair out of her face, nuzzling my nose against the crook of her neck. She smelled just like the flowers hanging off the gazebo ahead. Sweet and summery.

She shivered, her thigh going flush with mine as she crossed her right leg over the left. I lowered my hand from around her waist, needing to touch skin. I pressed my palm to the top of that thigh and rubbed my thumb in a circle just below the hem of her dress.

"You're a tease," she purred.

"And you're in love with me, so it's only gonna get worse." It was meant to be a joke but came across as honest. Real. And when she leaned her head back to look me in the eyes, I didn't see the *run* in her face this time. I saw the rawness of an *I love you too* on those lips I wanted on mine. She may not have spoken the words out loud yet, but two times now I'd seen their meaning in her gaze. And for now, that was enough.

Music started playing from a speaker somewhere behind us. A breeze lifted a strand of my hair that brushed against McKenna's cheek. She reached up, smiling as she grabbed the strand, then twisted it around her finger before she turned to focus on the reality of this day.

Our best friends were getting married.

As I stood and turned to look down the aisle, Kenna followed suit, her hand never leaving mine. Addie was at the end of a white runner, looking like summer and winter wrapped up in one white dress. She was gorgeous. I had to admit that, but nothing compared to the woman at my right. The one who'd stolen my heart. The one I couldn't stop looking at as what sounded like Adele played through the speaker.

I watched Kenna more than Addie. Her free hand went to her mouth and she cried, big, wet tears dripping down her face. But behind her fingers, I could see a smile on her cheeks. This wasn't just her best friend getting married, I knew that. But her sister too. Just as Addie had become my sister in a way.

Thinking of Collin and all he'd been through, I turned, finding his father by his side, an arm around Collin's shoulder before he took his seat. Mr. Montgomery looked at his wife as he approached, then back at his son, and finally to his granddaughter, who was already up and trying to get to her dad.

Like the hero he claimed to be, Max scooped Chloe up and set her on his shoulders. Lia sat next to him, dressed in a pink dress that matched Kenna's.

A groan sounded, catching my attention. It was a pained sound, like someone was trying not to explode with excitement. When I smiled and looked up, I saw Collin, this time with a hand over his mouth, rubbing furiously. He looked seconds away from falling at Addie's feet when she finally approached his side.

"Fuck this." Collin growled, grabbing her around the waist. He kissed her, and she kissed him back, and neither stopped, not even when the music did.

I shook my head, forgetting all my own senses as I yanked Kenna even closer. Her lips pursed, but then I kissed her cheek, and as if my mouth were magic, she relaxed against my shoulder, folding into me.

It was right where she belonged. Where I always wanted her to be.

The officiant cleared his throat when the kissing between Addison and Collin wouldn't stop. Whispering something under his breath, Max put Chloe down, and we all watched the little thing run toward Addie and tug on her white dress from behind. Grinning, Addie reached down and lifted her, cooing at how beautiful she looked.

Collin was the first to speak. "Not gonna apologize." He nodded once at the officiant before he continued. "Haven't kissed my girl since last night, and that's a long time to wait for me."

Addie tugged on the end of his tie with her free hand. "And we have the rest of our lives to kiss, silly."

I rolled my eyes, laughing a little. The two of them were weird as shit. And I loved them like family.

Collin grabbed Chloe from his soon-to-be wife, kissing the blond troublemaker on the nose before handing her to his mom. Mrs. Montgomery held her granddaughter's hand and offered her a sucker.

The ceremony droned on after that, and normal wedding stuff was said. Collin and Addie spoke some vows, but my mind was occupied with the woman at my side. Her eyes never stopped watering, her lips quivering too. She was crying, yeah, but they were happy tears. The only kind I ever wanted to see on her face again.

More words were spoken; rings were exchanged. I think Maxwell might even have cracked a joke, but my body, my mind, my everything was consumed by thoughts of Kenna and me having our own wedding one day. A day when I'd vow to her that I'd be her savior, no matter what happened, no matter where we were.

McKenna was my piece of forever.

As if she could hear my thoughts, she faced me, kissing me lightly on the lips.

"I love you." I couldn't help but whisper the words. I needed her to know my feelings, my thoughts.

Her fingertips lingered on my beard, as my fingers lingered on her face, and it wasn't until Max smacked me upside the back of my head that I realized the wedding was over. And McKenna hadn't run when I said those three words.

McKenna

Before I could say *I love you too*, Gavin turned around and smacked Maxwell's arm.

We stood and clapped as Collin scooped up Addie and cradled her to his chest. He all but ran down the white runner, nearly tripping as he darted around the corner of the inn. Eyes wide, I glanced toward the front of the altar, then back at Max, Lia, and Gavin. The two guys shared *a look* while Lia slapped her forehead and said, "My brother's a fucking idiot."

"Um, someone wanna fill me in on where they're going?" I was still trying to wipe my dang tears away. Heck, I didn't get to say congrats or hug my best friend.

"You don't wanna know." Gavin wrapped his arm around my waist. The four of us walked toward Collin and Lia's parents, along with Chloe, who was still content with the sucker she'd scored from her grandma.

"Um, yeah. I do." I dropped Gavin's hand and put mine on my hips, waiting.

"Oh, jeez, you two suck. I'll tell her." Lia punched Max in the shoulder and looked at me. "Addie told Collin they could try for another baby as soon as the wedding was over."

My nose scrunched up. *Ew.* Collin was such a douche bag. "So, what, he was literally going to take her up on it? As in, *right now*?"

"Yep." She nodded, then walked to her parents, hugging them something fierce. Not one of them seemed concerned with what had just happened.

What the hell was wrong with these people?

"You hungry?" Gavin leaned over and pressed his palm against my stomach.

I froze.

As did he.

Our eyes met, and then he grinned—just a little. It was the first time he'd touched my stomach like *that*. He must have felt what I'd been noticing for weeks. The tiny balled-up bulge.

"It's… Is that…"

I nodded.

His eyes widened. We'd been naked together a bunch of times over the course of the last month, but only today had the bulge finally made its appearance.

I cleared my throat, unsure of the warmth in my chest. Unsure if I liked it or wanted it gone. "It's a baseball with limbs right now."

He took another step closer. A look of concentration filled his eyes. The sun peeked from behind a cloud, haloing around his head and face while he stared down at his hand over my stomach. Awe filled his eyes as he spread his fingers, covering the small bulge that was our baby.

Our baby.

At the thought, I swallowed. Hard. The normal lump that appeared when I thought of this child slid away. The idea of having him or her didn't send me into the pits of regret anymore. Gavin and I had made some strides that I hadn't thought I'd be able to make with a man, which got me to thinking: *Could I have this baby with him after all?* The concept was so foreign and distracting that I almost didn't hear his question.

"Have you, um, felt it move yet?" His eyes narrowed

in concentration as he moved his hand around even more.

I shook my head, slowly, the sensation sending my heart fluttering. "Soon though. Apparently fourteen weeks is a good time for first movement."

His eyebrows arched. "Have you been, I don't know, reading up on this?"

I nodded. Again.

"I-I don't know what to say." His expression said it all, though, whether he knew it or not. I'd given Gavin a gift with that admission.

"Me neither." Mainly because I had no idea what I was doing. I just didn't want the feeling in me to stop.

He stepped closer, dropping his hands to his sides. But instead of pulling away, he kissed my forehead, inhaling. "I meant what I said."

"I know." *I meant what I wanted to say.*

"And you don't have to say it back. I—"

"Gavin, stop." It was my turn to press my hand against his face. "I love you too, okay?"

His eyelashes fluttered against his cheeks. "You do?"

"I do." The problem was, I had no idea what to do next.

CHAPTER

Gavin

Two weeks after Collin and Addison's wedding, I finally felt like I had a handle on my life for the first time in years. I was going to be a father—single or not, I wasn't sure—and I also had a fucking fantastic new girlfriend who loved me like I did her.

Life was good, even if it wasn't set in stone. But I had faith that things would play out as planned. Just wasn't sure where that faith was coming from.

We'd gotten a call from the Arlo PD asking for backup around three that afternoon. There'd been a five-car pileup on the interstate due to the rain-slicked roads, and Arlo's emergency crews couldn't handle so many transports. Thankfully, there were no life-threatening injuries to report, just a few needing stitches and a couple of possible concussions. When I was done there, I'd be on my way to Kenna's place.

The words coming from the radio slipped in and out of my ears, buzzing like background noise. Regardless of my good mood, my head still wasn't where it should be today, probably because I knew Kenna and her sister were out on the road, driving home from Chicago after seeing that museum. I probably should've called in and gone with them, but I didn't want to push my luck with the boss since I'd only been back to work for six weeks.

No matter. Kenna had promised to call when she got home—which according to my clock should be soon.

Twenty minutes later, we pulled up to the crash. Cops were scattered around the scene, taking notes and doing initial first care for the victims. Even with our wipers on full blast, the water was drenching, nearly blinding my partner, Lance, and me as we pulled up to the scene.

I grabbed my shit, covered myself in a raincoat, then jogged toward the truck where we were needed. It wasn't until I stood five feet away that reality set in as I took in the scene—more so the *truck*.

"No." Slowly, I shook my head, blinking, soaked, growing numb.

"St. James, let's go," Lance called to me from over his shoulder, his voice dark and distant.

I stared back at him, unblinking, willing him to handle this on his own because there was no way in hell I could do it.

No. Way. In. Hell.

Yet somehow, in the back of my mind, I knew it was inevitable. Knew I needed to see it with my own eyes.

One step, then two, and I was already at the bumper, my boots skidding to a stop along the wet pavement. My hands shook against my sides, my heart racing. I was completely numb by then, hands tingling around my pack strap. Even as I squeezed, as I pressed my nails against the flesh of my palm, I couldn't feel a damn thing.

Inside my chest, though, my lungs squeezed with every breath I struggled to take.

I knew that bumper sticker.

I knew that license plate.

I knew that goddamn, motherfucking truck.

The flashing emergency lights flickered through my vision, as did the music. Though nothing played outright, the memories sounded like sirens in my ears. The same fucking music he'd blared into that shed. That shed I suffered inside for months.

I squeezed my eyes shut, opening and closing my mouth. *Fuck. Fuck. Fuuuck.*

Rage blinded me. My fists squeezing. Lance was there, helping the accident victim stand, unknowingly helping the stupid son of a bitch who made me into the no-good, fucked-up guy I was today.

I breathed in through my nose again, then out through my mouth, not calm. Never calm. Yet the dizziness was too much, and my knees shook, forcing me to move forward just enough to hold on to the truck.

His truck.

My uncle.

He was still living in Arlo.

"St. James, gonna need the stretcher for this one after all," Lance called over the top of the door, his voice carrying through the rain as it pelted him in the face.

I might have nodded. Or maybe shook my head. Or maybe I didn't do a damn thing, other than turn around, walk to the ambulance, grab the stretcher, and push it back across the street, ignoring the way my hair stuck to my face, the way my rain jacket had slid off my shoulders, the rain soaking through my clothes, drenching my charged skin.

"Jesus, took you long enough." Lance laughed at me. He fucking *laughed*.

But I couldn't tell him what he'd done. Or what he was doing. I couldn't get close enough to do so. Because I couldn't, for anything, let my uncle see me cry. I couldn't see *him* either. There's no telling what I'd do, or say, or... *fuck*. He wasn't worth blood on my hands, but I wanted it there anyway. I wanted it so bad I could taste it.

I'd thought I was past this, that I had a handle on my shit. My mind. My *past*. But I'd also thought he was gone. Still in jail. Or dead. I'd thought he was out of my life for good, damn it.

Teeth chattering, I shoved the stretcher at Lance as hard as I could. Shoved it so hard that it squeaked, then fell to the side, splashing in the puddles.

"Jesus, man. What's going on?" Lance scowled at me, then the stretcher.

The other EMTs gathered around, but I could only look at the puddles. The rain falling in them, reflecting the flashing emergency lights.

It was getting colder.

The wetness soaked through me.

I couldn't look up. I couldn't see him. I couldn't—

"You okay, sir?" A hand was on my arm, a low voice.

That touch. That fake, soothing, *pitying* voice... I didn't know who it was. Nor did I care. I didn't care about anything. Nothing. Not a damn thing.

Then it happened, like a slow-motion picture screen.

The stretcher was righted, two men were there, and then he was out of the car, eyes the same watery brown I remembered. Like he sensed me standing there, he lifted his head, locking eyes with me across the road. I sucked back a breath, holding it. Waiting.

He squinted, blood dripping from his temple, but there was no recognition in his gaze.

The old man didn't know who I was.

I exhaled but couldn't stop staring. Not even when he looked away. Not when he smiled at Lance. Not when he got on the stretcher, rode by me, and nodded a small hello.

As he passed, my hands tingled for blood. I grabbed the white sheet and reached for him, though my mind begged me not to. I could end him. I wanted to. Jesus, did I ever.

But then a hand was on my shoulder, stopping me, a voice too. "Sir, I—"

"Don't touch me," I yelled, jerking my arm away, taking a step back, then another, until I ran into a body, another car, then fell on my ass onto the asphalt. *No. No, no, no. Not blood. Never blood.* I wasn't him. I wouldn't be. Couldn't.

People surrounded me. Voices loud over the rain. I dropped my chin to my chest, unable to look any longer. Unable to get the words out because I was scared.

I was so fucking scared he wouldn't let me inside the house again that night if I did.

That I'd have to spend another night in the shed, using garbage bags that smelled like piss and beer just to keep warm.

That I wouldn't be able to drink or eat for days.

That he'd play that music and flash those lights, and...

"No. Not real. Not real." I gripped my hair, knees to my chest, mouth agape.

Why wasn't he in jail? Why didn't I know he was out? Why, why, *why?*

My phone buzzed. It was the only thing I felt. The only thing that pushed me back to the here and now. And when I finally lifted my head, catching sight of the stretcher as it was pushed into the back of *my* ambulance, I realized something very important.

I wasn't okay.

I never would be again.

----◆----

McKenna

We were twenty minutes outside Carinthia when I got the phone call.

After spending all day at the museum and having a late lunch on our way back, I was exhausted and more than ready to get home and see Gavin. He was supposed to be meeting me at my place an hour after he got off work.

It was a good day—and I hadn't had many of those in a while. Sure, every moment I spent with Gavin was amazing, but the realization that I didn't need to feel reliant on a man to make me happy had made the day all that much more amazing. I could have it all. And it no longer scared me.

Hanna received especially good news today. It was in the form of a phone call from our mom, surprisingly.

Apparently, Hanna's ex was finally in jail, charged with assault and battery. Now he was awaiting trial with a bond that nobody was willing to splurge on. That meant my sister could go back home. And I couldn't be happier for her. Especially since she'd decided that she no longer would be living with our mother. It was time for her to spread her wings once and for all.

I touched the hands-free button to answer Addie's call. There was a twinge of disappointment that I hadn't heard from Gavin since this morning, but I attributed it to him having a crazy day at work. He was glad to be back, having a routine once more, and though our work hours didn't always coincide, we were making it work.

"Hey, Addie. What's up?" I asked, keeping both hands on the wheel. Thankfully, the rain had stopped, but the roads were still slick.

"Where are you?" she asked.

I stiffened a little at the worried pitch in her voice, glancing at my sister just briefly to see if she'd noticed. Hanna shrugged and turned the volume down on the radio, brows furrowed as I'm sure mine were.

"About fifteen or twenty minutes out. Why? What's up? Everything okay?"

"McKenna. Something's happened to Gavin."

I swerved the wheel, nearly hitting a pothole. My hands trembled around the wheel as I asked the only thing I could. "What?"

"He's okay physically," she clarified. "But he's gone… Nobody can find him. Something happened at work today. He had, like, a meltdown. He couldn't drive his ambulance from a scene, and the cops wound up taking him to the hospital in their squad car." She took a breath as fear gripped my chest, making it even hard to breathe. "After he got there, he just…took off. Left work, and now nobody knows where he is. Everyone's worried."

I sighed, secretly relieved that I knew exactly where he was, and automatically stepped harder on the gas. Hanna reached over and squeezed my shoulders, likely in support, but I couldn't look at her. What had happened to set him off?

"I know where he is," I eventually said, then cleared my throat to fight the frog inside.

"Okay, where? Collin and Max are freaking out and—"

"Tell them both what I just told you. That I know where he is, and then tell them I'm going straight there."

She mumbled something through the line, obviously not talking to me. A second later, she got back on and said, "Max wants to make sure you can handle it."

"What do you mean?" I scowled.

"Gavin gets really upset when he has one of these episodes, Kenna. They're just worried. Please don't take offense."

I nodded, though no one could see me, relaxing a bit. I was letting my emotions get the better of me, and if I truly wanted to be there for Gavin, I needed to prove I could handle this. "I'll be fine. Don't worry."

"Promise you'll call if you need anything?"

I loved my best friend. So much. "I will."

Hanna didn't say anything after I hung up with Addie. And I was thankful for that. Had I tried to speak, I was worried I'd crack. And right now, not knowing what I would be up against with Gavin, I knew I needed to save all the strength I could.

Exactly forty-five minutes later, after dropping my

sister off at my apartment, I pulled up to Gavin's river house, breathing a huge sigh of relief at the sight of his Suburban. On the other side of his truck, I saw another car. An unfamiliar one.

A shot of unease prickled my skin as I walked by it. Who was here with him? Who else knew his secret? Another woman, perhaps?

"Shut up, Kenna." I mumbled under my breath, yanking down the bottom of my T-shirt. Gavin was *not* Paul.

With a trembling hand, I opened the screen door and knocked three times.

A minute later, feet sounded on the other side, followed by the scuffle of a lock. Then the door opened, revealing an unfamiliar, older woman.

"Who are you?" I barked, claws out, ready to…to… to do whatever an emotional pregnant girlfriend did during situations like this.

The woman blinked, wrinkles lining her forehead and around her eyes. She wore her hair short and curled and was dressed in brown slacks and a cream-colored blouse.

She smiled up at me, her shoulders relaxing, her brown eyes warm. "You're real, then."

Eyes narrowed, I watched as she stepped back to let me inside. Instead of asking what her silly riddle meant, I asked the inevitable, no time to waste. "Where's Gavin?"

"Asleep on the couch. It's been a rough day for him."

I scowled at her back, hackles up. Regardless, I let her lead me in, hating that she seemed so at ease there. In the end, my concern over Gavin outweighed my jealousy by a million and a half miles.

Inside, the lanterns were all lit. I also noted that the fireplace was hooked up, the damp room warmed by the wood. But what tugged at my heart the most was a pale-faced Gavin on the couch, curled up under a blanket, fast asleep.

My eyes blurred at the sight of him. It was one of the most bittersweet moments of my life. He was okay, alive and breathing, yet the fear of what had put him there terrified me.

Silently, the woman sat on the coffee table behind me, the tiled surface creaking under her weight. I almost yelled at her to get off—Gavin had worked hard on that piece of furniture, damn it—but I managed to keep it together. Somehow. Whoever she was, this woman must have meant something to Gavin if she was there.

"He asked for something to help him forget. I gave him a Valium. That's why he's asleep now."

I blinked, taken aback by her words. "Forget what?"

"What he saw today." Sadness filled her eyes as she looked his way once more.

I swallowed hard, a hand to my belly. "What happened?"

"I'll let him tell you that when he wakes. He's been out for a few hours now." She cleared her throat and stood. "Follow me out? Now that you're here, I'm comfortable leaving him."

"Sure." Still uneasy about her relationship with my boyfriend, I leaned over and kissed Gavin's temple, my nose buried in his soft hair. It reminded me of Chloe's in a way, and I had to fight the urge to run my hands through it.

Just in front of the kitchen door, the nameless lady and I faced off. She assessed me, her eyes quickly zeroing in on my stomach. A small crease formed in between her eyes, but it didn't last long before our gazes met again.

"Who are you?" I finally asked, folding my arms. She was making me uncomfortable.

"My name is Heidi."

"Heidi…" I blinked, remembering that name. "Wait. As in Gavin's foster mother?"

She nodded. "I'm his psychiatrist as well."

"You're kidding, right?" Gavin's foster mother was his psychiatrist? *What the hell?*

"I'm not kidding." She grabbed a coat that was slung over the back of a folding chair, then slipped it on.

"Isn't that…*wrong*?"

"A conflict of interest, you mean?"

"Yeah." I waited for her to say *April Fools* in the middle of May, but it never came.

"Perhaps. But I've never treated him any differently than my other patients. After he came back from the Middle East, I was the one who encouraged him to seek therapy from a psychologist. When that was not enough, he came to me, asking for medicine. Now I help with both."

As a nurse, I found the entire situation to be strange. Typically, a patient did not go to family members for doctors. There again, Gavin trusted almost no one, so if he thought he needed help when simple therapy wasn't working, I was glad he had her.

"A man like Gavin may always need medicine." She paused, pulling her hair out from under the neck of her coat. "But he needs love and trust far more than anything else."

I nodded, looking to the floor, feeling her truth, deep inside.

I was the woman who could give Gavin that love. And he could be that for me too. Neither of us was perfect, but perfect was never what I strove for.

"I love him." It was the first time I'd admitted it out loud to someone other than Gavin. And it felt amazing.

A small smile graced her lips. When her eyes met mine again, they were glistening with tears. "Very good. Because he loves you too." She moved forward, hugging me against her chest. I let out an *oomph* of surprise, but the hug didn't hurt.

A painful lump lodged itself in my throat as she held me, and tears burned the corner of my eyes. I wiped them away, nodding against her, wondering if this was where I was meant to be all along.

The fact that Gavin had told this woman about me did something to me. Made me feel things I'd been avoiding for so long. Happiness. Hope. Contentment too. It's obvious Heidi loved Gavin like a son, and, well…

I breathed a heavy sigh, touching my stomach once more as the revelation hit me—harder than it had all month. It was a struggle to keep it together, especially having concluded what I suddenly realized.

I wanted to run back into the room and wake Gavin, tell him what I was feeling—what I'd been feeling since the wedding but couldn't find it in me to express. I'd worried it wouldn't last. That I was only caught up in the emotions. But now I knew the truth.

I wouldn't—*couldn't*—abandon him and this baby, no matter how scared I was.

Maybe I was a hypocrite for being so adamantly against children, only to suddenly want it all because of one man. But if I truly thought about it, the reasons why I'd never wanted them all stemmed back to one thing.

My mother and father. My life growing up.

Bottom line? I *wasn't* my parents. I knew that now. Gavin had been telling me that from the beginning. But the more time I spent with Hanna, the more I realized I liked being a person someone could love and count on.

I was McKenna Brewer.

The girl in love with Gavin St. James.

And I wanted us to become the parents we never had.

Once Heidi let me go and told me to take care of myself—and Gavin—I shut the door behind her and locked it, leaning back against the wood with another sigh.

"Kenna?" Gavin's voice cracked from the other room. I looked up, finding him just outside the make-shift kitchen. I moved in, not hesitating to comfort. To hug. To kiss.

"Hey," I whispered, raising a hand to cup his warm cheek as I approached. "You should go rest some more."

He shook his head, leaning into my palm. There, he shut his eyes and a sense of peace seemed to run through him. "I love you."

I smiled sadly, hating how he'd had to go through what he had. "I love you too."

"Hmm." He turned and kissed my palm, inhaling on a nod. It was as if those three simple words were all he ever needed to hear. But I knew they weren't. Things couldn't be that simple. We needed to talk—about today, his foster mom, and, most of all, my decision.

Taking him by the hand, I led Gavin back onto the porch, pulling the blanket up before he sat. He sunk into the cushions, urging me to follow. So I did. There was no place else I wanted to be.

Next to him, I put my head on his shoulder, letting this normalcy run through me. He and I together, this house, where memories would be made.

I'm not sure when it happened, exactly—when I'd realized how much he meant to me. Whether it was the night he carried me to bed, or the night we talked on the phone, or even the night he bought me new dishes. I loved how sweet he was to Collin's daughter, and how he spoke to my sister not as a victim, but as a human being. I loved him not only as my boyfriend, but also as the father of my child.

Before I could ask him about what happened today, he began to speak.

"I lost it at work again today."

"What happened?" I feared the worst. Another fight, perhaps? Either way, it didn't matter. If Gavin lost his job, I'd support him.

"I saw him."

"Saw who?" I took his hand in mine.

"My uncle." I shut my eyes as he paused, trying to keep my breathing even. "He was involved in a pileup on the interstate outside Arlo. I…" He took a heavy breath, the heat of it blowing over my hair. To show him how much I wanted to help, I squeezed his hand and simply waited for him to continue.

"He isn't dead. He didn't move away either. The

fucker wasn't in jail anymore, Kenna. He was there in that damn truck, and my partner... The guy was *treating* him. And I couldn't say shit, but I wanted to. I wanted to kill him. I imagined it in my mind. I wouldn't, but... he did that to me. He put me in that mind-set. And I hate him. So. Fucking. Much."

With a heavy sigh, I stroked his stomach, trying to figure out what to say as his body shook against mine. "Did he see you?"

"Yeah. He saw me, all right."

I winced at his bitter tone, wishing I could take his pain away. When he suffered, so did I. We were a package deal.

"Did he say anything to you?"

"No. The fucker didn't even seem to remember who I was. I haven't seen him since I was ten years old, but I knew him," he growled. "He was so damn happy, Kenna. And yet, here I am, hours later, letting him fuck with me all over again."

"Stop it right there, St. James." Quickly, I straddled his lap, needing him to see my face for what I was about to say. With his face between my hands, I told him the biggest truth in the world. "You are *not* letting him fuck with you. You're fighting back against that horrible man. Everything you've done since that time in your life has been like a middle finger shoved in his face, a loud screw-you. You get me?" I didn't wait for him to answer. There wasn't room for his self-doubt. Not anymore. "And whether you know it or not, you've made me so damn proud. *So* proud."

Tears filled my eyes—tears *always* filled my eyes anymore, it seemed. But I wasn't going to stop them.

Apparently, pregnant me was an emotional hot mess. What could I say other than embrace the bad to find the good.

"Me and your friends, who *are* your family… We love you *so* much, Gavin. And we will always be there for you, no matter what happens." I stabbed him in the chest with my finger, watching his throat bob as he swallowed.

"I'm never going to be normal."

I rolled my eyes and huffed, pinching him slightly in the ribs. "You think I care?" He grunted. "If you were this so-called *normal dude*, then I wouldn't be here."

"Yeah?" His mouth lifted on one side.

"Hell yeah."

He wrapped his arms around my waist and hugged me close, relaxing at the same time. "I'm gonna make the shittiest dad." His voice cracked with emotion, ripping me apart.

Slowly, I leaned back and kissed his forehead as I spoke. "Then I guess it's a good thing that this baby is going to have an incredibly shitty mom to go along with it."

Gavin pulled away and quickly blinked up at me, his mouth opening and closing in shock. All the darkness I'd seen in his eyes suddenly seemed to vanish at my words. It was a sight to behold, really. And though I knew I wasn't some sort of healer, nor did I have a magical vagina to instantly put this broken man back together, I'd at least like to say I was special enough to serve as semi-calm to his raging storm.

As Gavin was to me.

Or maybe we were both just *really* good at distracting each other.

"So, you…" he murmured.

I dropped my hands to his chest, flattening one palm over his heart. "Now's not the time to get wordless on me."

Gavin lifted both hands and covered the backs of mine. "The baby, Kenna…"

I nodded, never surer of anything in my life. "Let's do this."

Smiling wide, he dropped his forehead to mine, his entire face lighting up. "I didn't want to let you go," he said, pulling back to search my face again. "But I would have. I just…I need you to know that."

"You don't have to make that decision anymore." This time, my hands shook as I pulled one of his down to press it flat against my stomach. "Because we're in this together. Fuck our pasts."

"Yeah?" He smiled, eyes nearly twinkling.

"Absolutely, St. James."

CHAPTER  29

McKenna

GAVIN'S PHONE RANG THREE TIMES BEFORE I FINALLY ROLLED over to grab it off the floor. I didn't bother checking the time or even opening my eyes, because I knew it was early. Too early to be up on a Saturday.

He barely stirred behind me, likely exhausted from the emotional upheaval of yesterday. I'm not sure how we'd managed to sleep on the tiny sofa all night, but I wasn't going to complain. After yesterday, I'd decided I never wanted to be apart from him again. When it came to Gavin and me, I wasn't about to be reckless with another decision.

"What?" I groaned, thoroughly annoyed with who-ever the hell had the audacity to wake me after an all-night marathon of sex.

"Where is he?" barked Collin, the forever dickhead.

I rolled my eyes. "Hello to you too, asshole."

Collin chuckled on the other end, which had my heart steadying a bit. Early-morning calls usually meant something bad was happening.

I'd called them all the night before, assuring them that Gavin was good, safe, and with me. Max didn't question it. Collin grunted out a *good*, and Addie told me he was lucky to have me.

Really though, *I* was the lucky one.

"Need to talk to him."

Gavin stirred at my side, fingers grazing my hip. I shuddered, wondering if there was such a thing as too much sex while pregnant. That's one rule I'd be okay with breaking.

"There is this English word that most people use when they want something. Have you heard of it? Because you may think you can order my best friend around, but you can't sit there and—"

"Please," Collin groaned. "Lemme talk to my best friend."

I smiled at the small success, adding in a tiny fist bump. "Just so you know, for future reference and all, if you'd learn to use your manners more often than—"

"Addie's pregnant!" he shouted through the phone.

I froze.

"Now. I'm gonna need you all over here so we can talk about some shit."

My eyes widened, and I shot up off the couch, already grabbing my discarded clothes. "Let me talk to her."

Collin groaned. "You wanna talk to her, you call her on your own phone." In the background, I could hear someone's voice. Max, maybe? I couldn't tell.

"What's wrong?" Gavin sat up beside me, one hand along my lower back, the other reaching up as he stretched. His hair looked deliciously tousled, as if fingers had been run through it all night. *My* fingers, to be precise.

I mouthed, *Addie's pregnant.*

He stopped mid-stretch, reaching for his phone.

I rolled my eyes and stood, pressing my free hand against my naked hip. If he wanted the phone, he'd have to come get it.

His eyes did a long, slow swoop of my body, grinning when he reached my mouth again.

"Eyes up here, buddy." I winked, not minding at all. If he wanted to look at my naked body, so be it.

Smirking, he stood from the couch, his erection very noticeable. I licked my lips, ignoring Collin's voice as he hollered in my ear. Gavin in clothes was heavenly, but a naked Gavin was a dream come true.

With a smirk, Gavin reached down, giving himself a long, slow stroke with one hand, then grabbing his phone with the other. "Can't talk, Colly," he grumbled, only to hang up and toss the phone onto the table a second later. "That's what I wanted the phone for."

"Someone's grumpy in the morning." I giggled, palming his chest, loving the way his hand bumped my thigh as he continued to stroke his beautiful erection.

"Not grumpy. Just needy."

With a grin, I dropped to my knees before him, eyes up. "Poor baby. Guess I'll just have to take better care of you."

Then I pulled him to my mouth.

Gavin

After the best blow job of my life, Kenna and I got in the makeshift shower I'd created outside my river house, which led to me getting her off with my finger, only to bring her back in and make love to her on the shitty couch that was fast turning into the best couch ever.

Then we talked a little as we dressed and got ready to leave. About what had happened yesterday with my uncle, then a little about my foster mom. Kenna had suggested I take some more time off work, that she could help support me until I felt ready to go back. But that wouldn't happen. I loved my job. And knowing everything was falling into place for her and me, I finally had a reason to keep my head on straight.

After that, Kenna called to check up on her sister, while I gathered up some things to take back to my place and wash—like the blankets we'd used all night. The same blankets we'd dried our naked bodies off with after our outhouse shower.

By the time we made it to back to the duplex, Collin was pacing the floor, hands in his hair. "The hell took you guys so long?"

Kenna flipped him off and raced to the couch, wrapping her arms around Addie...who was crying. Shit. *Now* I felt bad for being late.

"I called you an hour ago." Collin jumped in front of me. "When I say I need you all to come over, I—"

"Shut up, Collin," Addie said on a sob. "Just...shut up."

The room went silent, other than the sound of Chloe babbling from her room and the air conditioner flicking on from outside. I looked at the clock on their wall. It wasn't even ten, yet I felt like I'd been awake for hours already.

As if it were his last moment on earth, Collin hurried over to Addie and fell before her on his knees. "I'm so sorry." He kissed her knees, looking pained as he lowered his forehead onto her lap. "I don't wanna upset you."

Kenna looked at me, then Addie, then Collin, before motioning with her head toward Chloe's door. I nodded, and she stood, following me. I pushed Chloe's bedroom door open, Kenna on my heels. She clicked the handle shut behind her and leaned back against the door.

"What in the ever-loving hell was that about?" she whispered, not wasting a second before walking to Chloe and pulling her out of her crib.

I grinned at the view, watching flustered, red-faced Kenna snuggle another piece of my heart to her chest— Chloe. "If Collin doesn't stop being a dickhead, I'm gonna shove my fist up his..." She blinked and looked at Chloe, whose head was bobbling back and forth between me and the lady who held her.

"Mama Addie?" Chloe asked me, blinking her still-sleepy, baby blues.

"She's talking to Daddy," Kenna said before setting her on the changing table.

"Dada nigh-nigh?" She looked up at McKenna this time, her lower lip puckering.

"Oh God. Don't cry, kid," Kenna groaned.

Shaking my head with a smirk, I came up behind McKenna, wrapping my arms around her waist. She was trembling, nerves from dealing with Chloe—and from Addie and Collin—had her internally freaking out, no doubt.

"Dada?" A tear ran down Chloe's face when she looked at me from over Kenna's shoulder.

"Daddy's getting your breakfast, Beaner." I reached

around Kenna's waist and rubbed a hand over Chloe's forehead while Kenna changed her diaper.

She fumbled with the Velcro tabs but kept at it, cussing under her breath the entire time. Collin would have a shit fit if he knew the language she was using around his kid, but Chloe had heard it all before. God knows, she repeated it plenty.

I'm not sure if Kenna was trying to prove a point to me, or what, but she didn't ask for help, just kept at it. And as I watched, I knew for a fact she'd have it down in no time. If not? I'd be there every step of the way to help. We were a team.

"You're a natural." I kissed her shoulder when she finished.

Chloe sat up on her own and reached for me. I pulled her close to me, thanking God I'd picked up my own balls along the way and gotten over my fear of kids and babies.

"You think it's safe out there?" Kenna bit her lip and looked up at me. I wrapped my arm around her waist as the three of us stared at the closed door.

I shrugged. "It got quiet."

"Which could mean a lot of things." Kenna grinned, a knowing look in her eyes.

"They wouldn't…" I shook my head and groaned. "Fuck that." I opened the door and walked down the hall, stopping at the sight. On the couch, Addie sat on Collin's lap, smiling. Max was sitting on the chair, and Lia was pacing in front of the table, shaking her head.

"I can't… Why would you do this?" Lia froze in front of Max, who looked half-asleep with one arm over his eye.

"What's going on?" Kenna asked, coming up the hall from behind me. She looked at the couch, at Lia, Max, and finally me.

Chloe wiggled, wanting down. She ran toward Collin and Addie, plopping herself on top of their pile.

"We have to move," Collin said.

The entire room stilled, including me. I looked at my best friend on the couch and my other best friend on the chair. He was selling the duplex? "Why?"

"It's bullshit, right?" Lia folded her arms over her chest and looked at me.

"Not like you ever even lived here." Collin rolled his eyes, moving to sit Chloe in between his lap and Addie's, who'd moved beside him.

"Move, as in out of the house? Sell it?" I asked, confused.

"We don't *have* to move." Addie looked at each of us, landing on Collin last. She huffed and grabbed his hand over Chloe's lap. "That's what I've been trying to tell him. We can stay here until the baby is older. It's fine."

Collin shook his head. "What if it's a boy? This is our first baby together. Don't you wanna decorate or—"

"How far along are you?" Kenna asked.

"That's the thing." Addie tossed her hands up in the air. "I *just* freaking found out this morning. I literally peed on the stick, came back in to tell Collin, then he was up calling this big powwow."

Chloe jumped on the couch as she normally did. Nobody moved to stop her, but I was itching to grab her. Pull her close. Protect her.

"He didn't even tell *me* what his plan was until fifteen

minutes before you all got here." She covered her face and groaned.

Max laughed from the chair, slapping his knee. "Colly, Colly, Colly. When are you ever gonna fucking learn?"

"Mouth." Collin pointed a finger at Max, frowning.

Max put his hands out in defense. "Yeah, yeah, whatever. Beaner's already got herself a potty mouth."

I shook my head. "You do what you want, Collin. But my advice to you?" I pointed my finger at him. "Don't ever wake my ass up in the morning like that again."

Frowning, I walked over to still-bouncing Chloe and sat her on the couch. I tickled her belly, smiling as she laughed. She said my name, over and over, her eyes twinkling. It really didn't matter where we all lived. All that mattered was that we stayed a family. Because that's what we were. A little dysfunctional at times, but a family all the same. The only one I'd ever known.

"You're really pregnant?" Kenna asked as if she'd just woken up.

I pulled Chloe onto my hip and turned to find McKenna crying. Addie jumped up, running across the room with a squeal. Together, they bounced around in a circle in the middle of the living room.

I scratched at my beard, looking at my buddies. Collin shrugged. Max rolled his eyes.

Lia flopped down on Max's lap, wrapping her arm around his neck. "Aww, look at them. Best friends, pregnant by best friends... It's like a reality show." She kissed Max.

"You jealous, Lee-Lee? 'Cause there is no doubt in my mind we can catch up, if it's what you want."

She grinned, then put her hands on his cheeks. "Nice try. But this baby-maker is not going to be baking tikes anytime soon."

The room grew loud, everyone talking or laughing. Everyone but Chloe and me, that is. I looked at the little girl in my arms, whose hands were in my beard, tugging softly. Her legs bounced against me, and her smile was like a ray of sunshine, as corny as it sounded. I couldn't help but wonder: Where would we be without her? She was what had held us all together. Kept Collin, Max, and me a unit even after we got out of the marines. The one thing that kept us sane when we were all struggling with our demons. They say kids change your world, and with Chloe, I couldn't agree more.

Chloe gave me Collin and Max. Chloe gave Collin Addie. She even gave me McKenna in a weird way. We lived in a twisted circle most might question…except for us, of course.

"I'm making pancakes," Max announced, smacking Lia on the ass.

Chloe cheered, throwing her hands in the air. I put her down, knowing she'd want to go see her other uncle now—hero Maxwell and his pancakes always won out.

Once Addie and Kenna finished hugging, I grabbed my girlfriend by the hand and tugged her close. She smiled up at me, wrapping her arms around my neck with a yawn, while I put my own arms around her waist.

"You really wanna do this with me?" I asked, thinking I'd dreamed up our conversation last night.

She scrunched her nose. "Do what, have pancakes?"

I kissed her smart mouth and moved my hand to her

belly, my voice dropping to a whisper. "Do *this* with me, I mean."

She pulled back enough to look around the room, her lips twitching with silent secrets and a wildness I'd never wanna contain. McKenna Brewer was my impulsive everything.

"Yes." She looked to me again, blue eyes sparkling and wide. "No doubt in my mind."

EPILOGUE

Collin

Two years later

IN THE BACK OF MY MIND, I KNEW THIS WASN'T RIGHT. BUT with two kids, and another on the way, we had to get it when and where we could, even if that meant a secluded alcove in the back of the reception hall at my best friend's wedding.

"You, sir, are insatiable."

I kissed my wife on the mouth as I stood, still tasting her on my lips. Sweet, warm...the spot between her thighs was one of my favorite places to be.

Her breathing was strangled, cheeks pink, and her eyes wide in the shadows. One good orgasm, and she'd nearly forgotten her mind...and the fact that Chloe had just taught her sixteen-month-old sister, Maya, how to say the word *fuck* during dinner.

"If 'insatiable' means getting you alone for a little while to eat your pussy, then I'll wear the title the rest of my life."

She rolled her eyes as I helped her pull up her panties, knowing she could hardly bend over. Little Man in her stomach was doing all sorts of shitty things to her back.

Still, a pregnant Addison Montgomery was the most beautiful thing I'd ever seen.

"Did anyone see us come in here?" She brushed her hands down the front of my suit, grinning against my mouth.

"Nah, they're all still eating."

She groaned and pushed her hand over the top of her rounded belly. "He's going to be punching his way out of me at this rate."

I lowered my hand, rubbing it against the curve of her seven-month pregnant belly. "He's got lots to catch up on with his sisters. Us Montgomery boys love competition."

One snort later, she was grabbing my hand and leading me out into the dark hall. "Yeah, and that's the problem. I can't afford to cut the school year short because your son has issues with being impatient like his dad. I *need* this job, Collin."

I kissed her soft lips once more and pressed my forehead to hers. "I know. You'll make it." She worked for the school district in Matoona, lead pre-K teacher—and fucking good at it too. Beaner stayed with her grandparents, both sides, while Maya alternated between Max and my parents—whoever wasn't busy that day.

Once we were in the reception area, I searched the room for our girls. Dad had them corralled in the corner, just in time for my best man's speech. Mom was likely getting more beer for Dad because our kids drove everyone to drink.

Max jumped in front of us, dark eyes suspicious and narrowed. "Where the hell were you two?"

I shrugged, no shame as I said, "Eating my wife's pussy."

"Collin!" Addie smacked my shoulder.

If I could've fucked her, I probably would've, but that'd be for later. When I had her alone in bed.

Max punched my other shoulder, then winked at Addie. "I thought you looked a little flushed, Short Stuff."

She rolled her eyes, but I saw her smile. The sass in her had me all but falling at her feet when she walked toward the head table. Nearly three years later, I was more in love with her than the day I dry humped her against the front door of our old duplex—the one Max and Lia were currently living in.

"You ready?" Max squeezed my shoulder and nodded toward Gav. He was sitting at the head table, Kenna in his lap, her white bridal gown sparkling, and their nineteen-month-old boy, Brody, snuggled against her chest. The mini-Gavin, with hair down to his shoulders, was pretty much the light of my daughters' lives.

Max and Lia had eloped about a year back, after breaking off the huge shindig my mom had been planning for them. Our mom was pissed, but Lia was happy, so she didn't hold too much of a grudge. Big weddings weren't for my sister anyway. And Max? He'd do just about anything to make her happy.

"Think so." I patted my suit coat and tugged out the piece of paper I'd written my speech on.

He nodded, that Maxwell grin lighting up his face. Missed waking up and seeing him in the morning, but I loved living on the river in the new house we'd just finished building next to Gavin and Kenna's even more. Max said he'd move to Arlo someday to be closer to us, but for now, they were fine where they were, just the two of them, especially when it meant more alone time as they attempted to get pregnant.

I shuddered at the thought, not wanting to think about my baby sister and her husband's sex life, even if the end result would be pretty fucking awesome.

Max handed me the microphone at the table. I tapped the end, gaining the room's attention. Once everyone was silent, I unfolded my paper, then decided at the last minute to ditch the programmed speech and speak from the heart. Addie would be damn proud.

I looked at her, then winked. She blew me a kiss and mouthed, *I love you.*

"When I first met Gavin, he was sitting in the bunk next to mine during boot camp. He didn't talk much. Barely even looked at me when I tried to talk to him. I thought to myself, something's wrong with this guy, so I kept away from him, until Max decided to make it his life's duty to befriend the quiet dude." I cleared my throat, looking down at Gav. He was shaking his head but smiled all the same. It could've been the fact that his wife was whispering in his ear. Or it could've been me. Either way, seeing him happy, when for so long he hadn't been, was the highlight of the wedding.

"Anyway, the three of us"—I patted Max's shoulder at my right—"grew to be friends. And then not long after, they became my brothers, sticking by me when life was so messed up I couldn't see straight." I rubbed my hand over my mouth, remembering that time, so long ago. "They became uncles to my daughter, the sole reason I survived nine months of raising a child on my own. I don't know what I would have done without them." I cleared my throat, a big ball of emotion lodged inside.

"I love Gavin like a brother. And this girl he made his wife today? Yeah, she's pretty amazing too." Amazing because she put up with him. His bad moods could be worse than my own. "And today, he got his happily ever after with the one girl who'd been able to make him see reality at its finest." Fuck, I sounded like an idiot.

"So let's raise our glasses, and give a toast to Mr. and Mrs. Gavin St. James." I lifted my glass in the air, looking over the tables. "May they be blessed with a house full of kids and a life filled with happiness."

"Cheers, Colly." Gavin toasted me, then Max, then the three of us pressed our glasses together. We drank it all down in one swig and set the drinks back on the table in unison.

One by one, we grabbed our ladies by the hand, hauling them to the dance floor. Some slow song played over the speakers as we moved, and a sense of completion filled me to the core. My wife in my arms, my buddies by my side...my two favorite little girls giggling from the side of the dance floor, watching.

There really wasn't anything else we needed. Life was pretty damn close to perfect.

"Fuck, fuck, fuck." Maya, with her dark-brown hair and her mother's brown eyes, jumped onto the dance floor, followed by a grinning Chloe, and my mom and dad chasing after them.

I shook my head and shut my eyes, pressing my forehead to Addie's with a sigh. She giggled—*God, did I love that sound*—and I couldn't help but laugh too.

Fuck perfection. It was overrated anyway.

ACKNOWLEDGMENTS

A few years ago, the voices of Collin, Max, and Gavin showed up in my head and didn't leave me alone until I told their stories. They put me through the ringer, probably more than they did their leading ladies, but I love them like they're my brothers regardless. Now that this series has ended—cue sniffles and tears—I feel like I'm losing a piece of myself. My only hope is that these three men and all their crazy antics have given you the same bits of joy that they gave me.

Recklessly Ever After was the hardest book for me to write thus far in my career. Mainly because of what Gavin went through. I channeled him for a long time and went into a dark hole of my own because of it. It wasn't pleasant, especially since I wrote this book while my husband was battling cancer. But Gavin pulled through his darkness, as did my husband with cancer, and in the end, I think I'm stronger because of it.

Seriously though… Depression has no cure, but there is absolutely no shame in asking for help like I did. Like *Gavin* did. Remember that.

On a lighter note, I have a million and a half people to thank, so I'll get right to it.

Chris. You know how much I love you. Without your support, your hard work, your devotion to me and our family, I wouldn't be able to stay home and write. Without you, I would be completely lost.

Kelsey, Emma, and Bella. My girls. You three are my light in the dark. And though you don't always understand my tears of frustration or my need to be on my computer for hours at a time when inspiration strikes, you love me unconditionally. Thank you for being the most amazing daughters in the entire world.

Mom and Dad. For obvious reasons. You gave me life and the guidance to be who I am today. Sometimes when it comes to you two, I don't have words to describe my love.

Jessica Calla…my sister from another mister. My #NMFTG partner in crime. Without you the last two years, I would have been floating in between projects with no guidance and a lack of confidence in who I am as a person *and* as an author. Thank you for giving me the gift of your friendship. Thank you for being the one person I can truly count on in life…even all these states away. Love you, J.

My critique partners, Katrina and Jen. You two ladies are THE best. Not only with your writerly guidance, but because you love me and put up with me and my neurotic tendencies. Love you both to the moon and back.

Special shout-out to some of my most supportive writerly friends out there. Michelle Hazen, Siobhan Davis, Kelly Siskind, and Lana Sloan… You four wonderful women give me joy on a daily basis, whether you know it or not. Thank you for your support. Thank you for being part of my heart.

The #amediting crew! I am so blessed to be a part of this tiny world we've all created. And though I'm usually the quiet one of the bunch, I appreciate knowing you all are there, ready to support me on a second's notice. Let's keep the momentum going for many years to come!

Stacey Donaghy. My agent. You've stuck with me thus far and accepted my...*tendencies*. Gavin, Collin, and Max wouldn't be out in the world without you. And I am so thankful that you continue to take a chance on me every single day.

The entire Sourcebooks crew, most especially my lovely, *amazing* editor, Cat Clyne. You all gave my characters life and you all took a chance on me as an author as well. For these two things especially, I can never thank you enough.

And last, but certainly not least, my fans. Whether you're getting Hot and Heavy with me on FB or sending me emails, messages, tweets, or anything of the sort, thank you for letting me tell my stories. Thank you for reading them. Thank you, most of all, for accepting me as the introverted author who really stinks at interactions but loves you all like no other.